THE DUTCHMAN'S DILEMMA

The
Dutchman's
Dilemma

MAAN MEYERS

M
MEYERS

BANTAM BOOKS
New York · Toronto · London · Sydney · Auckland

THE DUTCHMAN'S DILEMMA

A Bantam Book / August 1995

Copyright © 1995 by Annette Brafman Meyers and Martin Meyers

Book design by Susan Yuran
Map design by Aher/Donell

Library of Congress Cataloging-in-Publication Data

Meyers, Maan.
The Dutchman's dilemma / Maan Meyers.
p.   cm.
ISBN 0-553-09705-9
I. Title.
PS3563.E889D88   1995

813'.54—dc20

95-5207 CIP

Published simultaneously in the United States and Canada

Bantam Books are published by Bantam Books, a division of Bantam Doubleday Dell Publishing Group, Inc. Its trademark, consisting of the words "Bantam Books" and the portrayal of a rooster, is Registered in U.S. Patent and Trademark Office and in other countries. Marca Registrada. Bantam Books, 1540 Broadway, New York, New York 10036.

PRINTED IN THE UNITED STATES OF AMERICA

BVG   10 9 8 7 6 5 4 3 2 1

We dedicate this book to our niece,
Barbara Meyers.
In loving memory

For their experience and advice, we give thanks to John Milnes Baker; Annette Botnick, reference librarian at the Jewish Theological Seminary; to the librarians at the New York Public Library's Local History Division; and to the librarians at the New-York Historical Society Library.

And for their constant support and wisdom, we thank Chris Tomasino and Kate Miciak.

The Colony of Manhattan is bless'd with the richest soil in all New-England, I have heard it reported from men of Judgement and Integrity, that one Bushel of European-Wheat hath yielded a hundred in one year. Their other Commodities ar Furs, and the like. New-York is situated at the mouth of the great River Mohegan, and is built with Dutch Brick Alla-moderna, the meanest house therein being valued at One hundred pounds, to the Landward it is compass with a Wall of good thickness; at the entrance of the River is an Island well fortified, and hath command of any Ship that shall attept to pass without their leave.

Josselyn, *An Account of Two Voyages to New-England*, 1674

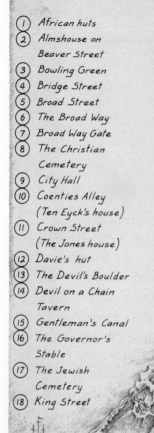

1. African huts
2. Almshouse on Beaver Street
3. Bowling Green
4. Bridge Street
5. Broad Street
6. The Broad Way
7. Broad Way Gate
8. The Christian Cemetery
9. City Hall
10. Coenties Alley (Ten Eyck's house)
11. Crown Street (The Jones house)
12. Davie's hut
13. The Devil's Boulder
14. Devil on a Chain Tavern
15. Gentleman's Canal
16. The Governor's Stable
17. The Jewish Cemetery
18. King Street
19. King and Queen Tavern
20. Asser Levy's Tavern
21. Asser Levy's Slaughterhouse
22. Lichtman's Bake Shop
23. Market Field
24. Mendoza Warehouse (Staple Street)
25. Racqel's Mikvak
26. Navarro's house
27. Old Soldier's Tavern
28. Queen Street (The Strand, also Pearl Street)
29. The Roome House and Store
30. Second Queen Street
31. Shellpoint
32. Stone Church in the Fort
33. Stone Street
34. Tonneman House and Barn
35. The Wall (Wall Street)
36. The Water Gate
37. Water Gate Road
38. Whitehall
39. Tonneman's willow tree
40. Wooden Shoe Tavern

North

EAST RIVER

BREUKELEN

The Mendoza Family

Abraham Mendoza
B. Unk.
D. 1666
M.
Sara

Benjamin
B. 1634 Holland
D. 1664
M.
Racqel Pereira

David
B. 1638 Holland
M.
Mariana Da Costa

Benjamin
B. 1666

Miriam
B. 1669

Abraham
B. 1671

The Tonneman Family

Maria Loudon
B. 1625 Holland
D. 1663

Pieter Tonneman
B. 1621 Holland

Racqel (Pereira) Mendoza
B. 1636 Holland

Anna
B. 1644
M.
Johan Bikker

Moses
B. 1665

Maria
B. 1666

Benjamin
B. 1670

Daniel
B. 1673

Johan
B. 1664

Maria
B. 1667
D. Inf.

Margrietta
B. 1670

THE DUTCHMAN'S DILEMMA

Prologue

The pearl-pale moonglow found the blade. Holding the knife so tightly his knuckles blanched, the Searcher felt the painful glint and shielded his eyes from the gnarled face in the moon that seemed to mock him. When the moon hid behind dark clouds, the pain dissolved.

But the Searcher would have the last laugh before dawn. Even without the moon the way was clear. Darkness was the dearest of friends.

Wild gusts of wind caught the Searcher's cloak, billowed it aft like a miniature sail, revealing his fine red coat.

A fragmented voice rode the wind. The sound was too distant for the words to be clear, but the Searcher knew it was the cry of the Rattle Watch, calling five and all well. The Rattle men were the Night Watchmen of New-York, that once was New Orange, that once was New Amsterdam, and always was Sodom.

The Night Watch's cry skimmed over the sleeping village, followed by others, responding, all a garble, just noise in the March wind.

"Sinners," the Searcher muttered. Soon enough, they would know the damnation of hellfire.

The night was pungent with game and dung. The knife in the Searcher's hand quivered for a moment, then the feral blade took on its own life, slashing the air. A large buck paused on a hillock, his antlers rising like the Tree of Life. Sniffing the air, the buck turned, its hackles risen, then disappeared into the brush.

Shadowed, hulking against the sky, the windmills offered little guidance, but the Searcher needed none. The moon returned in time to light his way.

From behind the closed shutters of Arian Cornelisen's Bread-loaf Tavern came a faint glimmer. Since midnight it had been the Sabbath. Cornelisen was tapping beer after hours on the Lord's Day. The Searcher vowed the tavern keeper would pay dearly for this transgression.

The way was clear. No dawdling now. God's work to do.

Or the Devil's, if need be.

Trees bowed against the fury of the gusty gale that sprang out of nowhere and roared up the Bowery Road. God and the Devil were angry indeed. The Searcher felt the glow of satisfaction. His mission was blessed this night. Or damned.

Ahead the City and the Water Gate. Both this and the Broad Way Gate were closed from sunset to sunrise these days, from six to six.

Slipping off the road and into the woods, the Searcher crouched on the cold ground. Carefully, quietly, he moved aside some shrubs. The Water Gate sentinel sat on his haunches, leaning against the massive iron-clamped door that led to the east side of the City, head lolling, punctuating the uneasy air with snorting snores. The guard's partisan and wheel lock were leaning against the large door too.

The Searcher kissed his blade, then raised it to the moon.

OTTO WERSTEN HELD the lamp still. No help for it; the lantern flame flickered in the wind and went out. He should have been grateful for the moon, but Otto hated nights like this, bright nights of the full moon, which his ma called the Devil's own, when the ghosts of the dead and the witches walked. He was grateful that this night was near over. Excepting that he needed some light to find his way, he preferred the comfort of the dark. He had developed a keen eye for dark-seeing, better than his mates. They called him Cat-Eye.

As always, Otto had come on duty at ten o'clock with his lantern, badge, wood rattle, and staff, and now he was ready for his bed. He set the lamp down and reached for the flask in the pouch hanging under his arm. In so doing he knocked his rattle from his wide leather belt. Muttering, he knelt and ran his hand over the ground. The cold cut sharply even through his wool mittens. There. Careful not to make a sound—that was all he needed, to alert the rest of the Watch when he was about to take a drink—he shoved the rattle back in its place at his waist. He took a long draught of brandy, hand holding his rabbit-skin hat, head tilted way back. So good. He wiped his lips with the sleeve of his threadbare gray duffel coat. The brandy brought a burning pleasure to his gut. What with dawn barely an hour away, and not wanting to take off his mittens, Otto didn't trouble to relight the lantern.

THE SEARCHER'S KNIFE stabbed the ground and dug at the earth. Standing, he threw clods of earth at the gate just left of the sleeping guard's head.

The sentinel swore and leaped to his feet, knocking over both his weapons. He scrambled for them, coming up with the spear first. "Who goes?" he cried.

The Searcher mewed like a cat.

The sentinel, his partisan pike pointing the way, came into the woods. "Here, kit, here, kit."

The Searcher mewed again and led the guard deeper into the woods. Then, with a shake of his head at the man's witless behavior, the Searcher circled round the guard and entered the sleeping City. All save one were oblivious of his coming.

SHUDDERING, OTTO CAT-EYE WERSTEN said a quick prayer, for he was a good Christian. He took one more swig of the flask, then packed it away. This night had been long. Longer than most, it seemed to him. He wrapped his thick Scots wool scarf once about his throat and pulled the flaps of his hat over his ears.

Otto's route took him down the Broad Way. He held his half-hour glass up to the cursed moon's light. The sand was almost all out of the top. Otto cleared his throat. He called:

"Half five the morning and all is well!"

Hard on his call, from over by the East River, Jan Kopper's call came to him on the wind, matching his. But Kopper's call was drawn out and with a richer tone. Always trying to go him one better, Jan was.

As he approached Stuyvesant's old home, the Great House, now called Whitehall by the beefeaters, Otto came to a trembling halt.

A horrible sound, a sound such as could come only from one of Satan's damned, overwhelmed Otto. The shriek enfeebled his body and dizzied his brain. He cocked his head and held his staff at the ready. Where had the hideous noise come from?

The Great House was the residence of Governor Edmund Andros's First Councillor, Nicasius De Sille. The Governor rarely came to Manhattan, happy to stay put in his regal mansion on Governor's Island in the Bay.

Apart from the Great House down a side path separated by a stand of dogwood trees and a high gate was a new structure, the First Councillor's carriage-house.

Otto ran along the stone path, clutching his staff. The gate was open wide. Cautiously, Otto approached the carriage house. The awful shrieking inside the building had ceased as abruptly as it had begun; he heard the terrified stamping and neighing of horses gone mad. Someone or something was hammering against the carriage-house doors. Otto shuddered again. God grant that it wasn't an evil spirit. Or maybe even the Devil himself.

In spite of his dread, Otto held his staff ready and dug his two feet firmly to the ground. As he reached out to open one of the large doors, both doors burst open. Something wet and hot splashed Otto's face. He was hurled to the ground as a crazed beast went galloping by.

The Dutchman's Dilemma

THE FORT OF NEW-YORK, James-Fort, was less than a quarter mile from Whitehall Street. Within the old Fort stood the Chapel. Built in 1642 and known as the Stone Church, it was the first house of worship in New Amsterdam. Then, it was dedicated to Dutch Reformed Christian worship. Now the prayers of the Church of England were said here.

Shadows leaped across the stone walls of the Chapel. The Reverend Charles Gordon held his lamp high as he made his way from the rectory to the pulpit. This was his time, the moments before dawn on a Sunday, when he enjoyed a personal communion with God in preparation for services.

But this Lord's Day was not beginning well at all. The preacher drew closer, his lamp before him. On the lectern, in the middle of the open prayer book, as if a page mark, lay a bloody sacrilege. "Dear God, preserve us," the Reverend Gordon gasped.

A ROOSTER CROWED. Otto's cat-eyes were fouled with something that blotted out the dawning sun. Mud? He drew his hand over them. Before he saw it on his mitten he knew; the smell of fresh blood gagged him even as he lay on the cold stone walk, half unconscious. He was soaked in it. Demented screams rent the air. Otto staggered to his feet. Was this blood his? He ran his hands over his body; no wound, no pain. The horse that knocked him down had doused him in blood. He rushed for the carriage house, whose doors now stood open, and ran into Richard Smythe, the stableman. Inside, horses screamed.

"What?" Smythe yelled.

Otto shook his head, spattering Smythe with blood. Mute with terror, he pointed with his staff toward the blood stench and the cries of the horses. Drawing the rattle from his belt, he whirled it vigorously to summon help for whatever abomination lay beyond the open doors.

Inside, two crazed four-footers were screaming and kicking holes out of their stalls in desperate attempts to get away from the death smell. Otto and Smythe had heavy going, their boots slurred through gross-mire. The early morning light blazed through the open doors and exposed the horror within. "Jesus Christ in Heaven," Smythe cried.

"Amen," Otto cried.

Smythe's hands took such a fit of trembling that Otto pushed him back. The Watch Man stepped inside the carriage house. The Governor's majestic black stallion, a gift from King Charles himself, lay slaughtered, its butchered entrails spilling onto the straw.

Chapter 1

Absently, Tonneman made wet circles on the scarred walnut tabletop with his mug. This place with its Dutch door, low, beamed ceiling, and long tables held memories for him. When Queen Street was called Pearl Street, the Old Soldiers Tavern had been Hendrick's and Joost's Pear Tree.

Tonneman took a sip of his tea, a draw of his pipe. He didn't take spirits anymore, hadn't for the past eleven years. Even if he wanted a taste of brandy, he couldn't get it here. In New-York there was no drinking Sunday and no drinking on any other night after the hour of ten. The only official reason for this tavern being open was that it had been designated the Post Station by the Common Council, a place where the rider brought the post after his long ride.

A man could have a beer for his thirst of a Sunday at home. It was the second and third drink that kept one from devotions, or necessary labor, that was against God and the tap law.

The leathery skin about Tonneman's eyes creased at the memories: He was Schout of New Amsterdam, and Maria and Hendrick were alive. But now Maria was dead and Hendrick was dead and Joost—it seemed a lifetime ago. Before the English.

The English had kept Tonneman as Sheriff. He grinned. Sheriff of His Majesty's colony of New-York. Quite an honor for a Dutchman. And that had been good. What with getting married again, he had been in need of a reliable income. It was more than ten years now since he and Racqel had wed, and they had done so before the mourning period for her husband Benjamin had ended. Benjamin's brother, David Mendoza, had used this breach, among many, as a further excuse to declare Racqel an outcast and denounce her to the other Hebrews. A grim smile came to Tonneman's lips. Racqel's marrying a Christian who would not convert was certainly reason enough.

Tonneman would have been content if Racqel had remained as she had presented herself, another man's childless widow, a barren woman. But then quickly, one on top of the other, a boy, a girl, and two more boys; suddenly Tonneman was a father again, many times over, and his life was filled with more joy than he could have believed possible.

With the boys had come the barbaric Hebrew custom of circumcision. Still, he'd agreed readily that his children would be Jewish. Only now, since she'd miscarried their fourth son four months back, during the excitement of the second Dutch reign when the City was briefly New Orange, his wife had once more taken it into her head that he, Tonneman, should be Jewish as well, so that death would not part them.

Ach. He relit his pipe from the candle on the table. Women. This was nothing new, really. During all of their years of marriage it always came back to the same thing. *Become a Jew. Do it for me. For the children.*

Racqel's own people shunned her because she had married a Christian. Well, most of them did. New-York had more people than New Amsterdam, perhaps three thousand by now. A small Jewish Community of thirty-five to forty souls thrived. But even now, every week one or another would reject Racqel with some cruel word or deed.

Their marriage vows had been Christian ones, performed in the Dutch Reformed Church in Duke Street, the Stone Church in the Fort now being English. Racqel had wept throughout the ceremony. After Moses was born in the autumn of '65, Tonneman made the crazy pledge to his wife that over the years had caused him so much woe: He would convert to her religion. And, if all he had to do was say aye, he would have. But he couldn't do what Racqel said he must do. He had too hard a head to learn those strange words or those strange things. He could not go through that Jewish baptism. And most of all, he could not put himself under the Jewish knife.

In spite of everything, over the years Racqel had taught the children to be Jewish. But the Jews of the City, for the most part, had turned their backs on her and her children.

Tonneman sighed. Other than this, they had a good life together. Their love had deepened and his desire for her was equaled by hers for him. He knew that.

His little Maria had followed Moses, then came Benjamin and Daniel. The miscarriage had been sad, but it was a part of life; his first wife, Maria, had suffered many. The good mixed with the bad, and all in all the Tonnemans were a family.

But Racqel had lost her other family, her community, and he knew that deeply grieved her. Sometimes, when he caught the pain in her eyes, it nearly broke his heart.

Their Christian-Jewish marriage didn't affect Tonneman in the least. After Maria's death in '63, much before meeting Racqel, he had practically stopped attending church altogether and he didn't go at all now. God forgive him.

He and Racqel had talked at first of sailing back to the Netherlands and starting over. Her father's kin still lived there; many were physicians as her father had been. Perhaps, under their supervision, she would be permitted to practice the medical skills her father had taught her. Tonneman had even resigned his position as Sheriff, but then his good friend Conraet Ten Eyck had come to him with a proposition.

So, he and Racqel had stayed and were glad of it. Tonneman, the former sailor, the former lawman, was now a businessman in partnership with his friend Ten Eyck. They were jacks of all trades in this town, be it called New Amsterdam, New Orange, or New-York. If a street needed paving, if City wells needed cleaning, or if the City wall needed mending, and it always did, they took care of it.

Ten Eyck and Tonneman were also Land Overseers retained by the City. They inspected fences to see if they were where they should be and if roads were in good repair. It was their job to make certain that citizens took care of the problems. If they couldn't do it themselves, Ten Eyck and Tonneman would, for a small fee, also supply workmen to take care of the problems.

The firm collected weigh money, acting as measurer of apples, onions, and turnips in New-York. They also condemned houses for pulling down and removal. And, for another fee, they would pull them down and remove them.

Of course, when it came time to decide who would deliver the Post, Tonneman and Ten Eyck were the men for the job. All this work was handled with a simple plan. Once they got the job, the two men hired somebody else to do the work.

Not only were they jacks of all trades, they were also masters of all trades. And though Tonneman didn't go to church, Conraet Ten Eyck did. This mollified the Common Council. The company of Ten Eyck and Tonneman was extremely successful.

As Post Master to New-York, Tonneman now sat nibbling stale crumpet cake and swilling tea early on a Sunday morning in Old Soldiers Tavern, instead of breaking his fast with his wife and children. The Post, which was usually in New-York by Saturday evening latest, had been delayed. So Tonneman waited for the rider, Jacob de Kees, to come through the Broad Way Gate from New England.

Two redcoats, no more than lads, were also patrons in the tavern, having come in minutes before. They sat at a table facing the closed double front door, their wheel locks propped against the table. As they talked, the pair seemed to be drinking tea swill, but all the time they nipped from their ill-concealed flasks. Their laughter blared.

Tonneman smiled. He remembered well when drink and boasting and boisterous laughter were his own nature.

"Tell me again," said one lad, who'd lost his right ear in some encounter or other, now offering his good left one to hear the tale.

His companion, a fellow with a broken nose, took a deep breath to arrest his laughter. "I said the preacher went up to the altar."

"Go on. What came next?" Torn Ear asked eagerly. "Say again. What was it he found on the altar?"

Broken Nose cawed and snuffled with glee. "Alas, he found a horse's *schlange* in his Book of Common Prayer!"

Chapter 2

"**M**ister Tonneman, sir."

Tonneman ran blunt fingers through his short-cropped, sand-colored hair and turned his attention from the callow soldiers. The orphan, Samuel Hankin, stood at his elbow. Not much older than young Moses Tonneman, Hankin supported himself by delivering messages.

The lad did not look like a ragamuffin either. For the most part, his well-tended clothes were gifts of mothers with growing children. Today he wore brown breeches, coat, and cap, which were very presentable. The once-white shirt was another story and needed a wash. Young Sam wandered the streets, continually offering his services. Most assignments awarded him a half penny or, if he was lucky, a penny. The plum of his existence was when First Councillor Nicasius De Sille gave him a shilling to carry a satchel.

"Yes, Samuel." Tonneman selected a half penny from his purse and gave it to the boy.

Samuel pulled his forelock and showed his brown teeth. The speech tumbled out. "Your man with the Post, Jacob de Kees, stands at the Broad Way Gate, sir. They hold him on the charge that he is working on the Sabbath."

Tonneman looked for the sandbox. When he couldn't find it, he spat on the floor, then heaved himself from the chair. The boy backed away. Standing eighteen hands and weighing fifteen stone, heavier by thirty pounds than he'd been when he was Schout of New Amsterdam, Tonneman was an awesome figure. Leaving a penny for his tea, he nodded to young Samuel as he went out.

His horse, Venus, granddaughter to the first one of that name, looked up from her nibbling at his approach. Tonneman led the dun mare and her small cart up the Strand to the Wall.

Just inside the Water Gate and across the road stood Asser Levy's tavern. The sign above the door was the standing figure of a lion. The leader of the Jewish Community in New Amsterdam and New-York was just closing his front door. Seeing Tonneman, Asser Levy smiled.

Although the butcher, who stood as tall as Tonneman, usually gave the impression of strength, today Levy appeared almost frail. Indeed, with his drawn countenance and baggy clothes, the butcher seemed to have lost a full stone since Tonneman last saw him.

Levy's coal-black eyes were deep set in a face darkened permanently from his early days under the Brazilian sun back in the fifties. Today the eyes blazed with some sort of sickness.

"Good morrow, Mister Levy. Do you have a beer for me this fine morning?"

"Ha, you mock me, Mister Tonneman. We both know you haven't had so much as a sip in years. And, while a Christian might get away with serving one beer on a Sunday in this City, a Jew would be crazy to ever attempt it."

"You're many things, Mister Levy, but you're not crazy."

The bearded man bowed to Tonneman.

Tonneman rubbed his nose. Every time he met Asser Levy he wanted to shout at the man for being disdainful of his wife and to beg Levy to take her back into the fold. But of course Tonneman didn't.

Levy asked, "You and your family are well?"

"More than well. Thank you."

The two men regarded each other briefly without words. Then Tonneman tugged on the mare's reins and rode west, not wanting to keep young de Kees waiting longer than he had to. It took five or six paces for Tonneman to realize that something had been different in Levy's manner. Levy, as the other Jews in the City, never acknowledged that Tonneman had a family. What was on that wily one's mind? Tonneman turned round but Levy was no longer in sight.

Wall Street was a short thoroughfare. He was soon at the Broad Way, which was high ground, and stretched north from Fort James, well into the woodlands.

At the Broad Way Gate Tonneman was pleased to see the Sergeant of the Guard was his old friend Frank Nesbitt. The Cockney was the epitome of a King's soldier, albeit in the pay of the Duke of York, smart looking as always in the uniform of the Musketeers— tunic, breeches, and stockings all scarlet. The buttons that ran down the sides of his breeches were black, as were his shoes. In contrast was the white shirt with a wide unadorned collar.

Every private soldier of the Musketeers, and there were one hundred of them at Fortress James, was armed with a musket and a short sword; all wore helmets and corselets, the sleeveless jackets of light metal that reached to the thigh. Slung from each shoulder to hip were leather straps. A half-dozen chargers, metal flasks of powder, hung from each strap. At the bottom of one strap was a leather wallet; at the bottom of the other, the sword.

Frank Nesbitt had been one of the advance party of English soldiers led by Brick-Hill when the English took New Amsterdam in '64. Although Tonneman and Nesbitt had met when each man was on the "other side," they'd come to a shared respect working together in the early days of British rule, when New Amsterdam became New-York and Tonneman was made Sheriff.

So it was with a wink and a nod and an affable promise of tobacco that Tonneman was able to prize young Jacob de Kees from the clutches of the English Army.

Tonneman loaded the three packets and the mail sack into his wagon. "Go home, lad," he told de Kees. "Get some sleep."

"I have to go to church."

Tonneman patted Jacob on the shoulder. The boy definitely looked the worse for wear. His first run with the Post, and Jacob had met up with a Connecticut snow squall and high winds, forcing him to take refuge in a barn, where he'd almost frozen to death.

That and the English at the Gate had to be enough for any man, let alone a tired boy.

With Jacob on his way to church or bed, Tonneman could head homeward with the Post. Pieter Stuyvesant had been one big sanctimonious pain in the arse when it came to religion, but the Director-General of New Amsterdam couldn't have held a candle to these beefeaters and their Sunday laws. In the old days, when they were fifteen hundred people living in the fifteen hundred feet between Pearl Street and the Wall, enforcing the law in New Amsterdam was left to Tonneman and sometimes his Deputy Pos. And to the Night Watch.

Now there were soldiers, a Sheriff and Constables, and the Night Watch, all ready to pounce if one drank or dared work on the Lord's Day. With that in mind, Tonneman walked Venus cautiously but quickly down the Broad Way, intent on following a circuitous route back to where he'd started on Pearl Street, beg pardon, Queen Street, and his house overlooking the East River.

The sun had been up for the good part of two hours; the sky was cloudless. The City was preparing for services at its several houses of worship. As he neared the Fort, he thought back to what he'd heard earlier in the tavern, and was tempted to stop in at the Stone Church and listen to the gossip. Nay, he would keep his nose clean. He would hear all about the pastor and his Sabbath Day surprise soon enough. For New-York, with eight Dutchmen for every two Englishmen or other foreigners, was in many ways still as it had been in spite of its new name and the Treaty of Westminster of '74. That being true, the gossip would come to Tonneman; he wouldn't have to go to it. Tonneman grinned. A horse's *schlange* in the Book of Common Prayer? The prank of schoolboys, from the sound of it.

With none of the work-a-day sounds to interfere, the air had a Sunday kind of noise. Tonneman preferred this country racket. The furious chatter of birds and the clucking, crowing of barnyard creatures, roosters and hens, and the occasional low of a cow. What he didn't like was the snorting oink-oink of the staggering number of pigs that vied with citizens for their place on the streets.

Tonneman turned off the Broad Way onto Stone Street, past Olaff Stevensen van Cortlandt's brewery, closed today, of course, but six days a week bustling with wagons and men.

Because of the dust raised by van Cortlandt's horses and wagons, the New Amsterdamers had demanded that the thoroughfare be paved. And so it was, and so it was named. The first paved street in the village. Now, on those six days, the wagons raised less dust on Stone Street. More noise, but surely less dust.

Tonneman crossed a small bridge, passing the luxurious homes of the wealthy merchants of the City all along the Broad Canal.

There was a feel of spring in the air. Tonneman's pulse quickened as it always did when he neared home. He had no need to flick the reins, for Venus, too, hurried.

He had built the white clapboard house atop the high stone cellar when he first came to the New World with Maria. It now bore little resemblance to its past. Then, he had been offered a plot of land on the Broad Way but had chosen this site on the East River, which was better shielded than the North River from the constant sharp southwesterly winds. Of course, property on the Broad Way was now worth more. But in those days he had not made good money decisions.

As Tonneman's new family grew, he had added two chambers to the house, and enlarged the great chamber. A real kitchen came next, in a chamber complete to itself. The roof had been retiled with red slate eight years earlier. Now it glowed coppery in the glancing sun.

Curly smoke wafted from the chimney serving the kitchen hearth.

Tonneman came through the yards of the other houses, edging past the winter gardens not yet planted with vegetables. A plump coney paused, mouth munching, twitched its long ears at Tonneman, and hopped off to a back lane.

He was aiming for the scullery door when he heard a happy

shriek from the other side of the house. Unmistakably, it was Benjamin, his second-eldest boy. Tonneman smiled. His children's happy sounds were a siren's call. He rounded the building and stopped short. He had a visitor: Captain Lodowyk Pos, Special Deputy to the First Councillor of the City of New-York.

Chapter 3

❦

The figure on the stoop was partially obscured by the limbs of Tonneman children climbing all over their honorary uncle. Nevertheless, when Pieter Tonneman appeared, the man was able to free his right hand and raise it in greeting. The years had treated Pos well. No line marred his agreeable face or his fine classic features. Not a jot of gray or white sullied his black hair and his fine jet beard. And his broad chest was only emphasized by his short stature.

"Begone, children, away," Tonneman commanded. "Uncle Pos is here to see me."

"Papi!"

"It's Papi!"

The children scrambled to their feet and came to attention. Tonneman ruffled each of three heads and planted a kiss on each brow. "Very good, very good. Now have your bread and honey and let your father and Pos talk business." Tonneman pushed wide the lower door for the children and shooed them inside.

The two friends stepped back, each still gripping the other's forearms, perhaps each looking back to a time when they had worked and drank side by side. When Tonneman had been Schout of New Amsterdam and then Sheriff of New-York, Pos had been his Deputy.

"So?" Tonneman said. They sat on the stoop. "To what do I

owe this unexpected visit?" Pos seldom found time to call. And certainly not at this hour of a Sunday. Tonneman knew that this was not a casual visit from an old friend.

Pos rubbed his nose and watched the gulls swoop over the harbor, as if seeking an excuse not to speak right away. Then he said, "The First Councillor wants to see you." He did not look at his friend.

Tonneman raised an eyebrow. "Here I am. The First Councillor can come and look at me all he pleases."

"This is important. He wants you to come to Whitehall right away."

"It's the Lord's Day."

"He's already been to church, and he knows you are a flagrant non-attender." Pos grinned.

"And what if I don't want to go?"

Pos sighed. He finally faced Tonneman. "Do it for me, my friend. We have need of your cooperation. I crave some harmony in my life."

Tonneman let his friend stew awhile before he answered. He was enjoying himself. "What's this all about?"

"He wants to tell you himself."

Tonneman laughed. "Of course, he would. Once an arse-hole, always an arse-hole."

Pos agreed in his heart, but since he now worked for the First Councillor, it would do no good to say such things himself. Still, times had changed. Their little village was now New-York town, and a man had to be flexible and change with the times.

A sudden wail pierced the restful quiet of the morning. Pos's eyes narrowed, his body tensed.

Tonneman placed a restraining hand on his friend's arm. "Heave to, you old warhorse. From the sound of those lungs, that's my youngest, Daniel. He's only two and soured on the world."

Pos laughed and relaxed. "So what do you say?"

"I say, come inside. I need to feed my hungry belly. I've been up since dawn waiting for my new Post Rider. And I'm certain you won't say no to some beer."

Pos winked. "On a Sunday?"

"My lips are sealed."

"What can I do?" Pos said plaintively. "You know me. I would not insult you by refusing your hospitality. But then we must go."

"Of course."

When Tonneman rose to enter his house, he thought he heard his wife's swift footsteps. It was quite likely Racqel had been listening to their conversation. Nothing escaped her keen observation.

In the kitchen, Racqel was pouring milk into a mug as if she'd been there all the while. Benjamin and Daniel rolled a ball of blue yarn at the gray cat, Ashes, trying to get her to wake up and play with them. Ashes, no fool, kept her eyes shut, continuing her snooze in front of the hearth. Now and then her tail flicked.

"A good morrow to you, husband." Racqel handed Tonneman a mug of milk and fixed him with a familiar look.

Tonneman kissed her lightly on the lips. "And a good morrow to you, my curious wife. See what I dragged in from outside." He loved the tilt of her chin even when it revealed faint disapproval at his behavior. What had he done now?

"Papi! Papi!" came from two young mouths. Daniel clapped his hands, gurgled, and scowled. The two eldest offspring, Moses and Maria, thought themselves too old to act like children.

"Moses," Tonneman said, "take care of Venus for me."

"Yes, Papi."

Smiling warmly at Pos, and ignoring her husband's teasing, Racqel stepped over the floor crawlers and the cat. "You are most welcome, Pos. You've been a stranger of late. Sit. You'll have some bread and cheese? Some fresh milk?"

"Thank you, Mistress Tonneman. Bread and cheese."

A pine table holding an earthen pitcher and bowl stood near the scullery door. From a rack on the wall above hung a piece of clean homespun. Tonneman poured water into the bowl and washed his hands with three quick rubs. Pos did not trouble himself to wash.

"Bring the man some beer, wife," Tonneman cried, drying his hands and hooking the cloth on the lower doorknob of the side door. "Before he expires."

"I'll get it, Papi." Maria, his nine-year-old, rushed to the door that led to the scullery porch and Racqel's garden. From a chest just outside, Maria drew a covered earthenstone pitcher, and with great care marched back with it. She set the pitcher on the table.

Tonneman beamed, and removed the cover. "Will you look at my young lady, Pos. Not a drop lost."

Pos grunted. "I admire that trait in anyone."

Maria curtsied. "It was covered, Papi. I couldn't spill it."

Tonneman poured Pos's beer into one of the empty mugs on the cherry wood table he had built himself the first year he and Racqel were together. "I still enjoy doing this," he declared, watching the foam rise. He pushed the mug to his friend. "Your health."

"Nay, yours." Pos quaffed the beer in one swallow.

Tonneman laughed. "Haven't lost your skills, I see."

Pos got to his feet. "Time to go."

"Nonsense. Time for me to have my breakfast." He poured Pos another beer.

Racqel moved to the bowl and washed her hands. "Blessed art Thou, O Lord, Our God, King of the universe, who has sanctified us with his commandments and commanded us to wash our hands." She had already eaten and had washed and prayed before that. This time her prayer had been as her husband's surrogate. He didn't know this; she never told him. Racqel said Tonneman's prayers for him all the time. Till the day came when he would do it for himself.

She wiped her hands on a cloth that had been drying on the door of her beehive oven, then said, "And you must have breakfast too, Pos." She carried the first platter, slices of bread and cheese, to the table. Then Tonneman's particular favorite: a plate of small triangular poppyseed and honey cakes. Though the festival of Purim had been over for almost a week, Racqel and their Jamaica servant, Alice, continued to bake them.

Daniel, seeing his mother's attention was elsewhere, tottered to the fireplace, which was in the Dutch mode, with no standing mantel framing the opening.

This wide, exposed hearth was dangerous territory for a small child; the fire burned flat against the wall under a hood that carried most of the smoke to the chimney. Protecting the fireplace wall and helping to preserve the heat, and also divert it into the room, was a large cast-iron fireback.

Attempting to get a better look at the fire, Daniel dropped to the floor. The child made a happy noise and crawled closer and closer to the flames, pointing his stubby finger. "Pretty."

"No, you don't!" Little mother Maria pounced on her brother and dragged him away from the fire. The child started to squall.

Tonneman took Daniel from Maria and tossed him high in the air.

"Now me," Benjamin insisted. He was all of five years.

Maria, Benjamin, Daniel, Moses. His children's names sang in Tonneman's heart. He liked this custom of the Jews. They named their children to honor their dead. Tonneman's first wife had been Maria and Racqel's first husband had been Benjamin. Moses had been Racqel's father's name and was now the name of the Tonnemans' ten-year-old son. And Daniel? Daniel had been named for the one who bearded the lion in his den, Tonneman's favorite Old Testament character.

Moses, back from stabling Venus, stood near the door to the scullery. The lad wanted to be picked up and tossed, but was too grown-up to say so.

As for Maria, she ignored them all. She didn't have time for such childish things. Taking advantage of Alice's absence at church, she was helping her mother cook.

Racqel set down a platter of potatoes. Before she returned to the hearth, she let her hand graze the nape of her husband's neck.

He grinned at her, placed Daniel on his feet, and gave Benjamin a lift. "Up, up, up, up."

"Higher, Papi. Higher."

"Me, more, Papi!" Daniel howled.

Now Benjamin was back on his feet, and Tonneman sat down to have his meal. "Moses, son. How are you this morning?"

"I am well, Papi."

"Have you had your breakfast?"

"Yes, Papi."

"Have you done your lessons and your chores?"

"Yes, Papi. The sun is up. Half the morning is over."

"He could be confirmed tomorrow," Racqel announced.

The lad made the smallest of frowns. He wasn't happy with some of the lessons his mother taught him, but he would never show disrespect. "I chopped five logs," he bragged.

"That's good," said Tonneman, picking up a hot potato. He bounced it between his weathered hands, cracked it, let the heat explode, then took a hearty bite of its flaky meat. He nodded at Racqel. His family all watched him chew and swallow, waiting. "Boy, Captain Pos is taking me to see the First Councillor in Whitehall. Would you like to come along?"

Moses's face lit up like a dry log in a hot fire. "Oh, yes, Papi, I would."

Racqel smiled. Her boy was becoming a man.

"It's settled, then," Tonneman said. He used the knife on his belt to cut a chunk of cheese.

"We really should be going," Pos protested. He helped himself to a slice of bread, and dribbled a blanket of honey on it.

Tonneman winked at Racqel and ate with great gusto.

But when Tonneman began his second mug of tea, Pos's patience frayed. "We don't want to keep the First Councillor waiting," he said anxiously.

Tonneman burped softly. He'd had enough to eat. He pushed his chair away from the table. It was time to stop making Pos pay for arse-kissing that snake.

THE FIRST COUNCILLOR'S house was but a stone's throw. Pos led the way as Tonneman and his son sauntered after.

An imposing white structure, Whitehall stood at the bottom of Queen Street, the part that was still known as Pearl Street. The structure stood gleaming in the morning light. To Tonneman, no matter its name or its occupant, this would always be Pieter Stuyvesant's Great House.

Pos lifted the lion door-knocker and let it fall once. The door was opened immediately by a tall African, a slave, with high cheek-bones and unsmiling eyes. "The First Councillor is waiting for you, Captain Pos."

The house was a formal affair, as if James, Duke of York, himself were in residence, and not in his home in London. The furniture was dark and imposing. Small mirrors with large frames carved from wood then covered with gold leaf abounded, reflecting Turkey carpets, blue-and-white china vases and plates.

The African, in his fancy satin breeches and teal waistcoat, led them down the hall to a door that was already open. As the rest of the house, this chamber with its silver candelabra and satin upholstered furniture was a great deal more sumptuous than in Stuyvesant's day, eleven years before.

"Well, you took your time." The First Councillor moved away from the window, where he'd been watching the Sabbath-silenced ships crowding the port of New-York.

It was true. Pieter Tonneman, private citizen, was not in a hurry to do the First Councillor's bidding. Especially since the First Councillor was his old nemesis, Nick De Sille.

Chapter 4

SUNDAY, 17 MARCH.
MORNING.

Like the city he governed, Nicasius De Sille had changed much over the years. He'd discarded the greasy lavender hair pomade, though not his lavender perfume, and donned a fashionable wig as easily as he'd discarded his loyalty to the Dutch West India Company and the Motherland and donned English manners.

Truth was, Tonneman thought, Nick's façade was slicker than that. Underneath, the man was still greasy, enough to have been the First Councillor for the previous English Governor, Francis Lovelace, and then, during the short-lived Dutch recapture of the town, for Dutch Governor Captain Anthony Colve. Now that the Dutch had finally ceded the City to the English, Nick cleverly continued in that position under the new English Governor, Edmund Andros.

Oh, how Nick De Sille, flaunting a luxurious mustache fashioned after that worn by the English King, Charles, out-Englished the English.

He had thickened amply in the torso, and though not as tall as Tonneman, he gave off an aura of power; after all, he was Governor Andros's right-hand man. More to the point, he had been a confidant of James's, Duke of York, for years, and he used his office, and the influence that came with it, to the fullest.

After the surrender of Fort Amsterdam in '64, De Sille had

bought three ships. De Sille vessels now carried European goods to Jamaica, exchanged them for African slaves, rum, spices, sugar, coffee, and cacao, and then returned to Europe. De Sille also shipped timber cut from both sides of the Hudson and cotton from the South to Europe.

As De Sille became more and more involved in the affairs of state, his wife, Geertruyd, became mistress of the fleet, in more ways than Nickie cared to admit. Geertruyd De Sille was often at sea, "To keep track of the profits," she liked to say. To get to know the sailors better, canny observers jested.

"And who is that you have with you?" De Sille filled the bowl of his pipe with tobacco from an ivory box, flamed it from a candle on a silver stick, and took a full draw of smoke. Through the cloud of smoke he exhaled, then smiled and answered his own question, "Your Deputy?"

Tonneman's nose wrinkled. It was that same nasty lavender shit Nick had always smoked. Tonneman would forever associate that fucking lavender with his own near-death eleven years before. The scent choked him.

De Sille didn't offer Tonneman a pipe, and for that small blessing Tonneman was grateful. He laid his hand on the shoulder of the boy at his side. "My son, Moses."

"Ah, yes. Are you going to lead us to the Promised Land, boy?"

Moses looked to his father. Tonneman nodded.

"I thought this was the Promised Land, sir."

"Touché, boy. Bloody touché."

The chamber reeked with lavender stink.

"Od's fish, but young Moses favors his mother's people," De Sille proclaimed through billows of smoke.

The boy did indeed resemble Racqel and the other Sephardic Jews of New-York, with his dark hair and olive skin. Only in his startling blue eyes and his sturdy physical frame did he look like his father.

"Moses, this is our First Councillor, Nicasius De Sille," Tonneman said. "Before he became so high and mighty, we were shipmates together on the *Princess of India.*" Tonneman's eyes engaged the First Councillor's as he said with the controlled anger that having burned for the past eleven years had tempered into steel, "Nick and Joost and I, we were the best of friends."

Nick smiled benignly. "Pos, why don't you show young Tonneman here the Governor's maps while his father and I chew on the old days?"

Again Tonneman nodded his permission.

Draping his arm over the boy's shoulder, Pos led Moses out of the chamber. "And I'll tell you all about the time your father and I out-drank the entire crew on the Spanish ship *Santa Rosa.*" His boisterous laughter could be heard even after he closed the door.

Tonneman watched De Sille through half-closed eyes, and waited.

"It's been a bloody while, Tonneman."

"It has."

"I find I have need of your confidential services," De Sille murmured over the pipe stem as he sat behind his handsome desk. He motioned Tonneman to sit. Tonneman chose instead to lean against the wall, next to the window that faced the East River, forcing De Sille to peer up at him.

"What kind of confidential services?" Tonneman frowned. His gaze was on a willow tree across the road. In the old days, when life was simple and he was a mere Sheriff, he'd spent much more time sitting under such a tree, just thinking. But life had become so complicated. He should get back to sitting under his willow tree. What was De Sille up to?

"There's been a vicious crime."

"Yes, I've heard," said Tonneman, guessing. "Privates in the prayer book?"

The First Councillor was taken aback. "God's blood, you know already. It must be all over the City."

"I would think so. You know how fast rumor travels here. Quite amusing."

De Sille flushed red. "It is not bloody funny."

"I would say that it's very funny indeed." Tonneman waved

away the smoke, dismissing De Sille's remarks with the same motion. "What does a ridiculous prank have to do with me?"

"Prank? Prank? Those God damn privates were originally attached to a stallion . . ."

Tonneman couldn't resist. "You're quite correct, not a prank. What we have here is an outrageous bit of horseplay."

The First Councillor grew redder still. "Enough of your bloody jocosity, Tonneman. That stallion was a gift from His Majesty to Governor Andros. This is more than a prank. This is a God damn crime against the King."

Tonneman thought for a moment. Nick had a point. "Your pardon, then, First Councillor. What does the Governor think about all this?"

A sneer began to form on De Sille's face. Thinking better of it, he smiled. "The Governor is unhappy. He sits out on his little Governor's Island in the Bay, suffering the insult."

"So. What does he, or you, make of this horse business? Revenge, do you think? Political?"

"I don't know. The villain wrote, 'Burn in Hell, English,' in the animal's blood, on the stall."

"In English or Dutch?"

De Sille nodded at the pertinence of the question. "English."

"What do you want of me?"

"I hereby commission you, in the name of the King, as special confidential examiner for the Crown."

"Not so fast, Nickie. What would my commission entail?"

"You will investigate this incident—thoroughly. It is important that we track down this traitorous villain and punish him."

"Why me? You've got Sheriff Gibb to take care of such matters. That's his job, let him do it. Gibb doesn't do much anyway."

"I want you, Tonneman. I know you. You'll report to me and only me. The Governor and I don't want this event to reach the ears of the King . . ."

Tonneman made a derisive noise in his throat. "Haven't you heard? Charles has his eyes and ears everywhere."

". . . until I've stretched this bloody villain on the gallows. My worst fear is that one of us will be blamed for it. Do it, Tonneman, as one countryman to another."

"And which country would that be, Nick?"

"The Netherlands, of course."

"Oh, are you a Hollander? Somehow I'd forgotten that. And I dare say, so had you."

Nick measured Tonneman for a moment, then said, "You'll be paid handsomely. And you will have the gratitude of the Governor and the First Councillor."

"Oh, no, you don't, Nickie. You're trying to pull me into some intrigue of yours."

Tonneman looked to the window again. Moses was throwing stones at the willow tree. Looking up at Tonneman, Pos pretended to choke himself. Tonneman tapped a fingernail on one of the leaded pieces of glass in the window. Moses saw him and saw Pos making his face, and grinned. Tonneman held up one finger, indicating he'd be right out. Moses's grin grew broader. "Sorry," Tonneman said to De Sille. "But I'm not the fool you think I am."

"Which fool are you, then, Tonneman?"

Tonneman's mouth tightened. He'd laid his own trap and walked into it. "Touché, Nick."

"Sit down, Tonneman. Hear me out. I'm asking a boon." But De Sille's manner was sharp, not the tone one expected from someone asking for help. Then, De Sille was never one to ask.

"Why should I do anything for you?"

"A pox on you, Tonneman. You bloody well *owe* me."

"I owe you nothing. I do not need you. I do not need your money. I have done well for myself." Tonneman strode to the door and looked back at Nick for a final word. "What's more, in case you haven't noticed, I do not like you."

Nick smiled. "Nor I you. God damn it, you don't have to like me. Take the commission. And contrary to your belief, you've become rich by my sufferance."

"What?" Tonneman was seething. "Ten Eyck and I have worked like slaves to fashion a business. Every license and every permission we received was hard fought."

"Nay." Nick shook his head. "Hard *bought*. Your partner Ten Eyck and I have had an understanding for many years. It's time that you understood too. You owe me, Tonneman. I'm calling in the debt."

"The hell you are," Tonneman shouted. He slammed open the door.

"Be back here by noon," Nicasius De Sille called after him. Then the First Councillor picked up the silver candlestick and refired his lavender tobacco.

Chapter 5

"What do you think?" Pos asked cautiously. His friend's face was a peculiar shade of red.

"I think you are a fine sort of friend for a Dutchman." Tonneman's words were odd, and his expression and manner odder still. He fixed Pos with a hostile stare and gestured at Moses. "Time to go, son."

"Good day, Uncle Pos," Moses said. What could the First Councillor have done to make his father behave in such a surly fashion?

Tonneman was indeed in a temper. The boy followed in his father's angry wake as Tonneman thumped along Queen Street, furious with Pos, De Sille, and most of all his devious partner, Ten Eyck.

The port was still; all the slips were occupied and other ships were in the harbor ready to enter and unload goods. But all waited on the Sabbath.

Only the gulls worked, diving in the East River for fish, their screams taunting, breaking the Sunday silence.

An egret, its long, graceful plumes shimmering, stood on the beach. It scrutinized the feeding gulls.

On a piling near the Ditch, the common name the Dutch had given the Gentlemen's Canal that flowed along Broad Street, a flock of plump pigeons settled and watched Tonneman and son. Tonneman kicked a loose bit of oyster shell into the canal.

Talk was that the Gentlemen's Canal, which flowed from the East River to the third bridge at Beaver Street, would be filled in because the farmers and Indians who set up stands along its banks left the Broad Street roads on either side foul with refuse and stole fire buckets from adjoining homes. Owners of the spacious homes facing the canal complained constantly about the condition of the area. The Common Council was currently debating the issue.

Tonneman knew who would win. New-York was controlled by the people with money, always had been and always would be. That he was finally fortunate enough to be one of them did not alter his dislike of the system. He crossed the canal at Bridge Street, his son lagging behind.

As they neared home, Tonneman spoke to Moses gruffly. "Tell your mother I've gone to Ten Eyck's."

The boy nodded, hesitated. "Papi?"

"It's all right, son. De Sille lied to me. I have to know why."

"About what, Papi?"

"Never mind. Go home."

Tonneman watched his son walk toward their house. The boy was gentle, like his mother, but he was a man for all that, and Tonneman was grateful to God, Christian and Jewish, for his second family. He continued up Queen Street, nodding to Sunday-clad New-Yorkers coming from church. Now that New-York was English, and it looked like for good this time, there was an assortment of different churches in town, even a Catholic one. Well, of course. James, Duke of York, was Catholic, wasn't he?

At Coenties Alley, Tonneman crossed the Strand and entered the narrow alley. The Ten Eycks had lived in this house at the water's edge since Tonneman and Maria first came to New Amsterdam. Over the years, they, too, had added a chamber. Pieter, Tonneman's godchild and namesake, was almost twelve and young Conraet would soon be twenty.

Inheriting his father's skill and dexterity, Conraet was a master silversmith. Indeed, the youth's talent was prodigious and he was continually employed, fulfilling commissions, leaving his father free to manage the concerns of the business firm of Ten Eyck and Tonneman.

Tonneman blew down the alley like an angry storm. The sight of Antje Ten Eyck, sitting on a bench outside her house, eyes closed, taking in the bright sun, stopped him short. A basket of mending was in her lap. Tonneman was devoted to Antje, loved her like a sister. She had been a good friend to Maria, and she had stood beside him, as had Conraet, when he'd fallen in love with Racqel.

Antje opened her eyes. "I could feel it was you. Like a fire. What has got you boiling this time?"

"Where is your husband?"

"On the dock with his smelly pipe. What troubles you?"

"Who said I was troubled?"

Antje set her sewing basket aside and stood, a plain, straw-haired woman with keen eyes and a keener wit.

"This is between him and me," Tonneman mumbled. He skirted the house and found his partner lying on his back on the dock, ankles crossed, smoking like a chimney. Ten Eyck seemed unaware that two gulls were dueling over his hat, which lay behind him.

"Ten Eyck! I have a bone to pick with you." Tonneman strode onto the pier just as one of the feathered creatures was attempting to fly off with Ten Eyck's hat. Startled, the two birds flew at each other, spreading their wings and cawing raucously. Into the East River went Ten Eyck's black Sunday hat, tugged by the ocean tide and buffeted by the wind filling its blue feather sail.

Ten Eyck sat up. "Now see what you've done. My good hat will feed the fishes."

"What I've done? Stand up, Ten Eyck. No, don't stand up, I might knock you down. Damn it, stand up, I said. Tell me like a man that De Sille lies, that you haven't been putting us in his debt all these years."

Conraet Ten Eyck got to his feet. His gaze went past Tonneman to his wife, who stood with arms folded, watching and listening. Antje had that I-told-you-so expression on her face.

Ten Eyck tapped his pipe on his boot and kicked the resulting ash into the water. "Would you condemn a man for greasing an obdurate wheel?"

"Spare me, partner."

"I had to, or we would never have gotten our start."

"Damn it all, Ten Eyck, I would never have allowed it. You knew. That's why you didn't tell me. How could you make us beholden to that scummy snake?" Tonneman's fists clenched. "Now he's got me exactly where he wants me. Right in the palm of his frolicking hand."

"I did what I had to do."

"Isn't that what Judas said?"

Ten Eyck's face paled. "That's a low blow, old friend," he said.

"To equal yours, old friend."

Ten Eyck reached his hand toward Tonneman's shoulder.

Without a word Tonneman turned away. He strode to the end of the pier.

Ten Eyck groaned. He saw that Racqel Tonneman had arrived in haste, a bright green shawl over her shoulders. Antje was explaining.

Racqel left Antje and hurried past Ten Eyck, her dark eyes on her husband's broad back. When she laid her hands on him, she felt every muscle tense. She rested her cheek on his back and half circled him with her arms. "Whatever this is, my love, we will see it through together. These are our friends. They mean us no harm."

Tonneman turned, kissed his wife's sweet mouth in front of all the world.

Antje took her husband by the hand. "Come, Conraet, I will make some tea and we will talk this out. Tonneman? Racqel? Do you hear?"

"I hear, woman," Tonneman blustered. His anger still boiled. He would not be beholden to any man, God help him. Neither De Sille nor Ten Eyck. "I will live with this because I have no choice. But your husband has a lot of explaining to do."

Chapter 6

Tonneman walked back slowly to the house in Whitehall, nodding to all like a man with not a problem in this world. As he climbed the white stoop to the right of the front door, he remembered another time he'd come to the Great House.

August of '64. Dawn. The deep gray sky had been streaked with yellow. A dry, cool wind was blowing. He and Racqel had just met the English officer Brick-Hill in Breukelen. That was when he'd learned for certain that the English intended to invade New Amsterdam. And for the first time he knew that he was in love with Racqel, a Jewish woman. But David Mendoza, Racqel's then brother-in-law, a true arse-hole, had dragged her away and Tonneman had not been able to talk to her for some time after that. Tonneman shook his head, remembering. But in the last analysis, his not being able to talk to Racqel had been his own fault, not Mendoza's.

On that morning, too, he'd come to this house to talk to another arse-hole. But to give him his due, that arse-hole had been a man. Yes, Pieter Stuyvesant had been a man.

Not De Sille. De Sille was a snake, a turncoat who had sold New Amsterdam out to the English to become one of them. It galled Tonneman to think that he must work for the man. But he would. He had to. The debt was there.

The heart-and-crown wrought-iron knocker with the *P.S.* monogram cut out on the backplate below the heart was no longer on the door. Instead, the knocker was the British lion. Beneath it were the initials *N.D.S.* Tonneman's smile was grim. Had Governor Andros not noticed De Sille's conceit?

Once more the door was opened by the same unsmiling slave. Tonneman wouldn't smile either if he had to work for De Sille. Ach, but he did have to. Well, no doubt he wouldn't be smiling for a spell.

Tonneman pushed past the African into De Sille's office.

"Tonneman, you're late." The First Councillor was filling his pipe with more of that lavender shit.

"I'll take the frolicking commission," Tonneman said.

"Of course you will. And should you succeed, I'll pay you fifty pounds."

"One hundred. And that will be the end of it. Whatever you and Ten Eyck have agreed to will be over. The slate will be wiped clean."

De Sille passed at his nose with a cloth from the sleeve of his silver-threaded coat as if he'd just taken snuff and sighed. "Agreed."

Tonneman looked De Sille dead in the eye, pursed his lips like a man ready to spit, then left the way he'd come.

Chapter 7

When Jacob Roome arrived in New Amsterdam in '63 with his wife, Judith, he used a small inheritance from his uncle Willem to purchase the solid wood-and-brick house on the Broad Way Road, just outside the Gate, from the Dutch West India Company. A year later, before the first coming of the English, he opened a store on the ground floor of his home. There he traded furs from the trappers for goods from the ships, and sold the goods to the people in town.

In spite of the vagaries of politics that transformed New Amsterdam to New-York, then to New Orange, and finally back to New-York again, Jacob Roome's life did not change. Six days a week he was in his shop, talking to people, making trades, or selling. On the Lord's Day he went to church.

So, by the grace of God, and the various Majesties of the Netherlands and Britain, his business thrived and he was blessed with three sons, all at once in '66, and cursed at the same time, for the boys' entrance into the world cost him the life of his dear wife.

Roome bought the indenture of a wet nurse, Eliza Davies, an Englishwoman. She and her son, Edward, then ten, were delivered to Roome in the summer of '66, ten days after his three sons were born. Miraculously the infant boys survived. Thank the good Lord.

Eliza Davies, a large, fleshy woman with a splendid disposition, was able to set his tumultuous household on a proper path.

At first her boy Edward was help in the store. Edward Davies could read and write English, soon learned Dutch, and gained an understanding of what made a fine pelt. Roome was so pleased with the boy's progress that he subtracted a penny a week from Eliza's debt.

Nine years passed and Roome's three boys, Jan, Dirk, and Willem, were fat and healthy. They were good boys who did their chores and helped in the store. And business was good.

When Eliza's indenture was over, she chose to stay. Roome viewed her decision as a gift from God. They married and Eliza bore him two lovely daughters, Inga and Ann. The family thrived.

Except for Edward Davies, Eliza's son. The boy was another story. Edward was neither happy nor content. Sometime after his fourteenth birthday he started acting strangely.

First there was all that drinking and carrying on with bad women. This behavior stopped dead after the Dutch retook the City. Then Edward turned to religion with such a fervor that the Roomes were relieved and gladly sent him to Hartford to study with the minister there.

When the English returned once and for all, Edward did too. Announcing that he would not live in a Dutch house, he built himself a hut on Roome's land. With money earned from trapping small game, Edward began to study with the new schoolmaster, Lester Crabtree. Edward had a dream. Someday he would be a minister of God.

This morning, as spring began to make its presence known, Jacob Roome walked through his fine house to his shop, feeling a great benevolence. This was not to last, for strange noises assaulted his ears.

"Yee you, yee you." Had a bird gotten caught within the shop? Jacob rushed to see.

Edward, tall as a tree, was naked as the day he was born, and rolling on the pine floor, rocking back and forth and bleeding from slash wounds on his hands and feet.

Roome reeled at the sight. "What in God's name?"

Edward's hollow face turned. His mad eyes blazed at Roome. He pointed his finger at his stepfather and cried, "Burn, traitor!" The crazed young man then threw the bolt of the front door and stumbled outside, scuffing Mistress Celia Van Ruyven and her daughter, Grace, and shocking them speechless. Off into the woods went the naked madman, snarling like an animal.

Roome prayed that no one would tell the Sheriff about Edward and that the young man would reach the shelter of his hut at the edge of Shellpoint in safety. Shaking his head sadly, he offered his apologies to the Van Ruyven women, who were huddled together under Roome's maple tree.

"Come in, please." Today was not the first manifestation of Edward's unnatural behavior. Last week it had been visions. Edward had stood at Bowling Green howling that New-York was filled with sinners and they must repent, else the town would burn to the ground in hellfire. Roome had been sent for. Somehow he managed to quiet his step-son and take him to his hut.

"That boy is a hazard," Mistress Van Ruyven declared, entering Roome's shop. "I heard he threatened to burn the City."

"God save us." Jane Winder appeared with her sister-in-law Carol Elkins and a male Negro slave who carried a large twig basket.

"He's no longer a boy," Roome told the women. "But I doubt that Edward would do such evil. He thinks he is Elijah the Prophet and sometimes, as today, the Christ."

"Take care, Mister Roome." Celia Van Ruyven shook her finger at the distracted man. "Back in the old country such pretensions would mean death at the stake by fire."

Her daughter Grace nodded vehemently. "Blasphemy. Criminal blasphemy. I understand he is a disciple of Beado."

"Beado?" Jane Winder, a bone-thin Catholic woman, crossed herself.

Catholics made Mistress Van Ruyven uneasy. Weren't they full of pagan ways themselves?

"Who is Beado?" asked Carol Elkins, a recent arrival from Britain. Her eyes were rounded by horror and curiosity.

"An evil man." Celia Van Ruyven shuddered. "Two years ago he claimed he had a holy command to kill, rob, burn, and destroy us. The Dutch council branded him and expelled him from the City. Now he howls at the full moon and the English do nothing about him."

Jane Winder fanned herself with a nose cloth. "Oh, my, my, my."

"Nonsense," Roome said. "Old wives' tales."

Mistress Van Ruyven cupped her right hand beside her lips and motioned all those in the shop closer. "Of course, you know, Mister Roome, about the blasphemy in the prayer book . . ."

"Say no more," Mistress Winder demanded. "We have all heard the shameful story, and proper women should not discuss it."

Mistress Van Ruyven glared at Mistress Winder. She shook her head firmly. "Francis Beado. He's the villain, I'm certain. They should hang him high."

"There was blood everywhere," Mistress Winder continued, disobeying her own restraints. "My husband knows the cousin of the mother of the Watch who went into the stable. Covered with blood."

Mistress Van Ruyven smiled diabolically at Mistress Winder. "I thought we weren't going to discuss it." She turned away from Mistress Winder and, prodding her daughter, went about the shop, seeing what she had need of that day.

Thus, Edward Davies's horrifying behavior was put aside for conversation more compatible to commerce. But Jacob Roome had difficulty keeping his mind on his business. All he could think of was that Sunday morning when the monstrous deed happened in the First Councillor's stable.

That day Edward had appeared in a frightful state as the Roomes were returning from church. His clothing was sodden with blood.

Chapter 8

Sheriff Thomas Gibb was napping in a chair in his office at City Hall. He'd just come from home and needed a bit of rest. He never got any from his wife and his six unmarried daughters.

Closer to seven feet than to six, and wide of shoulder, Gibb was gaunt of body and face. There wasn't a day when the Sheriff's back and feet didn't ache. He'd just eased his big feet out of his tight boots, when his Deputy, Eric Nessel-Vogel, came bursting in without so much as a knock.

Gibb took an unhappy look at his Deputy, then closed his eyes. "If it's trouble, Nessel-Vogel, I don't want to hear it."

"It's trouble. Big trouble."

"Who with?"

"Which do you want first, the rough or the smooth?"

Gibb sighed. No day of rest for him. "The rough."

"Edward Davies is running around naked, claiming to be the Christ."

Gibb, eyes still closed, raised his right hand and beckoned for more.

"That would fall under the rule about mutinous words and mutinous actions," Nessel-Vogel went on. "Not to mention sacrilege."

Gibb's fingers wiggled.

41

"At least five people have stopped me to say that the killing of the horse is a blasphemous ritual slaughter by the Jews. Three claim it was for blood for their Passover."

Gibb nodded. "I wouldn't put it past them. Except for Passover they need Christian blood not horse blood."

"Five others are certain that Francis Beado killed the horse and put the thing in the church."

Gibb's fingers wiggled again.

"Jan Keyser and Henry Backer."

"Whenever I turn around," the Sheriff groaned, "it's more trouble-making Dutchmen." Gibb was of the school who believed the Dutch required a regular thrashing so they would remember their humble station in life.

Nessel-Vogel, a native of Hesse, didn't react, though he knew that to Gibb a Netherlander and a German were all the same, which meant not as good as an Englishman. In sharp contrast to the Sheriff, the Deputy stood only several inches over five feet; he was so muscular, he didn't appear to have a neck. The muscles went from his shoulders to his head. Nothing and nobody distressed Nessel-Vogel. "You know that piece of land at Devil's Boulder, this side of Keyser's new tannery, which Backer's family lost when the Dutch were here and were just given back?"

Gibb hadn't opened his eyes. "So?"

"There's a dead cow."

"So?"

"Backer says it was on his land and he caught Keyser and his sons pulling it out of a stream."

"And?"

"Keyser says it was on *his* land, and he didn't kill the animal. Says he found it dead and he's entitled to the meat and the hide."

Gibb wiggled his toes. He opened his eyes and squinted at Nessel-Vogel. "Fine them each one beaver skin for fighting on the Lord's Day and forget about it. Damn. My back is going to be the death of me."

Disdainful, because the Sheriff never paid attention, Nessel-Vogel shook his head. "This happened today, not yesterday."

"Tell them to forget about it and leave me alone."

"They don't want to forget about it. And they refuse to deal with me. Each insists that you must be there."

Gibb had limp white-blond hair that straggled down his back. As he leaned forward to pull his boots on, his hair fell in front of his eyes. He flipped it behind him. The boots were a long reach and brought his aching back to mind. "There's nothing for it, then. I'll go out there. You go to Davies's hut. If you find Davies and Beado together and I convince Keyser and Backer to butcher that cow, we'll both be eating beef tonight."

"Of course," Nessel-Vogel muttered. "And pigs can fly."

Chapter 9

MONDAY, 18 MARCH.
MIDMORNING.

Since his back wasn't up to sitting a horse even for a short distance, Gibb decided to walk to Devil's Boulder, called so because of its immense size and depth. The rock's "roots" went so deep, 'twas said they went straight to Hell.

The lower section of the Broad Way was paved with cobbles now, and the town was beginning to look like an English village. The Dutch had the strange custom of building their homes out sideways, so they could load things in and out from the third floor through large side windows. A good English house faced front to the street.

Gibb hadn't been on his way for long, when a wagon, pulled by an old dun mare, went barreling past. "Halt," Gibb shouted to the driver. He chased after the vehicle, his back complaining with every step.

The driver pulled up. Dirt from the dusty road flew in the Sheriff's face. "What is it, Gibb?"

"That's all I need," said Gibb. "Another Dutchman to make my day right."

"And a good morning to you too, Sheriff Gibb." Tonneman was amused. He couldn't help but remember when he was Sheriff and he was kept hopping, chasing car-men in town.

"Tonneman, you of all people should know better." Gibb recited the rule. "Horses in the City are to be led—"

"Except on the Broad Way. There they can ride . . . slowly. I know the book, Gibb. I helped write it."

"If you know the damn rules, Dutchman, why can't you obey them?" When Tonneman didn't answer, Gibb said, "I ought to lock you up."

"It's not a jail offense."

"I'll fine you, then, you Dutch bastard."

"Mind your mouth. I could break your neck. Now, *that's* a jail offense."

Gibb knew he had said too much and all the wrong things. "Forget what I said. I meant naught."

"Forgotten," said Tonneman, forgetting nothing.

"But I'll have to fine you. That's the law."

"So it is."

A stab of pain coursed along Gibb's back. He leaned against Tonneman's wagon. "And I need this wagon to take me where I'm going."

"Have you lost your mind?"

"Be a good fellow, Tonneman. The word is that Francis Beado is the one who killed the King's horse Sunday night."

"Oh?" *There* was a candidate to sup with the Devil. Francis Beado. In December of '73, Beado, a Londoner, had been sentenced by the Dutch Provincial Council at Fort Willem Hendrick, as the Dutch had called Fort James, for coming to New Netherland without consent in order to disturb the good people thereof. Beado claimed to have a sacred commission empowering him, by fire and sword— his very words—to attack, rob, burn, and destroy the inhabitants. The Dutch had arrested him, staked him, branded his back with a red-hot iron, and banished him.

"And he was seen out near Devil's Boulder," Gibb lied. If he couldn't stretch his back soon, he would start screaming. "I wouldn't trouble you, but our wagon's got a broken axle," he lied again. "And you're riding in that direction anyway."

"If that's the case, get in." Tonneman was a practical man. If Mad Beado was his man, Tonneman would be rid of De Sille and that vile commission more easily than he could ever hope. And he *was* riding in that direction anyway.

"You mean it?" Gibb said. He climbed in painfully, happily surprised, and pleased at some relief. Pushing aside the bags of salt in the wagon, he attempted to lie flat, but his feet hung out the back.

"Comfortable, Gibb?" Tonneman called out. He urged the old dun mare Venus into a run.

"Halt and be recognized," cried one of the two red-clad Musketeers guarding the Broad Way Gate.

Painful as it was, Gibb sat up. "It's all right," the Sheriff shouted. "It's me."

The guards spat and shook their heads at the predictable fribbling antics of New-York's Sheriff.

When they reached Devil's Boulder, Henry Backer, Jan Keyser, and Keyser's three sons were standing over a cow carcass and yelling loud enough to make it rain. Behind them was an ass hitched to a high-sided cart, open at the back.

"Have any of you seen Mad Francis Beado?" Gibb asked immediately, to protect the lie he'd told Tonneman.

The elder Keyser and Backer shook their heads. The three boys stood silent, their eyes on the ground.

"This beef is mine," Keyser said, strident as always. "A pleasant morning, Tonneman."

"Mister Tonneman," young Backer said respectfully. Tonneman raised his hand in greeting. The boy and Tonneman shared a history together. When he was Schout of New Amsterdam, Tonneman had saved this boy from drowning in the East River.

Backer nodded to Gibb. "Sheriff."

Gibb got down off the cart and walked to the carcass. Bending meant more cruel pain, but he did so. He ran his fingers across the four-footer's hide and sniffed the air. "Killed early this morning, I would think."

"True enough," said Keyser. "But if I don't get her skinned and dressed, she'll start rotting."

Backer shook his head. "She's not yours to skin. First one government takes my land away, then another gives it back. Governments can do that. But things will have to come to a bad pass when I allow the likes of you, Jan Keyser, to add to my burden."

Gibb made an effort to rise from his awkward crouch. Finally he had to accept young Backer's hand. The Sheriff limped the few paces to the Devil's Boulder at the edge of the road and looked back at the dead cow. "It's Backer's land, it's Backer's cow."

"What?" From the sound of Keyser's outraged cry one would have thought he'd been branded with a hot iron.

Tonneman grinned. It was the same judgment he would have made. And he was glad it was Gibb and not he who had to take the brunt of Keyser's ire.

"Backer's land is bounded on the north by the Devil's Boulder," Gibb said. "I was there with Backer the day Conraet Ten Eyck surveyed the land and Ephraim Herman, clerk of the City court, signed the deed."

"Shit and piss," Keyser shouted, kicking the dead cow.

"Watch what you're doing, Keyser, that's my animal." Young Backer didn't hide his air of triumph.

Keyser made a rude gesture with his hand at his crotch and stamped off. The three boys lifted their eyes from the ground, looked at each other, scratched, got in the cart, and drove after their father.

Tonneman, who'd been sitting on his wagon all this time, climbed down and knelt next to the cow. Her throat had been cut and her head was twisted unnaturally to one side. He lifted the head and set it down again. He hefted her teats. He said, "This heifer's barely a year old." Like Gibb, he ran his fingers across the animal's skin. But then he felt the stone-strewn ground for several feet around. "Her hide's wet. The ground's dry."

Henry Backer looked toward the stream about ten feet west of them just into the woods. "That's where they found her. In the water."

Tonneman nodded. "Her throat's been cut and her neck is broken." What Tonneman wasn't saying was that the throat cut had been made by a very sharp knife. One didn't have to be a wizard to

47

see that. He knew for a fact that many butchers were careless about their blades.

On the other hand, by their own law, Jewish butchers had to use a knife that was twice as long as the width of the animal's throat, and without the slightest nick in it.

This severing was so precise, so fine, Tonneman was certain that if it hadn't been performed by a surgeon, it was done by a Jewish butcher.

Chapter 10

For the present, Tonneman was not inclined to share his thinking with the Sheriff. The thought had entered his mind that there might just be a connection between the two cuttings, horse and cow. He was cursed if he knew what the connection was. But there might just be one.

Gibb climbed back into the wagon, alongside Tonneman on the driver's box. By some miracle he was no longer in pain. In fact, the Sheriff seemed smug and righteous.

"What now, boss?" Tonneman asked.

Gibb eyed Tonneman with suspicion. He knew that the Dutchman was pulling his leg. "Nessel-Vogel went looking for Beado and Edward Davies at Davies's hut south of Shellpoint. You know where it is?"

Tonneman nodded and flicked the reins for Venus to go. He had invested his time in this already. He would play it out. Carl Luria would have to wait a bit longer for his salt.

The road to Shellpoint was circuitous. Up hill and down, twisting past jutting rock formations, cutting through deep forest and salt marshes. The route had once been an Indian warpath; it had been and still was part of the Indian trail established years before, to bring furs down from the north. Water from underground streams bubbled along the way. The streams and Shellpoint itself were treasure troves of blue crabs, turtles, and striped bass. But the streams were growing narrower every year as the wagon tracks grew wider. Soon enough the rabbit, squirrel, deer, beaver, bear, and red fox would find other places to play.

But for now thick clumps of maples, hickories, and red oaks were home to the animals and the partridge and quail. And the salt marshes were a haven for waterfowl, ducks, egrets, herons, and king-fishers.

On the far side of the huge pond, at the verge of the salt marsh, one could see the beginnings of a small community. Here the free Africans lived. Smoke puffed from chimneys and children's voices carried across the water.

Davies's hut sat on the near side. As Tonneman and Gibb came within sight of it, Nessel-Vogel burst from a thick clump of poplar off the trail. Tonneman reined Venus to a stop.

"Eric," Gibb called. "Did you find him?"

"No. He led me a merry chase, him naked as a plucked chicken. Disappeared into the salt marshes."

"Did you search the hut?"

Tonneman was listening, but his attention was on the road ahead, which seemed barely passable.

"No, sir. I went after him."

Gibb motioned to Tonneman to move the wagon forward. Nessel-Vogel led the way.

"He was doing some kind of Indian dance," Nessel-Vogel continued. "In front of his house. When he spied me, he ran into the woods. And I followed."

The woods grew so dense at this point, they nearly overpowered the road. But by ducking overhanging branches and waiting several times while Nessel-Vogel cleared the trail of rocks and forest-strewn litter, Tonneman could at last see, not the hut so much, but the smoke belching erratic and black from the wood chimney.

After a few more minutes of cautious driving, they finally arrived at the falling-down structure. A strange noise came from within.

"There's someone inside," said Tonneman.

"The loon must have doubled back on you, Nessel-Vogel." Gibb climbed out of the wagon, his right hand cradling the small of his back.

Tonneman jumped down and tied Venus to a hickory. She jerked her head at him, found a patch of grass within reach, and nibbled contentedly.

Rubbing the mare's nose, Tonneman reached into the wagon for an old friend. Oak cudgel in hand, he caught up with the two lawmen just as they threw open the hut door. Smoke poured out.

Gibb stepped back. "Damn it, Nessel-Vogel, get up on the roof. See what's blocking that chimney."

"All right."

Tonneman marveled at Gibb's ridiculous order and his Deputy's compliance. And they called *Davies* loony. He said, "Perhaps we should wait till we find out—"

The sound of coughing and choking stopped all conversation. Tonneman and Gibb passed a quick look, one to the other. In silent agreement they dashed into the smoky hut. Chance was with them. Only a few paces inside, a figure lay on the dirt floor.

THE SEARCHER was sorely disappointed. He had hoped to rid himself of both demons with one fell stroke. Ah, but though the mills of God ground slowly, they ground exceeding small. He understood his mission; soon enough he would destroy those set against God.

ANOTHER PAIR of eyes watched with great enjoyment at the sight of white men hurting each other.

BY THIS TIME Nessel-Vogel was high enough in a nearby oak to lower himself from an overhanging branch onto the flat roof of the falling-down house.

A bucket of water stood at the side of the hut. After Gibb and

Tonneman had dragged the choking man outside, Gibb grabbed the bucket and ran inside again. Glowing embers led him to the source of the trouble. He doused the coals and ran back out, coughing. Smoke made tears run down his face.

Mad Francis Beado lay on the ground, retching. His clothing was stiff with a dark brown stain. Tonneman leaned closer. The stain had to be blood. Tonneman sniffed. Beado stank of piss.

Gripping the neck of Beado's coat, Gibb shook him. "I should have let you die, you lump of shit."

Tonneman folded his arms. So much for De Sille's commission. Beado must be the horse killer.

From the roof, Nessel-Vogel gave a shout. Tonneman and Gibb looked up. Smoke coursed from chimney to sky.

Gibb released Beado, who dropped to the ground. Shading his eyes with both hands, Gibb shouted, "What was it? A bird?"

Nessel-Vogel ran the short length of the roof, then leaped to the overhanging branch he'd come by. Half sliding, half falling, he dropped to the ground. The Deputy's face was black with soot. Smiling like a demon, he lumbered toward them.

Beado stopped vomiting and sat up. Gibb put a large foot on the madman's chest and pushed him back down. "Stay, you murderer," the Sheriff ordered as if talking to a dog. "You're going to hang."

Seized with spasms of coughing, Beado's body twisted under Gibb's foot.

Nessel-Vogel pulled a mass of charred, sooty reddish colored rags from his coat pocket. "The chimney was full of these."

"Birds building a nest," Gibb said.

Tonneman shook his head. No bird ever tore those long strips. "More likely human engineering."

Gibb rolled his shoulders to ease his back. His boot was still on Beado's chest. Beado groaned. "Quiet," the Sheriff snarled. "You think someone was trying to kill this worthless vermin?"

Tonneman wiped his hands on his breeches. "Or Davies. This is Davies's hut."

"What murder?" Beado gasped, tried to sit up. His wild eyes

went from man to man. "I have not been in the City. I am forbidden to enter."

Gibb pushed with his foot; down went Beado, howling. "The King's horse," Gibb growled. "You murdered the King's horse and stuffed its privates into the prayer book at the church."

"Never," Beado swore fervently. "Never would I lift my hand against my lawful sovereign, or blaspheme my Lord God." Beado's tone was so sure, a surprised Gibb removed his boot and allowed the madman to sit up.

Tonneman studied Beado. His black hair hung in greasy strings to his shoulders. He was filthy, unshaven, his eyes bloodshot; he seemed more a creature of the underworld than of God's green earth. Tonneman's instincts told him the man was telling the truth. But he wanted proof.

"Prove it, Beado," Gibb demanded, echoing Tonneman's thought.

Beado leaped to his feet and let go a crazed-animal laugh that made the gulls cry out. He thrust both arms into the air and shouted, "Come dance with me." With these words he seized Tonneman by the shoulders and pushed him around in a maniacal caper.

Tonneman was amazed at the puny fellow's strength. He brushed Beado's arms away. "Name your proof, Beado."

Mad Beado pointed a gnarled finger at Tonneman. "Ask the Christ killer," he cried. "Ask the Jew—Mendoza."

Chapter 11

The wash was done and the wet clothes hung on the line out back. Racqel could take a breath and reflect a bit. Moses was outside with his books. Racqel no longer sat with the boy when he studied. Her son's intelligence was sharp and he had grown way beyond her ability to instruct. He needed a learned man, a teacher. Schoolmaster Lester Crabtree was fine for secular matters. But the teacher to instruct her son on how to be a man could be found only in the Jewish Community. To which she no longer belonged.

Daniel was sleeping, with Maria hovering over him. Alice, the free Jamaica hireling who worked every day but Sunday, was cutting carrots into the stew.

Racqel longed for a new house. This one was bounded by the Old Soldiers Tavern on one side and the City Hall and Jail on the other. But Tonneman was content here. Truth to say, it wasn't just this house that troubled her. It was her place in life. The money Tonneman now had was no solace. She wanted to be accepted again by her people.

Racqel sighed. "Maria, I have to go outside. See that the stew doesn't burn and watch the baby." She spoke to the child, but the words were meant for Alice.

"Yes, Mutti." The little girl was overjoyed to be little mother.

The tiny coffee-colored woman nodded and continued to grind pepper into the simmering stew.

"Don't add any water to the stew and don't fret Daniel too much."

"Yes, Mutti."

Racqel Pereira Mendoza Tonneman was an imposing woman, taller than most. Years and childbearing had rounded her breasts and hips, but she was still trim. Her blue dress was of the latest fashion: a close-fitting boned bodice that came to a deep point in front, elongating her already long waist. Her black hair curled naturally in ringlets and was covered with a small lace-trimmed cap of white muslin. Over her shoulders she wore a matching muslin and lace collar. Her long full skirt was divided in front, showing an embroidered underskirt.

Taking a cotton bag in which she carried her undergarments, Racqel wrapped her green wool shawl about her head and shoulders and left the house through the scullery door. She went past her hanging wash, through the garden, where Moses, sitting on a bench, was intent on his work. She patted her son's cheek as she went by. He grinned at her and bent once again to his study.

Racqel slipped behind the horse shed. She hurried down a path which she'd created herself by her secret walks over the years. The path took her back to Queen Street. She looked about, crossed the road, then walked quickly to Coenties Alley.

At the end of the alley, instead of going into the Ten Eyck house, she went into the woods, almost to the East River's edge. There Ten Eyck had built her a hut, a shed, actually. It was hidden from view by the overgrowth. This was the Ten Eycks' secret with Racqel. No one else knew about it. Not even Tonneman.

Next to the shed stood a rain barrel, covered with cheesecloth. The lightweight cotton protected against dirt but let the pure rainwater in. Racqel brushed some leaves from the cloth and entered the shed.

It was perhaps the only shed in all of New-York that had a wood floor rather than dirt. On the floor there was always dry wood waiting for her and large clay jars, a tin tub, and a slat bench.

Shelves held jars of soap, candles, a tinderbox, scissors, a comb and brush, and clean drying cloths. Racqel's private *mikvah* wasn't a splendid affair, nor had it been constructed under rabbinical supervision, but since she'd been denied the Community's own, her makeshift bath had to serve.

Jewish law prescribed that the water in the bath be alive, emanating from a natural source: rain, snow, ice. The *mikvah* was a pillar of Jewish life. To be a viable place, a town had to have a *mikvah*, a rabbi, and a physician. New-York had all of these, but the *mikvah* and Rabbi Alonzo Gomez had been denied Racqel. And she'd never had occasion to use the services of the physician, Solomon Navarro.

A new *mikvah* for the community had been built since her banishment. But Racqel knew it stood quite close to Asser Levy's fine house on Wall Street.

The outside of the new *mikvah* was made of fine Spanish yellow brick. She knew from her friend Rebecca Da Costa, the only Jewish woman who still talked to her, that the interior walls were covered with blue tile, also from Spain. It was a spare place made up of three chambers: a bath for the men and a bath for the women, where Jewish attendants served to aid the bathers. The African men who took care of the water and the fire entered only into the third, rear chamber. Here water was fed to the front chambers. Silver candelabra illuminated the two small rooms leading to the baths.

The women's ritual bath in New-York was a place where Hebrew women of the town came to make themselves pure and then to meet and talk, something Israelite women had done for centuries. The *mikvah* and all its joys had been denied Racqel since the day she married the Dutchman.

Racqel sighed for what was not and took up the tinderbox. Today was the twelfth day. She hadn't bled for the last seven. Today she would immerse herself and tonight she and Tonneman could be together. The years had not dulled her desire for him nor his for her.

She lit the fire, then went outside and relieved herself. Next, she filled her clay jars with fresh rainwater from the barrel. The shed was still far from warm, but she didn't like being away from her home for too long. She removed her wedding band and earrings, brushed her teeth, and cut her nails.

Then she bathed. Somehow she managed to submerge herself completely, even to the last strand of hair. The river would have been better for complete immersion, but it was too cold and too public. After her first ducking Racqel said the blessing, then submerged herself again.

HAVING CLEANSED and dried her body, having examined it thoroughly for any traces of dirt or stray hairs, Racqel dressed.

She was sitting on the bench, combing her hair, when she heard running footsteps. Someone was coming down to the water. Cautiously, she peeked out of her shed. The man stopped barely ten feet from her. Through the birch saplings near the river's edge, she could see him, crouched low. He dropped the sack he was carrying and slipped into the bushes. Seconds later she heard crackling noises, then saw him drag a small boat to the verge of the river. He tossed his sack into the boat and peered about. She held her breath.

When he stood, Racqel saw the man was tall, much taller than she, taller even than Tonneman. He seemed skin and bones under the red blanket he had wrapped about him. His face was drawn, but he had full lips, and small black eyes. Suddenly he stumbled. In his attempt to keep himself steady he dropped the blanket. Underneath he was stark naked. "Damn," he said like an Englishman, redraped himself, pushed the boat into the water, and rowed toward Breukelen.

Chapter 12

The strange behavior of the man in the boat, while intriguing, did not concern Racqel as much as the care of her children. She'd already spent too much time away from them. Murmuring a thank-you to God for her family, she rushed her comb through her hair and hurried home.

Maria was waiting for her outside, pacing, much as Racqel had often seen Tonneman pace. At the sight of her daughter, fear pinched Racqel's heart. "Is Daniel all right?" she asked, hurrying forward.

"Yes, Mutti. A boy brought this for you." Maria handed her mother a square of thick paper.

"Food, I want food," Tonneman bellowed, coming around from the garden and marching into the house.

Moses, just arriving from Queen Street on his way home from his lesson with Master Crabtree, joined in. "Food, food, food," the Tonneman men chanted.

Racqel glanced at the missive, tucked it into the sleeve of her dress, put her arm about Maria, and followed her men.

Tonneman, done with his speedy ablutions, was shaking his hands dry. His daughter ran to him and handed him the cloth from the hook. Tonneman wiped his hands and hung the cloth on the lower knob of the scullery door. He then bussed his daughter noisily. "That's my good girl."

The sun poured through the window, streaking the floor where Daniel lay fast asleep on his stomach on a blanket. "Food, food, food," said Benjamin.

"A good jest knows when to end," his father admonished.

"Yes, Papi."

"I smell bread," Tonneman said, "but I also smell salt cod." He looked to Alice at the fireplace, stirring the pot. The Jamaica woman giggled.

"That's for tonight," Racqel told him. "Salt cod and cheese and apples or pears from the cellar. Now I can give you stew. Alice, you can take the stew off the fire and feed the children."

Tonneman expelled a large breath of air. "Pity. I esteem salt cod."

"One does not esteem cod, husband."

"I do. I love my wife and I esteem my cod." He pulled her to his lap and kissed her.

"Tonneman," she protested mildly. "The children."

He nuzzled her neck, relishing the feathery touch of her hair in his face. "This is how we made them."

Slapping her husband's arm, she pushed herself up and away from him.

Tonneman grinned. "Very well, then. If I can't have you or my cod, I want my stew."

"I like that," she said with mock severity.

"So do I. My stew, woman."

"Have you had a good day thus far?"

"If one can count a day with Sheriff Gibb in it good, yes. But first I want to talk about yesterday."

Racqel was pleased. She had been waiting for him to share his thoughts.

After the to-do at the Ten Eycks' the day before, her husband had not spoken ten words to her. Tonneman had smoked pipe after pipe and stared into the fire, oblivious even of their children. This morning he had gone out without saying a word or having his break-fast.

"All these years we've been taking every contract we could from the City."

"Yes."

"I thought we were a cut above all the others and didn't need to cheat or buy our way. I believed we did well because of quick thinking, energy, and sweat. But it appears that Ten Eyck has been slipping a little *baksheesh* to De Sille all along."

Racqel took in a breath. She knew about such things from her years with the Mendoza family. She'd assumed only the Jews had to pay to do business in New-York. But then again, to the Gentiles, this was a Jewish family. "And that's why you had words with Conraet?"

"Yes." Tonneman's face was grim. "Nick's using that as a lever to get me to do a job for him."

"Is it dangerous?" she asked quietly.

Tonneman waved his hand. "No. Merely a nuisance. Somebody slaughtered the Governor's prize horse on Sunday."

"I know. I heard about it from some women who passed as Alice and I were doing the wash. Is it true what happened at the church?"

Tonneman nodded.

"How horrible."

Tonneman frowned. "De Sille wants me to find the miscreant. Today, as I was delivering salt to Carl Luria, Gibb stopped me, cited me the ordinance on horses being led in the City, and threatened to jail and fine me. Then he involved me with a triviality about a dead cow. Jan Keyser and Henry Backer were arguing about whose land it was on. The heifer had been in the water and someone had broken her neck and cut her throat."

"Perhaps she fell and broke her neck and then her throat was cut on a rock."

Tonneman took a hard look at his wife. She was right. Why was he surprised? She thought like a man. But it was unlikely; he dis-missed it. "At first I thought the cow had broken its neck and the blood was from a bone shard or"—he nodded to his wife—"a sharp rock, but then I saw that it was a clean blade slice. I wondered if perhaps someone had meant to butcher the animal and was called away. Then I realized that what was most significant was the throat cut. The knife that made that wound was sharp, very sharp. I'll wager there wasn't a nick in it."

Racqel's eyes narrowed.

"What?" Tonneman demanded.

Racqel shook her head. "Something, not yet clear to me. Let me think on it."

He stood and began to pace the chamber. "I don't have to think on it. That's the kind of throat-cutting surgeons do. Or Jewish butchers."

Racqel sighed. "Don't the Jews in New-York have enough problems without you blaming them for slaying a cow?"

"Why are you taking up for them? They've all but abandoned you."

"I am still a Jew, and that is the A and the Zed of it."

"Whatever you say, wife." Tonneman had been hearing this for years.

Racqel wrinkled her nose at him. "Whose land was the cow on?"

"Backer's."

"Then I'm certain Keyser wasn't very happy." She opened the door of the oven, slipped the wooden paddle under the three loaves, and brought them out, setting them on the side of the sink to cool.

Tonneman closed the oven door and bent to sniff the bread. "When is that simpleton ever happy? But that wasn't the end of the day's nonsense. Next Gibb roped me into helping him capture Mad Beado at Davies's hut south of the Shellpoint."

"Davies?"

"Eliza Roome's lunatic boy, Edward. Jacob Roome's step-son."

"Ach, him." Oh, my, Racqel thought. That's who I saw naked getting into the boat. Edward Davies. She pursed her lips. "There's more to it than that, husband. Nobody makes you do what you don't want to do."

Tonneman grinned broadly. "I thought it was done when we

caught Beado. We would nail the madman for the horse killing and I'd be done with De Sille and such folly. But Beado claims an alibi." Tonneman peered about for his pipe.

"Yes? Yes? Where are you going?"

Tonneman wandered into the great chamber. On the painted eight-cornered table he found a pipe and his tobacco next to the extravagantly carved silver box the Ten Eycks had given them as a wedding gift. He considered the box and the Ten Eycks for a moment, then ambled back into the kitchen.

"So who was Beado's alibi?" Racqel asked.

"David Mendoza."

Racqel pulled a face at the mention of her former brother-in-law, her first husband's brother.

"You think there's a connection between the two animals getting slaughtered, don't you?"

Tonneman drew his wife to him. She was beautiful and wise, all right. Wiser than most men. "Yes, I do," he whispered into her fragrant hair. "But I didn't say so to Gibb." Laughing, he shook his head. "Our honorable Sheriff screamed bloody murder when I made him and his Deputy and his prisoner ride along when I delivered salt to Carl Luria at his farm before turning back to deliver Beado to the jail." Tonneman packed his pipe with tobacco and lit it from the hearth.

"It sounds as if today began a bit better than yesterday."

"Tolerable. Gibb, that outrageous man, still demanded his fine. Ten shillings."

"Did you pay it?"

Tonneman laughed. "Not likely. I told him to collect it from First Councillor De Sille."

Chapter 13

While her husband was changing his clothes in their bedchamber, Racqel debated with herself. She fingered the paper in her left sleeve but did not take it out to read. It was an event for her to receive a letter addressed exclusively to her. The last had been from Cousin Sophia in Amsterdam. But this missive wasn't from Cousin Sophia. She touched the paper and almost brought it out. No. She would savor the edge of her delightful unknown for a while longer.

The man in the boat could be important, but Racqel had never told Tonneman about her *mikvah* and now was not the time.

A wry smile crossed her lips. When had she become a woman who kept secrets? Curiously, she took pride in this, sinful though it might have been.

When Tonneman came into the great chamber, he found his wife seated in the green velvet chair that had come from London, using his knife to cut the pages of a thin volume, *The Tales of King Arthur*.

Racqel had heard of Sir Thomas Malory's tales about the English King Arthur but had never read any of them. Here her cousin Sophia had sent the book to her more than six months before, along with the European balms and tonics Racqel had requested, and she'd hardly done more than lift the cover.

"What?" said Tonneman. "Reading in the middle of the day?"

"There's something I must tell you." Setting the book aside, she brushed the paper lint from her lap.

"I wish you wouldn't use my knife."

"I didn't dull it, I didn't break it." Racqel wiped the knife on her skirt and slipped it into the leather sheath at his waist.

"Help me with my neck cloth."

"You look quite handsome."

Tonneman grunted.

"I insist. You are a handsome lad, Pieter Tonneman." She walked around Tonneman, tilting her head this way and that.

Tonneman sighed. He was not one for fancy clothes. Usually he dressed the simple sailor he still was deep down, wealth or no. Today he had dressed like the owner of a ship. For he was that too.

He had a theory. Out in the country, farmers judged a man not by his clothes but by his land or the work he did with his hands. In cities, especially this City, clothes were the gauge. And if clothes were the measure of the man, and brought, if not respect, then attention, perhaps they would bring answers. With that in mind, he'd donned his finest clothes.

His coat, wine velvet, which fit snug across his wide shoulders, was open and loose to just below the knee, and with back and side vents that came to the hips. Large horizontal pockets were set about two inches from the bottom. The sleeves came to his elbows with deep turned-back buff cuffs. His breeches were the same buff color, and his stockings white silk. His black buskins gleamed.

Loose, too, and buttoned from neck to hem, was his buff waistcoat. He preferred it so. Unfashionable though it may have been, it allowed him freedom of movement. His yellow silk cravat, which he could never manage by himself, was hanging untied.

Tonneman reached out a huge hand and caught Racqel to him. He could feel her breasts against his chest.

She loved the smell of him and the solid strength of his large frame, and the way her body still fit so precisely with his. The night was so many hours away.

"Well? Have you forgotten my tie, woman?"

"Patience, husband." She tied the loops of yellow silk, adjusted the bows of the cravat. "There you are, my fine and handsome man."

"Bah." He felt confined in the coat, clumsy.

"I wish you would dress this way more often."

"And you could don one of those fine gowns from England which you've never worn and we could sit in our golden calash with an elegant blackamoor up on the box, and ride along the Strand and take tea with the Governor. Afterward, we can stroll along the Wall Street and up and down the Broad Way, nodding to the poor people."

"Fool," she whispered, stroking his throat just under his chin. She touched the bristly spot where his razor had missed. The heightened pulse of his heartbeat matched her own. "Will you be late?"

"I don't know. What was it you wanted to tell me?"

She ran her hand along his arm. "Near the Ten Eyck house, along the river, I saw a man pushing a boat into the water."

"Yes?" He kissed her forehead, her mouth, her earlobes.

Her breath came in short gasps. "I think he's your Davies man."

"How so?" His lips grazed the hollow of her throat.

She moaned softly and slipped away. She couldn't bear it. "Husband, either take me, here and now, or begone. Belay this torture, I beg of you."

By the Almighty, it was his most fervent wish, but there was too much to be done. Tonneman dropped his hands and backed away. Now he smiled. Belay? It amused him when she used his sailor's language. "Believe me, it hurts me more than you, my love, but I cannot accept your invitation."

Her eyes sparkled wickedly.

"Tell me what you have to say, temptress, so I can escape your clutches."

Racqel smiled and folded her arms. "This man was wrapped in a dirty red rag of a blanket. It fell away. Underneath he was naked."

Tonneman nodded. "Curious. I'll try not to be late."

"Is that all you can say? Your wife sees a naked man getting in a small boat for Breukelen, and your response is *curious*?"

When Tonneman grinned, Racqel had all she could do not to

smother him with kisses, he was so fair. And that's what he did at that moment. He grinned, and kissed her.

She pushed him away. "That's not honorable. I said go."

"I'll go. But if a naked man in the midst of March out in the cold isn't curious, I don't know what is." He set his tall black hat squarely upon his head and left the house by the scullery door.

Racqel lifted the bright yellow curtain covering her kitchen window and stared out after him. Where was he going? She'd forgotten to ask. And he'd managed not to say.

Now for *her* secret. She brought out the paper she'd concealed in her sleeve and felt a momentary snippet of guilt. This was not good. It was neither good nor proper for a wife to harbor secrets from her husband.

There was no salutation. The letter said:

I send you respectful greeting on this day and ask that you do me the kindness of calling on me at your earliest convenience.

Your humble servant,
Asser Levy

Chapter 14

MONDAY, 18 MARCH.
AFTERNOON.

Tonneman laid his two-foot oak stick on the ground and settled his rump into its well-marked place. This willow tree had been his private thinking place since his early days in New Amsterdam.

His clay pipe, packed with the plain rough-cut tobacco he favored, was glowing. He leaned back against the trunk of his tree, sucked in the calming smoke, then puffed out slowly.

Tonneman removed his hat and placed it on his lap. He looked up. The branches were spare this time of year. A few green buds showed above, but not the narrow spear-shaped leaves and the dense catkin spikes of small flowers that in warmer times fell as a curtain between him and the world.

How much longer, he wondered, would he be able to claim this spot? All around him buildings were going up along the waterfront. English-style structures, redbrick, three floors high and trimmed with marble, their fronts to the street.

A few story-and-one-half wood houses still remained. His was one. The first floors of many of these houses were used as shops or offices.

Shouts and hammerings penetrated his reverie. The port was crowded with ships from all countries. Babble had become a steady hum like a constant flock of birds over his island.

Opposite the City Hall a market house had been built on pilings over the water; next to it, also on pilings, the King's warehouse and customhouse had been expanded from the Dutch West India Company warehouse. Alongside it was the weighhouse.

Racqel was right. Already the wealthier were constructing homes beyond the Wall, north and east, along the East River and north and west along the Broad Way. The Wall itself was crumbling. Soon enough it would come down for good, and the City's expansion would be recognized. Perhaps he would use De Sille's fee and buy land north and build. But on the East River. He would miss it if he could not wake to its smells, its sounds, the sight of sailing ships. Deep down he was still a sailor, and he felt a sense of peace near, if not on, the salty sea.

He puffed thoughtfully on his pipe. The City was growing by metes and bounds. His children needed more space to run.

His children. Tonneman smiled. His eyes were heavy. Then he snapped awake, not pondering his brood, but De Sille. Damn that bastard and his commission. Much as Tonneman wanted not to, he had to give it thought.

Why should someone mutilate a horse? What sort of person? It would take thinking. Did this someone live in town? Or outside? If outside, how had he come past the sentinels at the gates? Easy—one, or both, of the frolicking sentinels had been asleep.

Tonneman knew, had known all along, what he had to do. He had to act as if he were still Sheriff. He had to ask questions. First he would have a chat with the Rattle Watch, who had discovered the dead horse. And then the stableman. He would inspect the site too, though he doubted it would offer much. And he would question the Musketeers at the gates, that was for certain.

If the mutilator was a City man, it would be a simple matter. One could keep few secrets in this town. Everyone knew everyone. And each knew the others' business. Of course, the Jews kept to themselves. They were a particularly secretive lot. Most, anyway.

If only he could have had a look at the horse's wounds. Were they as neat and precise as the slice across the cow's throat? Yes, he would ask questions.

As for that fellow Racqel had spied bare-arse-naked on his way to Breukelen, Tonneman didn't have to think twice. He would lay that in Gibb's lap. He was not going to drag himself to Breukelen. Though he could go on one of the buttermilk boats and pick up some buttermilk. No. Let Gibb or Nessel-Vogel go to Breukelen.

His mind slipped back to the main problem. The horse killing was not the handiwork of a sane man. Or he had a big hate. Against Andros? Against De Sille? Against the English? Against the King? That would make it a Dutchman. The odds were for that. Eight out of ten on the Island were Dutch.

His lids were drooping. As was the pipe. It fell from his lips. Damn, he hoped he hadn't scorched another shirt. Ah, well . . . He slept in the afternoon sun.

HE WAS AMIDST a herd of horses. They were galloping toward him, and all were bleeding from the throat. They came at him, threatening to pound him into the earth. Someone was shouting.

Tonneman opened his eyes to see two young workmen standing over him. One held a saw, the other a shovel. Tonneman waved an impatient hand. "Be off."

"You be off. We have work."

"Do it and leave me be."

"You're in our way."

"How's that?"

"The Governor's orders. We're building a new pier right where you sit."

Tonneman seized his cudgel. Both young men backed away, their hands ready. Tonneman smiled. He enjoyed the notion that two young men believed he was dangerous. He snatched his hat angrily, crammed it on his head, picked up his cold pipe, and heaved himself to his feet. "Are you going to cut down this tree?"

"Yes." The workman brandished his saw.

Tonneman nodded, laid his hands on the stout trunk of his willow for a moment, then pushed past the two young interlopers with a growl and headed for Whitehall.

Chapter 15

Racqel left her house and walked past the odious Old Soldiers Tavern, along Queen Street, which was crowded with dock workers and sailors unloading ships, loading barges and wagons. The sounds were deafening. The Strand was always busy, as was the canal on Broad Street.

Did someone call her name? Racqel stopped and turned. A barge was making its slow way from the East River up the canal. Men on the barge and on both sides of the canal shouted to one another. Several Indians talked to onlookers on Broad Street, either selling something or trying to cadge money, she couldn't tell which.

But she saw no one who might have called her. She resumed her walk. She would be there soon. Nothing was far from anything else in Manhattan. The Wall, what remained of it, was perhaps five hundred yards from the southern tip of the Island, where Fort James stood.

Commerce was a noisy spectacle. Racqel heard and saw it every day from her home. Dock men and sailors and buyers and tradesmen marched up and down and about doing what men of business did. She smiled grimly. What they did was yell and swear and argue, all the time. Or so it seemed.

She hurried her steps. Asser Levy's note had surprised her and gladdened her soul. Her heart pounded at the thought that he needed to see her. Asser Levy was an important man in the Jewish Community. Was it possible they'd had a change of heart and were telling her it was all right? That she could be a Jew again?

At the top of Queen Street, where the thoroughfare met the Wall and the Water Gate stood, she turned left. Just past the gate and across the road from the Wall was Asser Levy's tavern. It had no name, merely a large carved wood sign out front of the standing figure of a lion. Like the Old Soldiers Tavern, it was filled with loud-mouthed drinking men. Beside it was Levy's butcher shop, where in spite of her estrangement from the Community, she still bought her meat.

Levy's home was in the middle of Wall Street. Its size and construction proclaimed it as the home of a very rich man. Levy owned extensive property in New-York. East of his tavern and butcher shop were his slaughterhouse, situated on a pier in the East River, and his fine home, built in the Dutch fashion. He was one of the wealthiest people in New-York.

For a Jew, that is.

When one considered that Frederick Philipse, the Christian carpenter, often called the richest man in town, was said to be worth thirty times more, Levy was merely one prosperous man among many.

Racqel went up the three steps, lifted the plain brass knocker, and let it fall. After a moment or two, the door was opened. "Mistress Tonneman," Maria Levy, Asser's wife, said formally. "Thank you for coming so quickly."

Mistress Levy, a large and undeniably pompous woman, led Racqel through a beautifully appointed grand chamber and the huge kitchen to a small room just to the left of the oven. This room was always the warmest in any house and was usually kept as a nursery. But the Levy children were all grown and well married.

After giving the door a short tap-tap, Mistress Levy pushed it open. There, propped up in bed, a shawl over his shoulders, a velvet skull cap on his head, and a ledger on his knees, was Asser Levy.

"Husband," Mistress Levy said.

Levy closed the book. He removed his spectacles. "Ah, Mistress Tonneman, so good of you. Maria, tea."

Only after smoothing the quilted counterpane, which was in no need of smoothing, Mistress Levy left them. She did not close the door.

Levy scratched his head, a complicated motion that consisted of running his hand through his hair, finding the velvet cap, lifting it, scratching, and replacing the cap.

The butcher's hair was almost as black as it had been when he was a young soldier. It had started to speckle with gray in '64, when he was forty-two. The gray had remained just a scattering these eleven years. His beard, which was trimmed in the custom of a Spanish cavalier, gave force to the soldierly image. Though not a scholar, Asser Levy was a religious man and active in the synagogue on Mill Street for which he had donated the land. Racqel recalled her father's words about him. "Remember his name is Levy," he'd told his daughter. "And the *Levis* are a priestly tribe."

"You are well, Mistress Tonneman?" He spoke as if he were finding it difficult to breathe. On his left cheek, just above the beard line, was an unsightly purple welt.

The chamber smelled of human waste and sour breath, and Levy did not look the robust man Racqel knew him to be. She leaned forward to examine his bloodshot eyes. "More to the point, Mister Levy, how are you? You do not look at all well."

The butcher gave a weak chuckle. "I knew you were a better physician than these quacksalvers in town."

"I am my father's daughter. Had I known you were ill, I would have brought my bag."

"Can you cure my ailment?"

"That is not an easy question; therefore I don't have an easy answer."

He chuckled again, but this chuckle broke into a painful cough. "Spoken like a clever rabbinical student."

She put her hand to his cheek. "You have a fever."

"I've been losing weight. No appetite."

She placed her hand at the back of his neck. "Pain here?"
"Sometimes."

Her hand came away wet. "You're sweating a great deal." She
brought out a nose cloth from her sleeve and dried her hand.

He nodded, and resisted another cough.

Racqel poured water from the pitcher on the nightstand into
the bowl. There were clean cloths folded on the stand. She damp-
ened one and placed it on the ailing man's brow. "Hold this." He
did. "Aches and pains? Headaches?"

"My knees, my ankles. Pain everywhere." The damp cloth fell,
useless among the bedclothes.

"Are your bowels loose?"

"Mmm."

"How long has this been so? This feeling poorly?"

Sweat poured from Levy's face. His body shook. "Three, four
weeks."

She replaced the damp cloth. "Is this the first time you've ever
felt this way?"

"Yes." The cloth fell again.

Racqel began to pace, to the door and back to the foot of the
bed, then the confined width of the room.

"Stop already, you're making me dizzy."

"If I'm not mistaken, you already are. I would imagine you ac-
quired that bruise from a fall."

The butcher's hand went to his face, but he did not comment.
There was a long silence in the room, broken only by Levy's phlegm-
rough breathing. Finally Levy said, "Mistress Tonneman. Racqel.
Can you help me?"

"I can, Mister Levy," Racqel answered. "But why should I?"

Levy's feverish eyes glinted at her. "Because Torah demands it
of you. And I'll pay you handsomely."

"In what coin?"

The sick man stared at her. "Racqel, I can't believe this is you.
Whatever sum you ask, I'll pay."

If she were less of a gentlewoman, Racqel would have laughed.
Instead, she replied, "I don't need your money. I don't want your

money. My husband doesn't have your wealth, but we want for naught."

"I ask you in the name of your father, and his father before him all the way back to Abraham. You are still a Jew."

Color flamed in Racqel's cheeks. "Then why haven't you treated me as one? Why have you sent me beyond the pale?" Abruptly, she fell silent. Asser Levy was right: She was her father's daughter. "No matter," she said. "Of course I'll help you, because everything that I know says I must. But I am repaying spite with kindness."

Levy coughed, then sighed. "What can I say? Perhaps that wrong can be righted."

Racqel had been speaking in anger, not calculation. It had never occurred to her that anything she said would affect change, or that she might bargain with her physicking skills. Now, even though she knew she would help Levy no matter what, the idea came that she could use his gratitude to her children's advantage. She said, "Moses needs someone to help him study. He needs to know what it is to be a Jewish man. He is ready."

"That can be arranged," Levy said softly.

"And—"

"No more ands, Mistress Tonneman. Anything can be arranged. We can discuss your problems. Just cure me of this affliction."

"You have a fever and must stay in bed."

"I have a business to run."

"You'll stay in bed."

He narrowed his bleary eyes at her. "I was doing that before you came here."

"Alice, my servant girl, will bring willow bark for your headache and laudanum for pain. And I'll give you paregoric for your bowels. Between the laudanum and the paregoric you'll sleep well. And while you sleep, consider a Jewish mother and her four Jewish children who have been forced to exist without the love and strength of the Jewish Community. Who have been treated as outcasts."

Levy closed his eyes. His lips moved. A tremor shook him.

Racqel drew the counterpane to the tip of his sharp cavalier's beard. She rubbed his arms to keep him warm, then held the shivering man to her.

It was thus that Mistress Maria Levy, bearing the tea, found her husband in the arms of that pariah woman, Racqel Tonneman.

Chapter 16

Tonneman passed through the gate and took to the stone walk leading to the Governor's new stable. The earth bordering the walk and the walk itself were stained blood purple.

The trees, too, dappled with gore, bore witness to the catastrophe, as did the outside of the stable. All whitewashed brick, it was, marked with splotches of rusty blood.

An errant dogwood, aged and gnarled, leaned over the walk just shy of the stable. Tonneman ducked the low-hanging bough but not quick enough. The branch caught the crown of his tall black hat and hooked it from his head. Tonneman quickly turned on his heel and rescued his hat before it hit the ground. He glowered at the offending branch, then took time for a longer examination. It had been broken recently.

"That you, Tonneman?"

He looked up the path. The man he'd come to see, Richard Smythe, the Governor's stableman, was driving a pony cart toward him. As the cart came to a halt, the pony nuzzled Tonneman's waistcoat.

Tonneman knew Smythe, as he knew many in the City. Some he knew well, others only in passing. Smythe he knew only in passing. The clothes Smythe wore were of a fine cut, though ill-fitting and of yesterday's fashion. The blue velvet coat was much too long in the sleeves and hem, the brown breeches bagged at the runtish stableman's knees, and the ornate red hat full of yellow feathers sat on his ears. On his feet was the only apparel that made any sense, tattered canvas and leather boots. Tonneman labored hard not to smile. It was obvious what Nick De Sille did with his old clothes.

In the cart were three bony young black slaves. All wore poor excuses for clothes, thin cotton trousers and shirts that would have been more appropriate to a tropical island than New-York in March.

"Get started here," Smythe ordered them. "I want everything scrubbed down and white by nightfall."

The Africans pushed and pulled a tub of whitewash that sat in the cart. Tonneman noted that a ladder was leaning against the doors of the stable. Brushes were laid out on a low table.

"Wait," Tonneman said, gesturing with his cudgel.

"Sir?" Smythe's feigned respectful manner bordered on the belligerent. The man's left eye was walleyed. So much white showing made it appear that the little man was staring off in space, which only seemed to add to his insolence.

Tonneman came around the cart. The African boys were terrified at the prospect of opening the bolted stable doors. Or was it Tonneman's oak stick, with which he was gesturing so ardently, that frightened them? "I'll have a look around before you begin," Tonneman told Smythe. Good thing he'd come today. Had he delayed much longer, he would have found no evidence of the deed. Only whitewash.

"My master wants the stable like new," Richard Smythe protested.

"And it shall be," Tonneman told him. "But perhaps half an hour later. To quote the First Councillor, 'This stallion was a gift from His Majesty to Governor Andros and its death is more than a prank. This is a God damn crime against the King.' " Tonneman paused to let Nick De Sille's words soak in Smythe's puny brain. Then he continued. "The First Councillor will not complain if you tell him it was I who delayed your labor." With that, Tonneman strode to the stable doors and shot open the bolt. The doors crept open of their own accord. A small black creature with a white spine ran out, spraying the air with its acrid odor.

The slaves gasped. Smythe's hand fell on his stubby sword as the skunk disappeared into the shrubs.

Tonneman held his nose and stepped back. "God, that's awful. Before I forget, who took the carcass?"

"Jan Keyser."

Tonneman nodded. He pulled his nose cloth from under his vest and covered his nose and mouth. The stench was terrible. Swallowing his bile, he asked, "One horse, right? Only one horse was killed?"

Smythe nodded.

"How many horses were kept here?"

"Four. He left two crazed and one dead."

"What happened to the other?"

"The Night Watch told me he was nearly knocked down by it."

"What's the man's name?"

"Otto Wersten. All Otto saw was red, he says. Says the Devil rode that horse. What he saw was a red creature riding off on Cleopatra, Mistress De Sille's own mare. They found the beast at the Devil's Boulder the next day. Where else? She was so blood-mad, they tied her to two trees and I had to put her down."

Why the Devil's Boulder, Tonneman thought. Coincidence? Or pattern? He braced himself to enter the stable. The skunk had marked its spot as clearly as the horse killer had. None the less, the job had to be done. "Get me some light." When Smythe didn't move, he ordered, "Now."

"There are lanterns inside, Castor."

The youngest, smallest slave ran into the stable, both hands tight on his nose.

"Pollux, you and Gemini fill those buckets with seawater. I want this place sluiced out as soon as Heer Tonneman is done."

Tonneman noted the *Heer.* Was that meant to be offensive? God damn English.

Pollux and Gemini fell over each other in their hurry to get out. When Castor lit three lamps, rodents scattered, bringing up choking dust. The Governor's stable was a palace compared to the two-stall shed and carriage house where the Tonnemans' two mares were housed. However, today the palace was somewhat soiled. The dirt floor was carpeted with sticky straw all clumped up and disturbed. The parting gift of the skunk had obscured any odor of the blood that sullied the stable.

Tonneman stepped outside. The air here was no better. He spat and walked slowly around the perimeter of the stable. When he returned, Castor was raking the matted straw. "Not yet, boy."

The young slave stopped immediately, his eyes downcast.

Tonneman glared at Smythe. "Hold a light over my right shoulder," he told the stableman. He then traced the ground along the inside walls of the stable, Smythe hanging on his footsteps. The only sound was their scuffling feet in the straw. Castor stood perfectly still, afraid of doing anything that would upset either man.

There were four large stalls with half doors, which were open. A collection of water buckets hung in a row from nails against the wall nearest the outside doors; below them were a pitchfork and an assortment of brushes. A torn bag of oats lay on the floor, its seeds mingling with the rest of the filth, and from the display of droppings, it was also feeding the rodents.

Several large flies spun about Tonneman's head, nestled in his eyes. He drove them away with a flap of his hand, but they kept coming back. Richard Smythe was making grunting sounds behind him. "Lower the light," Tonneman commanded.

They had arrived at the stall where the King's horse had met its death. It swarmed with the activity of nature. The once-white walls were the color of stale port and were moving masses of maggots.

Smythe raised his lamp. "A pretty sight."

Tonneman thought to disturb the mess on the stall wall with his stick. He changed his mind. "Give me the rake," he called to Castor.

The boy swiftly complied. Tonneman gave Castor his stick to hold and raked the maggots from one wall of the stall, then another. There was the message De Sille had talked of: *Burn in Hell, English*, scripted in English. Tonneman traded the rake for his cudgel and made for the stable doors. He'd find naught here. God and nature had taken care of that. Once outside, he took his nose cloth from his face and used it to chase away the flies that had grown attached to him.

What with the skunk and the flies, he craved nothing more than to plunge himself into the sea. He shook his head. Though spring approached, it was still cool. Ah, so much for the finery he'd worn today. There was nothing for it, then, but to bury or burn it all.

Richard Smythe slumped against a tree and gulped air into his lungs. He reached into his pocket and pulled out a flask. He watched Tonneman for a moment, taking his measure. Then, insolently, the stableman uncapped the flask and took a greedy pull.

Tonneman wiped his eyes. He could have used a taste of brandywine himself right now.

Pollux and Gemini came up the walk, each carrying two buckets on a yoke. At the stable door the slaves squatted till the buckets touched the ground, then slipped out from under. They waited, staring at Tonneman.

"Go on, go on," Richard Smythe said, waving his arms. "Get in there and clean it up."

Pollux looked at Tonneman and pointed to something over Tonneman's head. Tonneman glanced up; he saw nothing but the pale blue sky. When he glanced back down, the slave boys were moving cautiously toward the stable. "What did you see?" he called after them.

"Your hat, sir," Pollux replied.

Tonneman removed his hat. Caught on its black band was a torn piece of crimson silk.

Chapter 17

"**L**eave my house, Jezebel!" Maria Levy stabbed an arthritic finger at Racqel.

"My dear." A flush climbed Asser Levy's neck. Sweat burst from every pore.

"*Out!*"

"You misunderstand," Racqel said, horrified. "The poor man was shivering with the chill."

Asser Levy's wheezes erupted into hoarse laughter. "Thank you for the compliment, wife, but the way I feel I couldn't tup my pillow."

An appalling eternity of silence followed. Humiliated, Racqel wrapped her shawl about her, anxious to be rid of the Levy house.

Then Mistress Levy granted her a frosty smile. "Of course. How terrible to misunderstand something so innocent. Please forgive me. . . ."

Racqel nodded. Mistress Levy's words were just that. Words.

Looming behind Mistress Levy was a servant girl bearing a tray. The girl's eyes told Racqel she'd heard the entire exchange. It would blow through the Jewish Community like the March winds.

"You'll stay for tea." Mistress Levy's icy words were not an invitation.

"Of course she will," Asser Levy answered for Racqel. He was looking at her with some sympathy. "Sit, please, Mistress Tonneman."

Racqel sat in a chair at the foot of the bed. Mistress Levy fluttered about her husband, plumping his pillow, straightening the counterpane, blotting the perspiration from his drawn face. Last, she perched next to Asser Levy on the bed, her head sharing his pillow. Racqel said not a word. Nor did the Levys. The ailing man held his cup with trembling hands, setting it on the silver tray from time to time when the sweat from his forehead flowed into his eyes. The tea was tasteless sump water, bitter in Racqel's mouth.

"Mistress Tonneman," Levy said at last. "Can you tell me what's wrong with me?"

"She's not a physician." Mistress Levy's spiny words cut Racqel to the core.

"Bah. Solomon Navarro wants only to bleed me." Levy looked at Racqel, waiting.

"Your wife is quite correct. I am not a physician."

Levy said, "Please, tell me what you think. Please."

"You have a fever. It must run its course. The medicine I have prescribed will help, I think."

Abruptly Levy began to shiver again. The tray on his lap shook. Mistress Levy removed the tray and glared at Racqel as if everything were her fault.

Racqel got to her feet. "Cool his fever with damp cloths. As now, when the chills are in force, he must be kept warm." Fitting her actions to her words, Racqel took the blanket from the foot of the bed and started to cover Levy with it.

"I'll do that." Maria Levy tore the blanket from Racqel's hands.

"Give him plenty of chicken soup. With garlic. Lots of garlic."

Mistress Levy sneered. "Tell me something I don't know."

Racqel was weary of the conflict. She quit the Levy household as it became a flurry of activity, with Mistress Levy shouting orders and servants scuttling about with blankets and hot bricks.

Her pace was quick as she went down Queen Street, her eyes lowered. The cruel accusation shamed her. *Jezebel.* She could still feel Mistress Levy's scornful eyes glaring at her, condemning her. To think someone would believe anything improper had happened when Racqel was only attempting to help her patient shamed her. Almost as much as if the impropriety had occurred. Racqel was oblivious of the soft blue of the sky and the clean fragrance of spring in the air.

The port along the East River continued a beehive of activity. Nothing was more important than the business of making money. Strains of many languages buzzed around her as workers grunted under their loads from ship to shore and from shore to ship.

She arrived home, her cheeks still burning, but now in anger. It was beginning again. Almost twelve years before, when her first husband, Benjamin Mendoza, went missing, some of the women acted as if she had driven Benjamin away and was a temptress waiting to seduce their men. She was an *agunah*, shut off from life. When Benjamin's bones were found, she thought she was free of that.

Tears of frustration stung her eyes; she brushed them away. Pieter Tonneman, the big, gentle Dutchman, New Amsterdam's Sheriff, had come into her life at that time and changed everything. She sighed. He had given her a great happiness. First his love, and then her family.

Racqel had thought—the Mendozas had convinced her—that she was barren, that there was something in her that kept her from having children. How wonderful it was when she realized she was pregnant with Moses. All those years. It had not been her fault.

She was teaching her children the ways of Judaism, and they were considered Jewish because they had a Jewish mother; they were also considered *mamzer*, the product of an illegal marriage. So now she was more shut off from her Jewish life than before. She was again an *agunah*. And so were her children.

In the great chamber Racqel found Daniel napping, a sweet smile on his face. His cradle lay in a shaft of sunlight. She kissed his brow and draped her shawl on the peg near the side door.

Upstairs in their sleeping chamber she poured water into the bowl, rolled up her sleeves, and washed her hands and face. At once she felt better, as if she had washed all the nasty suspicions and accusations away.

Alice was on her hands and knees in the kitchen, scrubbing the floor, while the pots on the hearth bubbled. Maria sat on a stool, embroidering a garden of flowers on a linen cloth. The house gave off a sense of cleanliness, industry, and peace. The child held up her work for her mother to admire. Lovely little delicate stitches. Racqel kissed the top of Maria's head. "You have a fine hand." Her daughter flushed with pride and resumed her sewing.

Racqel took her father's medicine box from a high cupboard in the pantry, where she also kept her mortar and pestle and the opium. Bundles of dried herbs, bark, and roots hung from the beams in her kitchen. She picked out the willow bark that she hoped would calm Asser Levy's aching head. This she ground down with her mortar and pestle into powder. She apportioned each separate dose into twenty small cloth bags.

She put a measure of opium into a jar and stirred a cup of brandywine into it. When the opium was thoroughly dissolved, she poured the tincture through a funnel into a small flask. The mixture was laudanum for her patient's pain.

More opium went into the making of the paregoric, along with aniseed oil and white crystalline from the benjamin bush.

"What a pretty smell, Mutti." Maria sniffed the vanillalike scent of the white powder. "May I have some of what you're making?"

"No. This is strong medicine for Mister Levy. One day soon I will teach you how to mix this and other powders and potions."

"I'd like that, Mutti." The girl watched her mother work for a few moments, then returned to her embroidery.

The paregoric went into another flask. Racqel placed the two flasks and the cloths containing willow bark into a small twig basket.

Alice had finished the floor and was on her way upstairs with a fresh pitcher of water and a clean bowl.

"Alice, when you come down, I want you to take this basket to Asser Levy's house."

The black woman bobbed her head and continued up the stairs.

"Maria will watch the hearth," Racqel called after her.

Outside, she could hear the boisterous cries of Benjamin and

85

the Anderson boy. Moses, she knew, was at Master Crabtree's house, studying letters and numbers with the schoolmaster. Her husband, no doubt, was seeing to his odious mission.

After Alice departed for the Levy house, Racqel poured the tea water. Tea that would taste like tea. As she sipped the strong brew, the incident with Mistress Levy weighed heavy on her mind, lingering there when she returned to her bedchamber.

She lit the bedside lamp and set it on her chest of drawers. Now she pulled the cord hanging from the ceiling that opened the door to the attic and brought the ladder in place. Carrying the lamp, she hitched up her skirts and climbed.

Lantern-light specters danced in the narrow space of the attic. But Racqel had no use for spirits. Excepting that of her blessed fathers, which she kept with her always.

Her father's old trunk was set in a corner under an India rug. Removing the cover, Racqel opened the trunk. Its latches were stiff with disuse. His tooled leather box was right on top. Inside, his papers, tied neatly with a black ribbon, had yellowed with age. The ink on them was brown and faded. She sat herself on the floor and read until the sun through the tiny round window told her that twilight was nigh. Unfortunately, she'd found no solution to the puzzle of Asser Levy's illness.

However, her studies were not a complete waste of time. Among her father's commentaries, certain words caught her attention. They stood out on the page as if circled in blood.

In case of homicide by an unknown hand, if the corpse be discovered in an open field, the elders are to take a heifer, break its neck, slit its throat, and cast it into a neighboring stream.

Chapter 18

Red silk. Tonneman fingered the slash of cloth. Removing it from the band of his hat where it had attached itself like a small bloody banner, he placed it in his waistcoat pocket. When had it joined itself to his hat?

In the stable?

No. The beams and ceiling stood too high.

Nothing jostled his memory. His hat hadn't . . . Ah . . . the tree.

Richard Smythe, truly an ugly weasel, shook his flask and watched Tonneman with his good right eye. Tonneman found it difficult to believe, but rising over the stench of the skunk, he could smell Smythe's rank odor. The stableman's sweat had the pungent stink of fear.

Of what was Smythe afraid? Tonneman walked the few paces to the ancient dogwood that had snared his hat earlier and pulled the broken branch to eye level.

The jagged break in the wood still held on to a strand of crimson thread. He plucked the thread loose and wound it about his little finger.

A night rider, traveling fast, perhaps unfamiliar with the lay of the land, would not have seen this branch before it struck and claimed a bit of—what? Perhaps a cravat flying in the wind? And who was to say that the crimson cloth came from the man he sought?

Tonneman, the merchant trader, had himself bought and sold silk. The swatch of silk in his waistcoat pocket was fine, the color rich. No workingman wore silk of this quality.

Rubbing the side of his nose, he realized that the man didn't have to be that tall. One bounce on a galloping horse could send a rider, even a good one, into the air. How high? Probably less than a foot. But what if the broken part of the branch were angled down? The rider could be a good deal shorter than Tonneman and still have been struck by the branch. Tonneman looked about for the broken-off end. But it was nowhere in sight.

At that point he recalled the mass of charred red rags Nessel-Vogel had found in Davies's chimney. Was there a link? Tonneman frowned. Unlikely. Then he chastised himself for lazy thinking. "Never assume," he told himself.

A breeze from the Bay disturbed the trees along the walk and reminded Tonneman how much he stank. He had to get home and get rid of these clothes, perhaps scrub himself with vinegar. After that he would plan his next move.

The odds were long, but he would do well to pay a visit to Staple Street with his trophy and ask some questions there. The tradesmen might help him track the red silk back to its source. And he knew he must talk to David Mendoza regarding Mad Beado.

Mendoza, younger brother of Racqel's first husband, had demanded Racqel's hand in marriage after his brother Benjamin's death. But Racqel had chosen Tonneman, the Gentile. And Mendoza had eventually married the Da Costa girl, Mariana.

For Tonneman, his and Racqel's union was a chain. A series of wonderful events that bound them together. He had loved his first wife, Maria, but Racqel was his great passion. And she had given him a new family, a clever and vociferous half-Jewish brood. For Racqel, their union had brought the joy of the children she'd yearned for, and, he knew, a passion as consuming as his own.

Yet Tonneman knew too well what that choice had meant for

his wife: cruel alienation from her people. They had treated her as an outcast, which never ceased to anger him. Much of this estrangement, Tonneman felt, was fueled by David Mendoza, who, though he had a young wife and a house full of children, was still bitter over Racqel's choice of husband.

Tonneman could feel Smythe's clear eye boring a hole in his back. He turned. "You seem in a quandary, Mister Smythe." Tonneman drew the patch of red from his waistcoat. "Perhaps you know the origins of this scrap of silk."

He pressed the tatter on Smythe, who shoved his flask into his coat pocket and raised both hands to his face. Clearly, the man was terrified. "Blasphemer," Smythe muttered. His hands shook as with a palsy. He backed away from Tonneman and the bit of fabric as if Tonneman were Satan himself and the unholy cloth a piece of the Devil's cloak. "Now we are all cursed—"

"Master?" A call came from within the stable as Castor appeared at the door.

Tonneman stepped closer to Smythe, almost treading on his boots. "I ask you again, do you know anything about this silk?"

Smythe's thin lips formed a canny smile. "One of yours."

"A Hollander?"

Smythe began to giggle. "One of yours for certain."

"If you know something about this, man, you'd best tell me," Tonneman said sternly. He snatched the man by his collar with one hand, lifted him off the ground, and shook him as a terrier shakes a rat. "Do you understand me, Smythe?" He shook the man again, then let him down, none too gently.

Smythe escaped to the stable. Then he spun around, his hand on the stable door. "It's them what practice witchcraft."

Tonneman rolled his eyes. "Who?"

"This place is rife with blasphemers." Smythe wiped his palms on his baggy breeches.

"Which place?"

Smythe sneered. "New-York. Blasphemers all. You must be rooted out."

"Bah!" Another loon. Tonneman walked away, well aware of the redolent smell of skunk surrounding him; how he'd like to shed his skin like a snake.

"Hey!"

Tonneman stopped, looking back. Smythe came a few paces along the walkway. "They all wear fine clothes, like as if they was lords. But you'll do naught about it."

"Who are you talking about?"

"Their leader, he wears such silk. A whoremonger's cravat. I saw him with my master, not a sennight ago."

Tonneman waved his arms in frustration. Smythe stumbled back, thinking no doubt he was going to get hit. "Give over, man," Tonneman roared. "What leader? Name him."

Smythe looked around before he spoke. His whisper was evil. "The Jew, Asser Levy."

Chapter 19

"Ow! Woman, you'll rub my skin clean off."

Racqel paid Tonneman little heed. A soft laugh escaped her lips, just enough for him to hear. As if to mock him too, the mares, Venus and Deborah, responded with aristocratic snorts and whinnies. They'd not been pleased with his pungent intrusion.

Tonneman was sitting, knees bent to chest, in a tin tub half-filled with tepid water as Racqel scoured him with vinegar and soap to rid him of the skunk stench.

While his children hovered outside the barn, Alice arrived bearing another kettle of steaming water. She and Racqel poured the hot water into the tub. Tonneman groaned. Racqel fairly choked with suppressed laughter. However, there was no stopping the children. They chortled with delight at the sorry sight their father made.

"Nasty," Maria was saying over and over again, a rose-scented nose cloth first covering her face, then young Daniel's.

"Stinky" was what Benjamin preferred. Daniel liked it too, for he giggled and clapped his little hands.

Alice retrieved the empty kettle and trudged back to the kitchen. Moses, always the serious one, leaned on a shovel, saying nothing, but his lips twitched into a grin when he thought his father wasn't looking.

Racqel stood and wiped her hands on her oversized yellow apron. "Have you finished?" she asked her eldest son.

As he'd been doing lately when both parents were present, the boy answered his father no matter which parent spoke to him. "It's done, Papi."

"Where?" Tonneman asked.

"In the woods."

"Did you dig down deep?"

"Oh, yes. Three feet."

"Good boy." Tonneman nodded his approval. "So much for my finery."

"This dropped out," Moses said, showing his father a bit of red cloth. "Is it important?"

The piece of red silk. "Yes. Racqel, keep it for me."

Moses handed the bit of cloth to his mother. She sniffed it delicately, then held it at arm's length.

"Very amusing, wife."

Alice returned. Even she, who never showed emotion, seemed to be enjoying herself. She had another full kettle.

"I believe you're all having too good a time at my expense. Go, find something useful to do," Tonneman growled in mock anger.

Reluctantly, the children dispersed.

Racqel took a small bag of herbs from a cotton bag in her apron pocket and scattered them in the bathwater. Then she and Alice poured most of the fresh water into the tub. Immediately, the steam rising from the bath was scented with lavender.

"Good Christ," Tonneman grumbled, "does it have to be lavender?"

"Do you prefer skunk?" was her tart response.

"You'll have me smelling like De Sille."

"Better De Sille than skunk, husband."

"I'm not so sure of that."

"I am. In the words of your children, 'nasty and stinky.' " Racqel poured the last of the water over his head and vigorously scrubbed his hair. "You might ask your new employer to reimburse you for your clothes," she said mildly. She sniffed the back of her husband's neck. "You're beginning to smell sweet again."

"Like a Frenchie." He reached a wet hand for her; she gracefully evaded it, took a large clean cloth from around her shoulders, and gently dried Tonneman's hair. There was no gray in it; it was still the color of fine sand.

"Ah, you can do that till Kingdom come, my love."

"And I would if we didn't have four curious children to care for." She handed him the damp cloth. "You're as good as new."

"And I hope to prove that to you," he murmured.

Racqel glanced at Alice and blushed.

Alice pretended not to hear. "Do you need any more hot water or cloths, ma'am?"

Racqel gathered some wet cloths and walked with Alice outside. "No, thank you, Alice." She handed the Jamaica woman the cloths. "Give the children their tea. We'll be right along."

"Ma'am," the woman said, bobbing her head. "We've near emptied the rain barrel."

"After tea, we will send Moses to find the water vendor."

When Racqel returned to her husband, she found he had dried himself and was now donning his old brown breeches. Racqel sat on a keg and watched him as he dressed. "I spent some time in the attic today, sorting through my father's papers. I think I would like to have them bound. His experiments with herbs are quite remarkable."

Tonneman nodded. He was thinking his own thoughts. He put on his serviceable old blue jacket. "A fine idea," he said belatedly. "Moses might enjoy reading them."

"I agree. I came across something in the papers that should interest you. A sheet separate from the rest. That's why I want them bound. If they are not, I'll surely lose them. This dealt with his observations on religious customs in the old country. I have no idea if the custom is still followed here or what the source is."

Tonneman's mind was on emptying the tub and eating his supper. "Religious customs?"

"It said that 'if there should be a murder in an open field, and the killer is unknown, the elders of a community are to take a heifer, break its neck, slit its throat, and cast the heifer into a neighboring stream.' "

"Ah-ah," said Tonneman. "You are such a helpful wife."

Racqel grinned at him. "That sounds familiar, does it?"

He grinned back. "Yes. Quite interesting."

"Was it a heifer?"

Tonneman nodded. "Near as I could tell, that four-footer never calved. Tell me the ritual again."

When she did, he said, "It doesn't help me with my horse case. But my cow case is closer to being solved."

"But it might mean you have a human case."

"Yes, I never doubted that."

"Have you made any progress in your mission for First Councillor?"

"Naught but the scrap of silk. Judas's noose! You haven't gone and buried it?"

"We wouldn't dare. Not after you told us to save it. Moses has knotted it to the barn door bolt."

A breath of fresh air floated into the barn from outside and the evening wind blew cool. After a day like today, Tonneman truly appreciated sweet air. He brushed at his hair, which had fallen over his eyes. "It might be from a cravat. Or," he mused, "it might have something to do with rags in a chimney."

Racqel frowned her confusion.

Tonneman shook his head. "Just an idle notion." He felt his face for his beard. "Our villain stole a horse. He rode it out of the Governor's stable after mutilating and destroying the King's stallion. I found the cloth. Nay, not so. The cloth found me. It flew from a dogwood branch near the stable to my hat."

"That's not much with which to begin an investigation."

"True. But it's all I've got." Tonneman pulled on his hose and shoved his feet into his every-day boots, which were many times more comfortable than his new, shiny boots, now rank and buried in a three-foot hole in the woods. "Except, this fellow might have a mark on his face where the dogwood bit him."

"Oh."

Tonneman eyed his wife. "You've seen someone with such a mark?"

"Yes. Asser Levy. On his cheek. But he's ill. He must have gotten the bruise when he fell. . . . He asked me to come to see him."

Tonneman shook his head angrily. "You went in spite of the way they've treated you?"

"Don't. He's really very ill. And from the look of him, I would say he was incapable of sitting a horse or wielding a knife this past Sunday. Too weak surely to go riding in the night."

Tonneman, remembering how he thought that Levy hadn't looked well when he'd seen him on Sunday, nodded. But he was not prepared to cross the butcher from his list this quickly, especially not after what that walleyed weasel Smythe had told him.

Still, it was a fact he never realized until he married Racqel: Christians were always quick to blame the Jews for any trouble. Tonneman admonished himself not to leap to conclusions. Perhaps this time a Jew really was at fault.

He was most definitely going to keep Asser Levy's name on his list of suspects.

Chapter 20

"**D**on't you see?" Racqel insisted as they approached the house. Her husband was staring at her, a blank expression on his face. "A murder has taken place. There's a dead man out there somewhere."

Tonneman was a good husband and never smirked at his wife. Well, almost never. This time he did. "Wife of my heart," he said. He took her hand and led her up the stairs. "I love you till the end of time. But sometimes you just don't listen to me."

"What do you mean?"

"Of course I see. Didn't I say that my cow case is closer to being solved?"

Racqel's brow wrinkled. She nodded. "Yes, you did."

"And you said, 'But it might mean you have a human case.' And I said that I never doubted it."

She sighed and pushed open the door to their bedchamber. "Yes, you did. I got so excited with my conclusion that my thoughts flew to the winds. I'm so dull."

"Dearest Racqel, if there's one thing you are not, it's dull."

She shook her head. "Exactly the right thing to say. These are the times you amaze me, Tonneman. When you act the perfect Jewish husband. And think like a Jewish scholar."

They went into their bedchamber. He looked about for a pipe as he pondered her remark. "And what does that mean?"

She fluttered her hands, dismissing another argument before it began. "That you accept something so archaic as the cow ritual. And so Jewish."

He narrowed his eyes at her. "Is this another scheme to get me to convert?"

"No. I'm talking about the dead heifer. But since you ask, what would it harm? I wouldn't expect you to be any better a Jew than you are a Christian. You don't go to church. I wouldn't expect you to go to synagogue. You did promise."

"I agreed that the children would be brought up as Jews. I did not agree to learn hundreds of rules for which there is no purpose and to allow some barbarian with a beard to hack at my baubles with a dull knife."

"You don't understand. To the Jews of this City I am unclean. I can't live with that. I feel empty inside. I love you, I love our children. But I need more. I need my God."

"God is always with us. Even I know that."

"I need to feel God's presence." Racqel's chin thrust forward as it did when she was angry.

"Yet," Tonneman said quickly, going back to the original thought, "if we're correct, there's a dead man out there. A dead *Jewish* man."

His wife nodded. But she had not forgotten. Racqel needed to be what she had once been. She would pack away her need for the present and unpack it again when she felt the time was right.

"And other Jewish people know about it. Perhaps as many as ten."

Racqel nodded again. "A *minyan*. Or more. He's not out there in the open, rotting. He's been buried. He would have been buried as soon as possible. Before sundown of the day he was found."

"How many Jews are there in New-York?"

"With or without me?"

"Racqel."

She shrugged. "Thirty-five."

"With so few, it would be easy to tell if one is missing."

"Unless," Racqel said, "the dead man is a stranger."

"Good." Tonneman rubbed his jaw. "So we are perhaps talking about a large part of the Jewish Community concealing a murder."

"Or only a few. Also, you are going to have a difficult time getting people to talk about it. Jews have an aversion to speaking of death."

"Yes, I've seen them spitting through their fingers." He waited for her chin to thrust forward.

There it was. "And Gentiles have no superstitions?"

"Of course not. We are a noble breed, through the grace of Jesus Christ, our Lord."

Racqel did not comment. Instead, she asked, "What are you going to do?"

He grinned. "I'm no longer Sheriff. Dead men are Gibb's problem. And he's stupid enough without twisting his head with your theory about the dead cow. Let's keep that to ourselves. While I pursue the killer of horses, it won't take much effort to sniff around about the killer of cows. Or Jews."

"Be prudent. If it should come back to us and it turns out to be someone prominent in the Jewish Community—"

"Such as Asser Levy?"

"Bite your tongue. If you pursue this too keenly, I—we—will never be accepted."

"Not we," he said gently, and watched her delicious chin thrust again.

"You're a stubborn man, Pieter Tonneman. Don't you want to lie beside me when the Messiah comes?"

"I thought He'd already come."

Her dark eyes sparkled dangerously; the chin thrust farther.

"Perhaps I can broach the subject with your beloved brother-in-law, since one of the things I should do is verify Mad Francis Beado's story that he was with David Mendoza on Sunday."

Racqel looked pained. "Don't tell him I found mention of the ritual." Chance meetings with her former brother-in-law troubled

Racqel. Mendoza was a violent man who clung to his grudge. "Pieter, I continue to worry that there might be a connection between the cow and the horse."

"I agree."

"If so, my people will be branded with it."

Tonneman studied his wife's face. She seemed desolate. What wasn't she telling him? Perhaps it was just that going through her father's papers had brought sad memories. He took her hand. "Are you thinking of your father?"

"I think of my father all the time." She looked at Tonneman and tears sprang to her eyes.

"What is it?" He sat on the bed and patted it for her to sit beside him.

She sat, grasping the down-filled quilt, her lips pressed tightly together. From below came the voices of their children, Daniel's hungry cry above the others.

He brushed dark tendrils from her face. "Well?" She smelled of sunlight, perspiration, and spices.

"I told you that Asser Levy sent for me today."

Tonneman waited. Racqel would tell him in her own way.

"He was at first hot with fever, then shivering with a chill. I attempted to keep him warm in my arms while waiting for blankets."

Tonneman's brain understood. Still, her words sent blood to his head and made him feel like the old days on spirits.

"His wife saw us. She called me Jezebel. Oh, she apologized. But the maid heard. It will be all over the City and we will be shamed."

"You and Asser Levy? Horse shit."

"My people will take it as gospel. So will yours. I am not accepted by either. They want to believe the worst of me."

"Mistress Tonneman." Alice was calling from downstairs. "A gentleman to see you and the mister."

Tonneman rose from the bed and offered Racqel his hand. "We'll face the arse-holes down as we have in the past. Come, let's see who our visitor is." He led her down the stairs.

In the great chamber stood a stubby man with owlish eyes. He wore a small black mustache and a neatly trimmed black beard. Except for the bright cravat at his throat and the red heels on his fashionable black shoes, he was dressed completely in black velvet, including the low-crowned hat in his right hand. His cravat was also red. Red silk.

Racqel recognized him at once. Solomon Navarro, the physician, had been in New-York only since '73, arriving directly after the Dutch had retaken the City. Dutch rule had lasted a mere six months, but in that time Navarro, who'd been a poor physician somewhere in Johnny land, had become a rich man. He had been promised a good income by the Jewish Community in Manhattan, and it had come to be. But, in truth, the physician appeared richer than any medical practice could have made him.

Perhaps, Racqel thought, her medicine had helped Asser Levy. Or perhaps it had killed him. "Mister Navarro," she said, stepping out from behind her husband as they descended the last steps.

"Sir." Navarro's black eyes were slit with fury. He ignored Racqel and spoke to Tonneman. "Your wife is not a physician. She is a woman. These two things more than disable her from treating patients. Especially *my* patients. She is naught but a witch."

Tonneman's roar was a sound that stopped all other sounds. He crossed the short distance that separated him from Navarro. Towering over the physician with his fists clenched, he had all he could do not to hammer the man into the floor. "What did you say?"

But Solomon Navarro did not retreat. Scoring Tonneman with his eyes the physician said, "Your wife has been treating one of my patients. It will cease." The little man turned on his fancy red heels.

And as he strode to the front door, he snarled, "Or she will live to regret it."

Chapter 21

He staggered out of the woods and plunged directly into the pond. The biting cold of the water woke him from a deep stupor in the act of drowning. His cloak caught on an underwater shrub and, as if possessed, sought to strangle him. With an indifferent motion he jerked free, leaving the cloak, engorged, floating on the surface of the water.

When had he left the house? What had sent him out this time? There was no memory for him to draw on. The last he could remember were embers glowing in the fireplace like eyes in the darkness. Then, his book on his lap, he had drifted, drifted, to sleep.

And now this.

So it was happening again. A powerful shudder shook his body and he was suddenly aware that he was standing in the pond, chest-high in cold water. He splashed his way to land and fell to his knees.

He did not know if he could bear it. He couldn't explain what he did on his nightly meanderings. That he was bewitched, he had no doubt. But this time he would not let them drive him out. Evil was all around him. His fallen angels, the two he loved so ardently, had become demons, demons he must destroy. And the hidden witch had to be rooted out and burned.

The night clamor of the beasts and birds surrounded him, shrouding him in velvet. He lay shivering on the winter grass until the thumping in his heart subsided. Sitting up slowly, he pulled off his shoes and emptied them of water. His grimy toes poked through his white hose, showing gray, like so many little tadpoles.

Where had he been? What had he done? He patted his left side. No baldric, hence no sword. Save for Sunday, he never went about unarmed. No knife either. For this he offered a prayer of thanks.

Reshod, he stood, feeling the shoes pinch his feet. Overhead the full moon rolled in the star-studded sky, crooning to him, singing, "Come closer, my son, closer, closer."

He reached up, his hands almost in prayer. "Yes, Father, I will come." No! What was he doing out here in the night with the birds and the beasts and the spirits, and perhaps the red Indians, who could see as clear in the night as they could in the day?

An owl hooted; he heard the whir of feathers. When he cast his eyes about, the moon reflected on the water-lit path. It was then he realized where he was. Shellpoint.

He shook the water from his clothing, as a dog would, and followed the trail.

All at once something seized his foot and he went flying. Crack. His head hit a tree; his face scraped along the bark. He knew, even as the blood ran down his face, that he'd tripped on a half-buried root. As he rested against the smooth trunk of his attacker, the sweetness of his blood came to his lips and he savored it. He was grateful the tree was birch and not oak.

But now he felt the chill. Not the spring wind. Something else. Something evil. It crept through his veins like death. His limbs shook. He was a leaf in the wind waiting for the powers of the night to buffet him to Kingdom come.

He needed to be safe. Home. He had to get to his room, to his bed. That he was damned he had no doubt, but not until he fulfilled his mission. Not until he meted out a sinner's share of his damnation to the source of his pain. He had to find the blasphemer. Rising, he made his way home, stripped to his pale, mottled skin, and fell into bed. But not to sleep, not yet. Now the fever came, washing his bloody cuts with scalding salty sweat. And the racking pain in his fingers, his arms, and his legs. Retributions for his sins. The Devil's whips. Or were they God's?

At dawn, when he awakened, he knew he would have no memory of this nocturnal excursion. He would have just his bloody, wet, and stained clothing, which he would burn. All except his red coat. He must preserve his red coat as well as possible so the blasphemers, seeing him in it, will know him as God's vengeance.

He wouldn't remember. But he would know. It was merely a matter of time before this evil sickness became worse. He had to find the fiend who was doing this to him. He had to find the witch who had cursed him.

Now did he sleep, only to dream of the fires of Hell.

AT SHELLPOINT, the night obliterated all evidence of the intruder. The music of the forest could be heard once more.

The water lapped gently at the bank. Nearby, nature embraced one of its own creatures. Rising from the boulder, where he'd crouched perfectly still since his sharp hearing had detected the intruder, the watcher ran his left hand over his almost hairless head till it touched the lock of hair at the top.

He spat in the water. The pond was his once more, as were all the creatures in and around it. He was so much a part of his surroundings that no one would have noticed his presence, save another like him.

Soundlessly, he walked to the place where the intruder had fallen from the woods into the pond. He continued walking until the water was almost to his waist. He was abreast of the floating cloak. There he paused, his hands over the waters. As if he'd become water himself, he slipped below the surface, barely rippling it.

Within five heartbeats he emerged, the trophy he sought in his hand. He walked to the land and laid it on the winter grass. Perhaps the insects heard his faint grunt. Perhaps the birds saw the slits of his eyes or the baring of his teeth glinting against the moon.

The stranger had interrupted his meditations. But Man Who

Walks Like a Fox had his compensation. This blue warrior belt that the Europeans called a baldric was lavishly ornamented with the different tinted glass stones, not the jewels these whites prized so dearly. The sword it held was not so colorful, but it was three feet of good double-edged steel with a fine pointed blade that could kill an enemy quickly. He would keep the blade and perhaps sell it. Or, better, he would kill with it.

Chapter 22

Tonneman had spent the afternoon of the previous day dedicated to the City Council's business. Business that brought additional money to Ten Eyck and Tonneman.

Tonneman, as Land Overseer, inspected new fencing and the road repair the City Council required of farmers whose land bordered the Bowery Road and the Broad Way Road. Although some farmers did the work themselves, others hired Ten Eyck and Tonneman to handle the chore for them. It had been a moderately uncomplicated and nicely profitable afternoon.

On this day he was on the Governor's business. That meant he was working for De Sille, which only soured him more. Or perhaps it was really the Duke of York's business, since this was his domain, though he'd never set foot in it. Still, it was all the King's business. Tonneman was certain His Royal Majesty had not been informed that his handsome gift to Governor Andros had been so abused. Ah, these English. Life had been much simpler before them.

The physician, Solomon Navarro, had been much on his mind. Tonneman feared no man. But threats against his wife troubled him greatly. Especially when what was threatened was something he could do nothing about.

And there was something else about Navarro to consider. His

red silk cravat. The cloth it was made of could have been the sister to the bit of red silk that had attached itself to Tonneman's hat.

Tonneman rose at dawn, which was always his way. His sleep had been troubled, and he awoke with an aching head and his old longing for spirits. Hitching up his breeches, he thrust his craving aside, albeit with a craven reluctance, and thought about what had to be done.

To be rid of De Sille and to be back to his own serene, well-ordered life, Tonneman had to discover the horse murderer. And yet he understood too well that his serene, well-ordered life would never be the same. His friend and partner Ten Eyck had been greasing De Sille's palm all these years.

Damn! How much of his money had gone into De Sille's coffers and fostered that wily bastard's schemes? Had it purchased those ships that were making the First Councillor even richer? Tonneman had heard that De Sille was buying flour mills. What did he know? De Sille had always galled Tonneman. And the thought that De Sille was using Tonneman's money galled him even more.

He ate his grits porridge, then bread and cheese, and pickled fish with green peas. In a dark humor he drank his tea, muttering one or two words and only in response to questions, and scarcely acknowledging his children.

Abruptly he pushed his chair from the table before he'd finished eating and was out of the house.

"Where are you off to in such a fine humor?" Racqel called after him.

"Hard day ahead. I'm for a gossip or two."

She tilted her head for a moment at his answer, then went back to rolling out pastry while Alice prepared the fish. Before dawn Alice had taken her angle rod to the bottom of Queen Street, caught some bluefish. They would have fish pies for their midday meal.

Tonneman didn't believe in interrogation. He preferred gossip. He'd learned over his years spent as Schout and then Sheriff that he got more from people if they didn't know they were being questioned. People, especially New Amsterdamers–New-Yorkers, didn't like to answer direct questions, but how they esteemed a good gossip.

His first stop was the Old Soldiers Tavern. The public house was empty save for two bleary-eyed Musketeers and another, asleep or drunk, with his cheek on a table, his arms at his sides. Tonneman attempted to talk to the two who were half-awake, but they would have none of him. The barkeep, Russell Mitchum, never looked up from his whittling.

Tonneman was about to leave, when Jan Keyser appeared. The tanner was aging like his hides, his skin looking like brown wax and more leathery as the years went by.

"Good morning, Keyser." Tonneman spoke with more good humor than he felt. Keyser was a weasel, a liar, and a cheat.

The little man shivered. "Buy me a drink, Tonneman? I've got a chill."

Tonneman grunted. "Why not?" The man's audacity never ceased to amaze him. "Mitchum?" He raised his voice. "Mitchum."

The tapster looked up, startled. Apparently, like the soldier, he'd been asleep too. He stumbled to his feet.

"A beer," Tonneman said.

A glint came to the tanner's eye. "I have a raging thirst for a kill-devil."

Mitchum stood there whittling, waiting for Tonneman and Keyser to decide what the drink would be.

"And why should I stand you to rum?"

"You owe me, Tonneman. You could have pushed Gibb to deciding in my favor. And because I've been sick and deserve a kindness."

Tonneman was amazed to hear such talk from a man who'd never offered a kindness to anyone. Alas, expecting logic from Keyser was like expecting milk from a bull. He drew the piece of red silk from his coat pocket. "Is this anything you recognize?"

Keyser frowned but didn't answer.

"Well?"

Keyser wiped the sweat from his forehead and slapped it on his greasy buckskin trousers. "No." The little man cleared his throat. "I hear you're working for His Royal Arse-Kisser, De Sille. That he's got you looking for the killer of the King's horse." The tanner barked a single sound meant to be a laugh.

"Did you get that carcass?"

"You know I did. Bad messed up, it was. But there's something most don't know." He watched Tonneman slyly.

"And what's that?" Tonneman motioned to Mitchum. "A rum and a cider."

"Spirits?" Mitchum asked, setting aside his knife and his whittle branch and shambling to them.

Tonneman raised his eyebrow. The barman served Tonneman his non-fermented cider and Keyser his rum.

Spittle appeared in the corner of Keyser's mouth. His hand shot out for the wooden cup like the tongue of a snake. Tonneman seized Keyser's bony wrist. "Now, why have I bought you this rum?"

"Because we've been friends lo, these many years. Didn't I help you solve the murder of Hendrik Smitt in '64?"

"No. Go on."

"All the cutting and hacking down below of that beast made it impossible to get a clean hide, I'll tell you."

"Get to it. The stallion." Tonneman was fast losing his patience. He squeezed the tanner's wrist for a moment, then threw it aside.

"Besides all that." Keyser's voice dropped to a harsh whisper. He rubbed his sore wrist. "On the beast's forehead was cut an upside-down triangle. The Devil mark. Some say it's an Indian thing, some say the Africans. Me? I lay it on the Jews."

"Do you now?"

The tanner nodded and drank his rum straight down. "No offense, but it's a Jewish plot."

"Is that so?"

"Indeed. The Jews are planning to steal Manhattan from the English and the Dutch. Look at the way they're pushing their way into decent Christian business. Damn that Asser Levy. Do you know he's doing tanning now?"

"That sounds reasonable. He's a butcher. All that cowhide going to waste."

"Not reasonable to me. Oh, no."

"What are you complaining about? All the game skins are still
yours. Levy's not allowed to touch them."

"He'll find a way. Remember I said that. They're a crafty lot,
Jews. They killed that horse, that much is obvious. Devil worshipers.
Oh, they love blood. Use it in all their rituals. Didn't your wife ever
tell you about that False Easter of theirs? How they kill any firstborn
Christian children they find running loose and drain their blood and
use it to bake unleavened Passover bread. And put the blood on
their Jewish doorposts to fend off the Angel of Death?"

"Then why kill horses?"

"Not for me to understand the heathen mind." Keyser mopped
his head again. "Christ, it's hot. It's started, Tonneman. They'll be
killing Christian children next. Mark my words."

Tonneman's instinct was to throw the vicious little bastard
through the door without opening it. Instead, he clenched his jaw
till his teeth ached, dropped sixpence on the bar, and left the tavern.
Tonneman was so sick of Keyser and his stupid talk that he walked
all the way to the Wall and back again along the Broad Way to the
Christian cemetery before he remembered what he was supposed to
be doing.

The day was shiny, as if God himself had used a polishing cloth
on it; birds sang from every treetop. Tonneman's mood brightened.
In spite of his resolve to let Gibb handle the matter, he decided he
should go straight across to Breukelen on Harry Price's buttermilk
boat, ask if anyone had seen Davies, then ride back on Harry's boat
and have the milkman deliver him and twelve jugs of milk to Coenties Slip. That way he and Ten Eyck could keep two jugs for themselves and sell the rest, thereby not wasting the journey. Combine
the trip with business.

Ach, what was he talking about? Tomorrow was Market
Day. Harry Price, the buttermilk man, would be there himself,
peddling his own. So much for a quick profit in buttermilk. But
there would be people from Breukelen at the Market Field. He

could ask his questions about Davies without making that damn trip.

He stopped in at Lichtman's bake shop for a crumpet cake, which he had learned to enjoy since the English. A few steps north of Lichtman's was the Devil on a Chain Tavern. Tonneman walked into the cool darkness. He could just make Pos out in the shadows, holding down a stool, his giant hand about a large wooden cup.

"Good morrow, Tonneman," Pos called.

"You must have the eyes of a cat."

"Beer and spirits. Good for the sight. How goes your quest?"

"It's not the Holy Grail I seek, that's for certain." Tonneman nodded to Reed Winship, the barkeep, and sat on a stool next to Pos. "Any talk of blaming the Jews for this horse nonsense?"

Pos made a great show of drinking, but Tonneman could tell his cup was empty.

"I see."

"Sorry, Tonneman."

"No need. You didn't cause it." Tonneman left the Devil on a Chain, his mood more dour than before.

Dust rose southward along the Broad Way. That had to be workmen digging up the street in preparation for paving. Since he knew that they were his and Ten Eyck's workers, that Ten Eyck was overseeing this job, and that it meant money in his pocket, Tonneman was pleased. But thoughts of his partner made him frown. The two of them would have to work this problem out.

Not today though. Along the wide avenue of the Broad Way and down and up the narrow side streets, between one tavern and the next, Tonneman made a point of chatting with everyone he met.

Ilsa Laughton, a Philipse who had married an English merchant, thought it was terrible about what happened in the Stone Church. She blamed it on the Africans.

Jane Winder had a different view. Mistress Winder thought there was too much talk in the town, in the world, in fact, about the proper way to love God.

If there was one thing Tonneman did not want to hear, it was a sermon. He tipped his hat, prepared to move on.

But Mistress Winder wasn't having any. "I am Catholic. I say this proudly. Weren't we the first to love Jesus? Does someone have the right to tell me that I'm a bad Christian?"

"No indeed," Tonneman offered by way of farewell.

"We must love each other. Don't you agree?"

"Of course."

Numbed by her chatter, Tonneman tipped his hat again and finally broke free, only to be accosted by Charles Lanchester. Lanchester, a short, stooped man who'd been a sail maker till he broke his fingers and lost his dexterity, wanted to ask Tonneman about a job, fixing fences or the like. "Or," Lanchester added as Tonneman tried to keep moving, "I could ride for you. I could carry the Post to and from Boston." After showing Lanchester the bit of red silk and getting a negative answer, Tonneman told him to go see Ten Eyck about work.

Charlotte Seixes was concerned only about talk that the Jews were responsible. "I realize that you are a Christian, Mister Tonneman, and that your wife is no longer Jewish, but something must be done to stop this hurtful talk." Tonneman never got a chance to ask her about the red material because she talked so fast and was gone before he could think to ask.

The clothmaker, Harold Furth, told Tonneman the silk might have come from India, because of the faint smell of sandalwood that lingered about it. Furth had also heard tell that one of the Gate guards was to be court-martialed because someone came through the Water Gate early on Sunday, and the military believed it was the horse killer.

Fred Zinn, the cobbler, showed Tonneman a pair of a man's silk shoes that matched the red silk Tonneman was holding and that Zinn had just finished for Nick De Sille. While Tonneman pondered this interesting piece of information, Zinn filled his ear about how shaken up Otto, the Rattle Watch, was. And how he, Fred, was glad he had a trade and didn't have to wander town at night, when the witches were out.

Witches, Tonneman thought. What next? He reminded himself that he had to talk to Otto and the Sunday morning guard at the

Water Gate. And that he should find out if Nick owned any clothes to match his fine new red shoes. Impossible. Why would Nick do his own horse in and then hire Tonneman to investigate?

He stopped; he told himself he wanted a pipe. But that was a lie. What he was wanting was a drink. All these years and still thirsty.

The sensation on the back of his neck was like a shock of ice. The short hairs growing there began to bristle.

There was no denying what it meant.

Tonneman watched the New-Yorkers bustling past him, all concerned with their morning tasks. Then he looked behind him. All he saw there was the rising dust of the road workers.

None the less, he knew he was being followed.

Chapter 23

Tonneman headed toward Broad Street and its stone walk, reckoning if he couldn't see his tracker, he might hear him. But to no avail. Back on the Broad Way again, he picked up on his tavern walking, from the very English King and Queen Tavern to the purely Dutch, Wooden Shoe Tavern. Both were already filling with morning drinkers eager for their first drop of spirits.

At the Wall he turned right toward Asser Levy's tavern. What was the matter with him? Had he lost his touch? He certainly wasn't going at this in an orderly fashion.

Tonneman was curious as to how Asser Levy got the bruise on his cheek Racqel had told him about. He should have gone to Levy's house on his first pass.

If he ran his business like this, he and Ten Eyck would have been in the almshouse on Beaver Street long ago. Still, now, thinking it over, with Levy sick in bed and not a stern presence at his own tavern, the patrons might be more willing to answer Tonneman's questions about the slaughtered animals, the horse and the cow.

Asser Levy's tavern had only eight patrons. Not a *minyan*, thought Tonneman, pleased at his Jewish joke. A *minyan* was the ten men required by Jewish law to conduct a religious service.

The main topic of conversation seemed to be one Ezra Cohen,

who had gone missing. Now, this was more like it, Tonneman thought. Who was Ezra Cohen? Could he be dead? And the reason perhaps for the dead heifer?

Tonneman beckoned to the scraggy-bearded tapster. Asser Levy's son-in-law was known to all as Zedekiah the Sneezer.

"Tell me about this Ezra Cohen."

Zedekiah sneezed and sniffled into a huge nose cloth. He shrugged. "What's to tell? His wife can't find him."

One of the men cackled like a hen. "Becky Cohen wouldn't find me neither if I was married to her."

Tonneman bought a cider and ambled about the chamber. Two men were arguing with noisy heat.

"It was the *St. Charles*."

"No. The *Ste. Catherine*."

Others offered opinions.

Tonneman recognized the argument immediately. It was about the first Jewish settlers who had come to New Amsterdam. Though the incident had occurred a mere twenty-one years before, people constantly argued about the details, such as the name of the French ship and where the twenty-three Jews had boarded the vessel.

In 1654, in the town of Recife, the Dutch surrendered Brazil to Portuguese soldiers. Fear of the Inquisition led many of the Dutch who had settled in Brazil, Jew and Christian alike, to return to the Netherlands.

Sixteen ships left Recife. One version of the story had all sixteen heading for the Netherlands. Another stated that two ships did not, and that one of them, the Dutch schooner *Valck*, had been bound for Martinique.

Either way, the *Valck* was captured by Spanish privateers, and eventually the twenty-three Jews on board her were either rescued by a Frenchman, Captain Jacques De la Motthe, or they met him in Cuba.

De la Motthe contracted with the Jews to transport them to New Amsterdam on board his ship. The other argument was the one Tonneman had overheard: Was De la Motthe's vessel named the *St. Charles* or the *Ste. Catherine*?

Tonneman picked the longest of the clay pipes from the rack on the bar and broke off the tip. As he packed the pipe slowly with tobacco from the bar, he let the different conversations float around him. One piqued his interest more than the missing Ezra Cohen or the name of a French ship.

Zedekiah the Sneezer, who thought he could whisper, spoke to an ancient white-haired, white-bearded man who had just tottered into the tavern. "Grandfather, don't say anything about the two trappers from Albany," he cautioned in Gudezmo, the Spanish the Jews took with them when they left Spain during the Inquisition in the fifteenth century and which they still spoke amongst themselves.

"What about the trappers from Albany?" Tonneman demanded in the same language.

The tavern suddenly went quiet. It was as if some signal had been given.

Tonneman took a moment to light the pipe from one of the candles on the bar. "When were the trappers from Albany here, Grandfather?" he asked softly.

"Who are you to ask?" someone shouted.

"You all know me. I'm Pieter Tonneman."

"That and a penny will buy you a beer," the shouter said.

Laughter followed the remark. Then silence again.

Tonneman wanted nothing more than to talk to the ancient grandfather, but each time he looked at him, the old man fairly cowered on his stool.

So here it was: He had only two choices. He could leave. But he wasn't quite ready to do that. Tonneman took the second choice. He moved closer to the old grandfather and the men who had drawn protectively around him. "Did you fellows hear about the dead heifer near the Devil's Boulder? Its neck was broken and its throat was cut."

Tears began to fall from the grandfather's eyes. "A shame, a terrible shame. They were here Friday early."

"Be still, old man." The shouter again. Who was he? Tonneman craned his neck but could not see.

The old man was crying freely now. This upset Zedekiah the

Sneezer considerably. He sneezed. And sneezed once more. With this explosion his black silk cap was tossed off his head. Zedekiah picked it up and returned it to its place atop his frizzled brown hair. He stammered, "They were, they—they—"

"They were what?" Tonneman demanded.

"Strangers to everyone and Mendoza wasn't in his warehouse."

"Mendoza?"

There was a collective groan. The Sneezer had really put his foot in it now. He continued. "Yes, they were trappers for David Mendoza. They were looking for him. When he wasn't there, they left their furs in his warehouse on Staple Street and came here. They asked about Sabbath services."

"They were Jews, then?"

Zedekiah's pale green eyes swam in moisture. He looked at Tonneman as if he were a madman. "Why else would they ask?"

"Had you ever seen them before?"

"No."

"Did they eat and drink?"

Zedekiah nodded, then sneezed four times.

Tonneman waited till the tapster recovered himself. "And did they come to Sabbath services?"

"Don't answer that," someone cautioned.

"None of his business," another cried. "He's not Sheriff anymore."

The grandfather mumbled something in *Gudezmo.*

"What was that?" asked Tonneman, turning his attention to the ancient.

"Strangers, dressed oddly," the old man replied, his voice thin. "Alike enough to be twins. Their hair was the color of carrots. Tied with ribbons."

"What color?" Tonneman demanded.

The old man's face pinched with trying to remember. "Blue. And red."

Tonneman showed the old man his bit of cloth. "Like this?"

"Could be. They wore skirts."

Tonneman frowned. "What do you mean?"

But the grandfather had closed his eyes and by Tonneman's reckoning was pretending to be asleep.

Tonneman took a breath. Again he asked Zedekiah, "Did they come to services?"

"No." Zedekiah's hands shook violently. His nose cloth fell to the wood floor. He picked it up and blew his nose.

Like Gabriel's trumpet, thought Tonneman. He was surprisingly fertile with jesting thoughts this day. "Have you seen these men since then?"

"No."

Tonneman became aware that he was surrounded by the patrons of the tavern. They stood in a tight semicircle about him, Zedekiah, and the white-haired grandfather. "Then why were you telling the old man not to speak of them?"

"Because they looked like thieves. I didn't want to be associated with thieves."

"Are you a good Jew, Zedekiah?"

"You have no right to ask," a voice called.

The barkeep bridled and glared at Tonneman. "You dare talk to me about that?"

"I apologize. I merely wanted to point out that lying is a sin. Especially when you're not very good at it." Tonneman touched his hat with his fingers. "Good day."

Tonneman could feel the hostility of the crowd, mean as barbed needles. He was armed with sword and knife, but he'd neglected to carry his cudgel today. A mistake he vowed not to repeat as long as he was on this damned case for De Sille. He had no compunction about drubbing this lot with his staff, but he hadn't the stomach for sticking any of them. He took a final draw on the clay pipe, set it on the bar, and started for the door. The crowd parted for him, shuffling but otherwise silent as he left the tavern. The crumbling wall across the road cast an irregular shadow in the late morning sun.

As he stood before the tavern door, listening to the babble inside, Tonneman just made out the two men who had been talking about the ship that had brought the first Jewish settlers.

"It was the *St. Charles.*"

"Idiot. The *Ste. Catherine*. Were you there, Saul?"

"No, and neither were you. For your information, all of the twenty-three went back to the Netherlands."

"Except Asser Levy."

"Then leave me alone and ask Asser Levy."

Good advice, Tonneman thought.

Chapter 24

But Tonneman put off his visit to Asser Levy. He headed due west from Asser Levy's tavern to the North River.

In a small pocket along the North River just inside the Wall were the taverns favored by trappers. Here they would congregate when they came down from Albany and other points north to trade their furs.

He visited every tavern. It would have been easier with a glass of brandywine in his hand, and more pleasant with some in his belly. Since becoming sober, he'd found that taverns could be tedious places for one who didn't drink.

Tonneman listened carefully, but nowhere did he hear further mention of the two Jewish trappers.

Passing through the Broad Way Gate, he set off for Staple Street. Like the East River, the North River was dense with ships.

On shore, the streets were bristling with commerce too. The major thought on most people's minds was what to buy and what to sell and how to make a profit.

Beyond a patch of woods was the warehouse district of Staple Street. Here, David Mendoza conducted his business in the same place his family always had on this island. The Mendoza building was a one-story wood frame warehouse-office. Along with his European merchandise, Mendoza stored the furs he bought from the trappers and Indians.

A fine yellow carriage with a pair of bay geldings stood in front of the warehouse. The driver, also in yellow, sat at the ready on his box, picking his nose.

Tonneman stepped into the warehouse. By the sunlight that fell through one high window, David Mendoza and a well-turned-out Englishman stood examining bundles of pelts.

Mendoza interrupted his conversation with the Englishman midsentence. "Many pardons, Sir Henry." To Tonneman he said, "What can I do for you?" He spoke as if he and Tonneman were old friends and had just broken bread the day before. Without waiting for Tonneman to answer, he went on. "If you'll excuse me, I would like to finish my business with Sir Henry."

Tonneman nodded and stepped back outside. A loud noise drew his attention to the side of the building, where a door was swinging in the wind and slapping against the warehouse wall. An arm reached out and pulled the door closed.

Tonneman walked past the door to the shore of the river and looked across to the rugged hills of New Jersey. The smell of spring was in the air. The last of the snow had almost disappeared and the ice in the river was gone. He glanced at the warehouse in time to see Mendoza's customer come out and leave in his yellow carriage; Tonneman returned to Mendoza's office.

The years had steadied David Mendoza and strengthened his body. Judging from the stories about his wealth, they had sharpened his mind and his business acumen too.

It was obvious from the way the square black silk cap graced Mendoza's head that he considered it a crown. Tonneman had oft heard Racqel speak thus of David Mendoza's arrogance. In the rare moments when she chose to speak of her former brother-in-law, it was always with bitterness.

Mendoza stared benignly at Tonneman. "Yes? What is it?"

"Two trappers came from the north this past Friday. They brought skins for you."

"If you change that number to twenty trappers, I would agree with you. Also, I do business only in the morning on Friday." Mendoza picked up one of the many lamps that illuminated the warehouse and walked to the back of the large chamber, stacked with goods from floor to ceiling. He disappeared behind a wall of carpets. "I'm very busy," he called, "and I can't stop my work to talk."

Tonneman followed Mendoza behind the carpet wall. Mendoza was seated at a long desk that had a chair at each end. He was writing in a huge account book. A Jewish youth with fuzz on his cheek stood to his right. The youth was too old to be one of Mendoza's sons.

"I regret disrupting your day, but this won't take long."

Mendoza set his quill down. "Are you then Sheriff again?"

"No. I'm working on a private commission." Without thinking about it, Tonneman fingered the slip of cloth in his waistcoat pocket. He pulled it out.

"Acting for whom?"

"I'm not at liberty to say." Tonneman showed the bit of silk to Mendoza. "You deal in this sort of material?"

Mendoza took the piece of silk and rubbed it between his palms. "It is similar to some I've sold." His nose twitched. "But mine was less fragrant." As he handed it back, something flickered in his eyes. "I misspoke. There was a consignment from India, inferior stuff, more than a year ago. I believe Mister Jacob Roome and I made a trade for the labor of his wife, she being a fair seamstress. I have a business to run, so if that is all, I bid you good day."

Very interesting, thought Tonneman as he placed the scrap of cloth in his purse in order not to forget it again. He would have to have a talk with Jacob Roome. He pressed Mendoza once more. "The trappers?"

"Which trappers?"

"The ones who left their furs with you, went to Asser Levy's tavern, and were never seen again."

"I suggest you ask the people at Asser Levy's tavern. Or Asser Levy himself."

"I'm asking you."

Mendoza offered Tonneman a cold smile. He motioned the

young man away with an impatient lift of his chin. "I buy or trade for trappers' furs." Mendoza raised his hands. "And that is that."

"These were Jewish trappers."

"In that case, I wish them good luck. Now, if you'll excuse me." Mendoza picked up his quill, and his nose went deep into his ledger.

"One more thing."

Mendoza did not look up. "You're keeping me from my prayers and my luncheon," he said impatiently. He set the quill down and sighed. "I eat the midday meal early. If that's all right with you?"

"None of my concern when you eat. But I do need to verify Francis Beado's story that he was with you on Sunday."

"He was. Good day, Tonneman."

"At what hour?"

"From the early morning before the sun rose, till noon."

"Why?"

"Why what?"

"Why did Beado come to see you?"

"To sell me three beautiful red fox pelts. Good day."

"It took six hours to sell three skins?"

"Beado is an exacting bargainer. Good day."

Tonneman watched Mendoza for a short time, then left his office. The scratch of the pen over the paper followed him as he walked the long, cramped course through the goods and the furs back to Staple Street.

Sounds of men working filled the air from the surrounding streets and down to the waterfront as ships were unloaded and reloaded. From the Old Dutch Tavern in the unnamed alley nearby came the sounds of men delighted at their play and drink.

Mendoza's warehouse was a conglomeration of several structures, some joined, some not, added on over the years as the business had grown and prospered.

It was in the smallest of these additions, one connected to the main building, that Tonneman had seen the arm closing the door. Instinct spurred him to investigate.

He dodged a cart being pushed by a boy who was so tiny, the boxes piled high on the cart blocked his view and he had to keep peering around the side of his load. The boy rolled his cart into one of the side additions, but not the one Tonneman was interested in.

A wagon drawn by an aged brown plow horse with white feet pulled up outside Mendoza's main doors. Two men began unloading bolts of fabric.

Tonneman rubbed the back of his neck; his skin was crawling. Whoever was following him earlier was still with him.

Chapter 25

TUESDAY, 19 MARCH.
MORNING.

Tonneman had worked at enough occupations in his lifetime—seaman, lawman, merchant—to know that when he had a premonition such as this, it was best to pay heed.

Everyone along the road and on the side roads seemed to be in his proper place. As on the East River, trappers and Indians shared the busy thoroughfares with merchants and traders.

From the corner of his eye Tonneman caught a movement, followed by a glimpse of a face looking out at him from the small side building attached to Mendoza's warehouse. A spark flared in his brain; the face disappeared, but the memory clung. Tonneman had recognized the face.

The face reappeared, this time with a hand; was the hand beckoning to him?

Tonneman felt for the knife at his belt. He did not draw it. If he was going to do this sort of business, he'd have to restore old habits. He sorely missed his oak cudgel.

The small building was a long box with one door on its long side. Cautiously, he put his head inside the door. It was only a spare antechamber. Nothing human here. A three-legged table held a low-burning lamp, a cup, a plate scraped clean. Roasted fowl. Chicken, by the smell of it. But if so, where were the bones? Tonneman lifted the cup. Traces of beer. Recently poured beer at that. His stomach rumbled.

Tonneman took the lamp from the table, turned up the wick. It was hard to say if this building led directly to the main warehouse. The answer lay behind the second door.

He removed his hat and pressed his ear against the panel. No sound. Only the continual work noises coming from the street.

Setting his hat back upon his head, he held the lamp high and opened the second door. This led to an otherwise dark chamber whose expanse he could not yet determine. He stepped across the threshold.

A crash of pain sent Tonneman reeling into the darkness. Reaching up to protect his head from another blow, he dropped the lantern. Whether the chamber went darker or he was slipping into unconsciousness, Tonneman couldn't tell. He groped for balance.

Surprisingly soft but strong hands seized his throat and dragged him to the floor. Tonneman gasped for air, cursing De Sille. If the bloody bastard were here, Tonneman would surely have killed him.

Fury against his attacker and De Sille gave Tonneman renewed strength. He rolled over, then got to his knees. But his attacker stayed with him, never loosening a powerful grip.

Tonneman crashed over backward, wheezing. A door slammed. And another. His attacker was gone. It had been a trap and he had walked right into it. Damnation! Tonneman cursed De Sille again, and then he cursed Mendoza. The trader's mention of prayers and food had reminded Tonneman of how hungry he was. Now? During this? Yes. He needed food. And prayer?

He felt about in the dark, searching for the lantern, but found nothing. He heard only his own labored breath; the distinctive odor of death crowded him.

Feeling his way along, he finally found the door he'd come through. He shoved it open. The door to the street was open too, and lit the area somewhat vaguely with sunlight. It was enough light to see the man who'd beckoned to him crumpled like a sack of feathers on the wood-strewn floor. A long knife was stabbed into the back of his neck, the tip protruding from under Edward Davies's chin like a lost and bloody tongue.

Racqel had been wrong; the boy hadn't gone to Breukelen after all.

Chapter 26

TUESDAY, 19 MARCH.
MORNING.

"There was a notice on his door that he's ill, Mutti."

Racqel looked up at her son, shading her eyes. She dusted the dirt from her hands. Daffodils and tulips were just starting to send little green shoots up through the ground. The branches of the apple and peach trees seemed to swell and soften, already beginning to convert to spring. Her garden was going to be lovely.

Racqel offered her son her hand and rose, shaking dirt from her apron. Although she wore a bonnet, the sun glanced warm on her face. Maria, who'd been working beside her, stood and dusted her hands and shook her apron in imitation of her mother. The girl squinted at the sun, then at Daniel, who sat in the dirt, looking for pebbles. Scooping up her wriggling brother, she took him to sit under her favorite apple tree, out of the sun. There, Maria plumped down next to her baby brother and cooed to him. But Daniel would have none of it. He screamed lustily, "No, no, no," and, after making several tumbling attempts, finally stood and ran after a large ant.

Racqel brushed her oldest's fine dark hair away from his face. "You didn't inquire what was wrong, Moses? Perhaps he's in need."

"The sign said 'I'm not well. Please do not disturb me.' It was signed L. Crabtree. When I asked Mistress Jones, the woman he lets the room from, she just kept repeating that she didn't know anything, but she's very hard of hearing and doesn't see well either. Do you think I should have gone in? I thought I should, but Mistress Jones kept saying, 'Go away. Go away.' "

"Has she ever acted like this before?"

"No, Mutti."

"Mistress Jones is an old woman. We'll fix a basket of food and pay a call on your Master Crabtree. He may be too proud to ask for help, so you and I will provide for him. In the meantime, why don't you go up to my bedchamber and study? Afterward Benjamin could use your help. He is building a house with straw." She smiled. Benjamin had a talent with his hands, as Moses with his mind. "Ask Alice to make a basket for your unfortunate schoolmaster."

"Yes, Mutti." Moses slung his canvas bag over his shoulder and went inside. Once he was out of sight, Racqel allowed her concern to show on her face. Had something frightened the old woman? Racqel had seen her at the Market Field over the years, and though age had slowed her and her hearing was gone, Mistress Jones seemed to have a kind nature.

"Huloo, Racqel!"

Antje Ten Eyck came around the house followed by her younger son, Pieter, named for Tonneman, his godfather. Pieter at ten was already half a head taller than his mother. There was another special connection for young Pieter Ten Eyck with the Tonneman family. It was Racqel who'd delivered him one hot August day while the English were laying siege to New Amsterdam, demanding surrender.

Pieter brandished a net full of wriggling bass. "See what I've brought for your supper, Aunt Racqel. I'll clean them for you if you like."

"Well . . ."

"Let him," Antje said. "It will do him good."

Maria caught Daniel before he gobbled up the ant and brought him to the Ten Eycks, struggling and kicking in her arms. All at once Daniel quieted. He was studying the fish.

"And perhaps," Antje continued, "Maria can help." Antje winked at Racqel.

Pieter's face grew red just as Maria's did. "Oh, Mutti!" each cried.

Racqel swallowed a laugh. "Of course. Maria would be happy to help. If we can prize her away from Daniel."

On hearing his name, Daniel looked up from the dangling fish. Racqel took him from Maria's arms; he began to howl again. "My, Daniel," Racqel exclaimed, "what powerful lungs." She blew in his ear. He giggled. "Maria, go help Pieter with the fish." As Pieter and Maria went into the house, Racqel grinned at Antje. "We'll have them married soon if you have your way."

"Is that so bad?" Pulling up her skirts, Antje settled her broad bottom on the stoop. "Ah, the sun feels good."

Racqel opened the bosom of her dress to receive her son's hungry lips.

Antje frowned. "You never give up. You're not going to bring your milk back, the miscarriage spoiled that. And he's getting too old for the teat, Racqel. Enough, for Jesus' sake."

Racqel grinned at her friend. "You know by now I never do anything for Jesus' sake."

For a moment Antje did not reply. She scrutinized Racqel's face, then said quietly, "You are not yourself." Racqel merely gave her a sad smile. "Is it the baby you lost?" When Racqel still didn't speak, Antje continued again. "That husband of yours is still mad at mine, is he?"

Racqel readjusted Daniel, who had begun to nod off. "He hates being beholden to De Sille for more reasons than I think even I know. Let's have some tea."

In the kitchen the women sat knee to knee, speaking quietly while the sated Daniel slept in Racqel's arms. They watched Alice fill a small basket of bread and cheese for the ailing Crabtree. From the scullery came the soft murmur of their youngsters' voices.

"My Pieter and your Maria," Antje said thoughtfully, "I think will bring our lines together. We shall be sisters."

"We are already." Racqel shifted the sleeping child in her lap.

"Then why don't you tell me what's troubling you?"

Racqel stood and folded Daniel into his cradle. "Will you walk a ways with me, Antje?" She covered the child with a thin blanket and kissed his damp forehead, combing his feathery blond hair with her fingers and replacing his little blue cap. "When he sleeps he's such an angel." Racqel called into the scullery, "Keep watch on Daniel, Maria."

"I'd best be home, then," Pieter said, appearing in the kitchen with Maria. His eyes never left the girl.

"If that's what you wish," Antje said, teasing her smitten son.

Confused, Pieter flushed.

Antje shook her head. "It's really true what they say about Dutchmen. We have no sense of humor. I'm only going for a little walk with Racqel, Pieter. So you can stay with Maria and I'll stop back for you."

"Oh, Pieter," Racqel said, "yesterday at your lessons, did Master Crabtree seem not well?"

Pieter frowned. "He was as always, Aunt. Except for his hands. They shook worse than ever. He kept breaking the chalk on the slate and talked to himself in a language I didn't understand."

The women wrapped their shawls about their shoulders, fastened their hats. Racqel picked up the basket that Alice had covered with a bright bit of green homespun, and the two friends walked out onto Queen Street. They strayed, as if by special design, to admire the view of the East River. Gulls swept in curves across the sky. Ships blanketed the Bay with their billowing white sails. Breukelen and Long Island seemed close enough to touch, and the sun bathed all with a white-yellow glow.

"For all of it, this is a piece of heaven we live in. Eh, Racqel?"

Racqel agreed.

Now the two old friends turned westward on Broad Street along the canal and thence to the Broad Way, where they walked on wooden walks along the side of the road. The Ten Eyck and Tonneman workers were paving the Broad Way with cobble. With the ends of their shawls the women protected their mouths and noses from the stink of tar and the billows of dust coming out of the half-paved road.

"Good day, Mistress Ten Eyck, Mistress Tonneman," the workmen called.

They nodded to the paver, an egg-bald man with an oft-broken nose.

"Mistress Ten Eyck?"

"Yes, Mister Pijnenborgh," Antje said.

"Mister Ten Eyck said he was going home for some beer."

Antje made a face at the thought of her husband coming home to no wife. "I'm in trouble," she mumbled as they walked on.

"I doubt that," Racqel said.

"So?" Antje prompted, returning again to the subject of Racqel's disquiet.

"Ach, where to begin?" Racqel murmured.

"At the beginning."

"After all these years of a comparatively peaceful life, my Tonneman is once again hunting criminals."

Antje wrinkled her forehead.

"I hate to mention this, Antje, but because of certain kindnesses he has extended to Tonneman and Ten Eyck, the First Councillor claims an obligation from our husbands."

"What kind of obligation?"

"De Sille demands that Tonneman find whoever killed the Governor's horse on Sunday."

"Shit."

"My feelings exactly." Racqel sighed. "There's more."

"If that husband of yours is causing you sorrow, I'll personally box his ears."

Racqel laughed. The picture of Antje, whose full height brought her barely to Tonneman's chest, attempting to box her husband's ears was too funny.

"What, then?"

"Asser Levy's wife called me a Jezebel." Racqel fell silent. She had the uneasy feeling that people were watching her.

"Wait," Antje said. They were approaching the Devil on a

Chain. On its threshold, carrying a clay jug, was young Maarten van Dam. "If I have to hear more of this, I need some beer. Huloo, Maarten. What's that you have there?"

"A double-beer for my father," the young man replied.

"What's that cost?"

"Three p. a quart."

"I'll give you four for it."

"Done," said young Maarten. He handed the quart jug over to Antje, took the coins she proffered, and dashed back to the Devil on a Chain.

Racqel stared at her friend. "Why did you do that?"

"Because I'm thirsty." Antje pulled out the wooden stopper and drank from the jug.

Racqel was astonished and embarrassed. Bad enough Mistress Levy was telling lies about her. Here she was standing in the middle of the Broad Way and her friend was drinking beer.

"Now," said Antje, lowering the jug. There was a wicked smile on her lips. "We'll walk slowly to Master Crabtree's residence and you can tell me the entire story."

Antje offered the jug to Racqel; Racqel refused. Instead, she fussed with the napkin that covered Master Crabtree's bread and cheese. Carts and carriages rolled past them. The sun was leaving noon and making its way toward evening. Racqel sighed. "Let's walk faster. I want to see how Master Crabtree is faring and be back in time to have the midday meal with the children, and perhaps even my wandering man."

"All right. Tell me what happened with Mistress Levy."

"Mister Levy is sick. He sent for me, probably over his wife's objections. Jezebel, she called me." Racqel's lips trembled.

Antje took the basket from her friend. "You are not responsible for small minds."

"Small minds can keep me from my people."

"Ach, Racqel." Antje shook her head.

The two women continued walking in companionable silence. Everywhere around them structures were going up: houses, City works, shops with large wooden signs indicating their craft or wares.

As the women passed through the Broad Way Gate, a Musketeer nodded to them.

"Good day," the women called.

In spite of the problems plaguing her, Racqel couldn't help but reflect that the old Wall was in such poor condition, it might as well be gone. It leaned in places like a drunken sailor; elsewhere it had crumbled to splinters and dust.

Just past the Wall, streets had been laid out and marked with stones. King Street already showed newer houses, built in the English fashion. Here and there among them stood a few older Dutch farmhouses. Beyond King Street was Second Queen Street, followed by Crown Street. On Crown Street stood the only remnant of what had been a large farm belonging to the Jones family. Old Mistress Jones had outlived husband and children. The widow had been selling off parcels of land until she was down to the small plot on which the farmhouse stood.

She took in lodgers, especially those who were not opposed to helping her around her house and what was left of her land.

Lester Crabtree, a shy man and a gifted teacher, had arrived in New-York the summer before, just after the English returned, and advertised himself as a schoolmaster. Crabtree did not object to using some of his time to repair the hinge on Mistress Jones's back door or nail down a floorboard or two that drifted.

"Ay, how our small village changes daily," Antje said over the noise of industrious carpenters. The two women stopped to watch the framework of a good-sized house go up.

A cart rolled by, hit a bump, and dislodged a basket of apples from its open back. Before anyone could say a word, four porkers plunged into the dirt road ahead of Racqel and Antje, snorting and grunting, and made fast work of the apples. Not content with the fruit, they finished off the remains of the smashed wicker basket.

Across the road Racqel and Antje could see Mistress Glenda Jones napping in a chair in front of her house, oblivious to the din. The old farmhouse had recently been painted yellow with blue shutters.

"She is deaf as a stone," Antje said. "Poor thing."

"Just as well. The peaceful countryside is no longer peaceful. I hate to wake her."

"Well, let's not. We can go inside and look in on the schoolmaster and be gone without her ever knowing it."

Mistress Jones herself was adding quite nicely to the noise with her whistling, growling snores.

The women grinned at each other, opened the farmhouse door, and entered. The kitchen was a very orderly place of some size. A rabbit stew simmered in an open pot on the hearth.

The other side of the kitchen led to the great chamber, low-ceiling'd and filled with sturdy furniture. A narrow staircase led upward.

Racqel went to the foot of the stairs and called, "Master Crabtree?"

There was no response.

Antje said, "He's on the second landing. Let's go up."

"Master Crabtree," Racqel called again, taking the basket from Antje.

No response, neither a muffled footstep nor a breath.

"Oh, well, up we go." Antje set her beer jug on the green-painted floor and lifted her skirts.

Racqel followed her up the steep stairs, sniffing. A peculiar smell hovered on the second story. Disconcerted by the odor, she walked right into Antje, who'd come to a full stop in front of her. "What's wrong?"

"Too dark. We must go no farther without light."

"Wait here," Racqel said. She descended the stairs and went back to the hearth. There on a table she found a candlestand with a good bit of candle left. She lit it from the hearth and returned to the foot of the staircase, where she found Antje sitting.

"There's a God-awful smell up there, like death himself." Antje shook her head.

"Come, come, Master Crabtree may need our help."

"I think he's past that," Antje said with a sigh. But she followed Racqel up the stairs.

The smell came strongest from the last door in the narrow corridor. Racqel covered her nose and mouth and held the candle up to the door. Both women gasped.

Across the door, scrawled in red, was the word <u>BLASPHEMER</u>. There was no notice of illness. Instead, nailed to the door with a bright tenpenny nail, dripping blood, was the very private organ of another stallion.

Chapter 27

David Mendoza sneered at Tonneman with cold contempt. He set down his quill. The young man at his elbow stood mouth agape. "It has naught to do with me."

Tonneman removed his hat and touched the back of his head. He felt a swelling, but no blood. Cats were yammering inside his skull and his throat was tender. Carefully, he set his hat back in place and repeated what had caused Mendoza's sneer. "There's a dead man in a lake of blood on the floor of your smallest outbuilding." He noted that neither Mendoza nor the youth bore any trace of blood. Nor did either appear in any way disarrayed.

Mendoza picked up his quill.

The boy moved the standish under the pen.

"The building you speak of is leased to Jacob Roome." Mendoza dipped his pen and wrote in his ledger. He raised his head and locked eyes with Tonneman. "You will please leave."

Their mutual enmity was distracted by the panting breaths of the boy, whose wan face had turned quite red.

Mendoza jumped to his feet, all the while speaking soothing words in *Gudezmo* to the lad. He rubbed the boy's quivering back. Slowly, the agonized breathing subsided. "Better?" he asked the boy in Dutch.

The young man nodded.

Sitting, Mendoza stretched his arms and yawned. In English he said to Tonneman, "Asthma." Then gently, in the same language, "Aaron, find Sheriff Gibb and bring him here. Do not run."

"Spare the boy the trouble," Tonneman told him. "I'll do it."

"You are more than kind," Mendoza said with exaggerated courtesy, and returned to his thick ledger.

Tonneman left them. What had happened between him and Mendoza? He knew only that they would undoubtedly take their shared rancor to the grave.

Let Gibb handle it, he thought, disgruntled, as he trudged across town toward the Water Gate Road, which would take him to Queen Street. It was Gibb's problem, not his. The death of Edward Davies had naught to do with Tonneman. "Listen to me," he said aloud. He knew he was as wrongheaded as Mendoza. The notion made him touch the back of his pate again. The lump was now the size of a pigeon egg. Carts passed him, loaded with logs cleared from the forest land, their rumble making his sore head throb. Ten Eyck had wanted to get into the lumber business but Tonneman had rejected the plan. Now, with people building farther and farther north, he was having second thoughts.

Davies had been a likely suspect in the horse killing, and now he was himself killed. Was Davies killed for any of numerous, and yet unknown, other reasons? Or had he died because someone was afraid of what the wild young man might tell Tonneman? And had he been running off to Breukelen to hide, and returned to meet his death, or had he never gone at all?

A barrel-filled cart thundered past him, raising dust, then stopped. "Mister Tonneman? Do you need help, sir? You look as if you've been chased by a mad bull and he caught you."

Tonneman glanced down at his clothes. They were covered with blood. At this rate he wouldn't have any clean clothes left. Tonneman removed his ruined jacket, torn and stained with the unfortunate boy's blood, rolled it, and tucked it under his arm.

The driver was young Jacob de Kees, his Boston Post Rider. Tonneman could smell the beer in the barrels. As it mixed with the scent of blood that had remained in his nostrils, once more he thought of Edward Davies. "I am well, Jacob. Someone else's bad fortune. Tell me, have you heard anything about this horse ado on Sunday?"

"Forgive me, sir, but yes. There's talk the Jews did it. For their Passover coming."

"Lord help us. Keep it between us, but I'm looking into this. So if you hear anything else, let me know."

"You know I will, Mister Tonneman."

"Shouldn't you be on your way to Boston?"

"Yes, sir. As soon as I drop this load at Soldiers Tavern."

"Then be gone."

Jacob de Kees drove off, flicking his hickory stick smartly at the brawny gray mare.

Tonneman watched Jacob de Kees and his cart move away, wondering if perhaps he should talk to another Jacob. Jacob Roome, Davies's stepfather. And the young man's mother too. No, damn it, he would not be the bearer of news of someone else's bad fortune. That was Gibb's job. Christ's bloody hands. *Tonneman, living the burgher life has made you a coward. You were there. You tell her.*

The shed that marked the back end of the Jewish cemetery lay ahead of him. Originally the cemetery was a small place; now graves pushed against the fence. Tonneman paused. His eyes searched out the stones of Benjamin Mendoza, Racqel's first husband, and Moses Pereira, the physician, her father. Tonneman had not known either man.

He stepped over the low fence and walked among the graves. Soon he spied what he was looking for. Under an aged chestnut tree someone had filled a fresh grave. And there had been no Jewish deaths. At least none that had been spoken of before today, and none today on his round of taverns. With fewer than forty Jews in New-York, he could be fairly certain.

Someone had strewn twigs and leaves over the grave so that the new-turned earth would not be noticed from the road. This confirmed it. Some part of the Jewish Community had to know about the dead man—the one Racqel suggested the cow had been killed for. If there was a dead man. It gave Tonneman something further to ponder as he started down the road toward Queen Street.

One of three men could be in that fresh grave. The missing Ezra Cohen. Or either one of the two carrot-haired trappers from Albany. Maybe all three were in the grave together?

Tonneman scowled. The Jews would have 578 laws saying why he couldn't dig up that grave. And Gibb would say he didn't give a frolicking shit about a new grave in the Jew cemetery.

Tonneman himself felt the act profane, but the only way to find out for sure was to dig. He ran back to the cemetery, found a shovel in the shed, and went to work.

The earth was soft and crumbly; still, it was a job. But his labor proved well worth his efforts. The pine box was barely three feet down, and when he prized it open with his knife, he discovered a body, wrapped in a winding sheet. Undoing a shroud was work better left to God and maggots, but the stitches came undone easily enough.

The corpse was a man with carrot hair, which included a beard and mustache. He was naked and quite clean for a trapper. Still, from his hair, he had to be one of the two they talked of in Levy's tavern.

There was a blade wound in the chest. Tonneman turned the body. There was no wound out. Perhaps a knife rather than a sword had accomplished this killing. Much good that did him.

The dead trapper's orange hair stopped below his ears, except for a long braid that traveled halfway down his back. The braid was tied with two ribbons. One, dark blue; the other, scarlet red.

Tonneman respectfully replanted the man in his grave. "Rest in peace," he said with the last shovelful of dirt.

AT THE JAIL in the City Hall building, he found Nessel-Vogel, sword out, body extended, practising parries and thrusts.

The Deputy stood erect and gaped at Tonneman. "What's happened to you?"

"It's what happened to Edward Davies that you have to concern yourself with."

Nessel-Vogel laid his sword on the plain pine table and removed his baldric. "Damn thing doesn't hang right. What happened to Davies?"

Tonneman placed his rolled-up jacket on the table next to the sword. "He's as dead as a doornail. In one of Mendoza's outbuildings on Staple Street. Where's Gibb?"

"How—" Nessel-Vogel looked pained. "I reckon I ought to go on over—"

"Nessel-Vogel!" The shout could only be Gibb's, and it was coming from just outside.

The Deputy had scarcely time to put his baldric back on and was sheathing his sword when Gibb slammed through the door, followed by Antje and Racqel. "Move, Nessel-Vogel," the Sheriff shouted. "The horse killer has done in the schoolmaster."

"We don't know that for certain." It was Racqel, trailing Gibb, and Antje was behind her. "Tonneman!" Racqel rushed to her husband. "You're hurt."

"Not my blood," he assured her, kissing the anxious hand that reached for him.

"Thanks be to a generous God," said Racqel. "What happened?"

Gibb shouted again, this time at Tonneman. "What the devil are you doing here? I'm more than a little tired of you getting under my feet."

"Get ready to be more tired. Davies is dead at Mendoza's warehouse."

"My God," said Racqel.

Tonneman would not look at his wife. "There's more. A fresh body now lies in a fresh grave in the Jewish cemetery. I dug him up."

Racqel gasped. Gibb merely narrowed his eyes.

Crossing to the Queen Street window, Racqel stared vacantly at the ships in the East River. What her husband had done was sacrilege. Now they would never let her back into the fold.

Tonneman needed a pipe. All he could taste on his tongue were blood and dirt. "The new corpse is a man with carrot hair and a knife wound in his chest."

Gibb rolled his shoulders and jerked his neck. This was not going to be good for his back, and he was getting damned sick of Tonneman sticking his nose in Sheriff's business. "Nessel-Vogel, get over to Mendoza's warehouse. The chap in the grave will have to wait. Tonneman and I will go to the schoolmaster's."

Nessel-Vogel grumbled, "When did Tonneman become your Deputy?"

"It's the schoolmaster, Tonneman," Antje explained, seeing the question on Tonneman's face. "Someone wrote 'Blasphemer' in blood on his door. The stink was enough to make my eyes . . ."

Racqel stood with folded arms, staring at her husband hard until he, chagrined, said, "I'm sorry, but digging up the grave was something I had to do. There was a murder not reported—" He held his hand out to her.

She saw his throat, which was starting to color purple, and took his hand. She loved him, but his admission had filled her with dread.

He grabbed both her hands and held them. "Racqel?"

She shook her head, mute, pulled her hands away.

Tonneman nodded. "Is Crabtree dead too?"

"We don't know," Racqel answered. "His room was a horror. Blood everywhere. The smell was hideous."

"And," Antje added, a glimmer of a smile tugging her mouth, "nailed to the door was a horse's bloody thing."

"Jesus' balls!" Gibb snorted. "But no sign of Crabtree?"

The women shook their heads.

Racqel continued. "Blood covered the sill and the window was open wide."

"That's on the second floor in the back," said Nessel-Vogel.

"How do you know?" Gibb demanded.

"I know it," Nessel-Vogel said. He smirked contentedly.

"We went downstairs," Racqel said. "From the blood and marks on the ground, someone jumped or was thrown from the second floor window." She nodded at Nessel-Vogel. "In the back. Besides the blood on the ground, I could see blood on the house just under the window."

The Deputy shook his head. "She just had it painted."

"How do you know that?" Gibb demanded.

Nessel-Vogel adjusted his baldric. He didn't answer the Sheriff.

"We'll go to the warehouse," Gibb said, "where we know we have a dead man. Then we'll search for the schoolmaster."

"That may not be prudent," Racqel said. "There was a trail of blood across the new lots leading toward the Broad Way Road. The trail should be followed and quickly. For all we know, Master Crabtree may still be alive and in need of our aid."

Gibb frowned. The woman was right.

In the distance came a peal of thunder.

"We must hurry," Racqel urged. "Before those blood marks disappear."

"That's rain coming," Antje informed the Sheriff, taking Racqel's arm. "Let's go quickly before everything washes away."

Nessel-Vogel stamped to the window. After a moment he said, "No lightning I can see. It's far off."

"But it's coming," said Antje.

"It would be better," Tonneman said softly to his wife, "if you returned to our house and saw to our children."

Chastened, and confused, Racqel thought to comply. Instead, she thrust her chin forward. "Alice will feed them."

"Move, Nessel-Vogel." Gibb was already outside, shouting back to them. "Tonneman is right. We don't want these women getting in our way. Tonneman, are you with us?"

Tonneman grabbed his soiled coat from the table. Racqel's eyes accused him of sacrilege and betrayal. Antje's expression was as unyielding as his wife's. The back of his head felt as if it were about to come off. "Go home, both of you. You have no business in this. It's man's work."

Neither woman budged.

Tonneman touched Antje's arm. "Will you talk to her? If you stay, Racqel will stay."

Antje's sharp blue eyes glinted at him. "Tonneman, I love you like a brother. You may tell your wife what to do. And you may be vexed with my husband. But you are not giving me orders, no matter how sweetly you put it. My husband and sons can take care of themselves. I'm going to follow the blood. Are you coming, Racqel?"

Antje was already out the door and on the street.

Chapter 28

From the direction of New Haarlem, rolling over woodland and swamp, came the low snarl of thunder. The three men climbed into the Sheriff's wagon. A small crowd had gathered, mostly of car-men, a few sailors, and young lads of the City who worked the docks. Wood, the miller, who was loading kegs into his dray with mighty heaves of his one good arm, stopped to call, "What's wrong, Sheriff? Are the Dutch coming back?" He ended with a high, whining laugh, so strange to hear from a man his size. A few in the crowd sniggered.

"More likely the Swedes," offered the seaman helping Wood.

"Move, Nessel-Vogel!" Gibb shouted, irritated. Everyone in this town thought himself a jester. "Be quick about it."

Nessel-Vogel flicked the reins. The startled gray gelding jerked forward and tore into a gallop. The cloud of dust raised on the dug-up ground along Queen Street left Racqel and Antje just as startled and, even more, angry as the fine grit settled over them and the wagon moved away.

The wagon nearly tipped over when they turned left at the Wall. Tonneman noticed four or five men standing in front of Levy's tavern.

"My back, you yap," Gibb screamed at Nessel-Vogel. "Do you want to break it?" The Sheriff was not pleased.

Nor was Tonneman. And there wasn't a thing he could do about it.

"Slow down, Nessel-Vogel," Gibb ordered as they approached the Broad Way. "We'll never see the blood at this rate."

"But it's not there to see yet. The house is in Crown Street." The Deputy spoke with almost condescending patience.

"Slow," Gibb ordered. "What if he came this way?"

"I'm slowing." Under his breath the Deputy added as they rode through the Broad Way Gate, "First he says fast, then he says slow."

"Hoy, Gibb," called the sentry. "In a race with a turtle?"

"Shut up," Gibb muttered. He was in misery.

Mistress Jones was sitting in her chair, awake now, and with a contented smile on her pudding face. Waving her arm, she seemed delighted to see them. She straightened her bonnet and beamed like an expectant child. If anything was amiss, you couldn't tell it by her.

The Sheriff got down from the wagon with care and stretched his arms above his head. "Nessel-Vogel, get into that house and take a look. Tonneman and I will investigate out here."

"What is it, Sheriff?" Mistress Jones eased herself up from her armchair and waddled to the edge of the porch. She peered at them. "Sheriff. Mister Tonneman, good day to you."

Gibb, having spied a dark red trail coming from around the corner of the house, ignored the old woman.

"Sheriff?" Her caw was a crow's call.

"A small problem with your tenant," Gibb shouted loud enough to rouse the dead. Surreptitiously, he signaled to his Deputy.

Nessel-Vogel trudged into the house.

"What? What?" Mistress Jones leaned toward the Sheriff, nearly losing her balance.

Gibb saw that the blood led to the Broad Way Road from behind the house. "You tell her, Tonneman." He followed the trail.

Tonneman stepped up on the porch and led the old woman back to her chair. He patted her shoulder. "Stay here," he shouted.

She complied with some confusion and sat with a loud sigh.

Oh, for a deaf woman, Tonneman thought, obedient, with no opinions.

At the back of the house Gibb found the site where the mass of blood had soaked into the ground; he studied the bloody shingles and the second story window above him.

By this time Tonneman had joined Gibb. Nessel-Vogel put his head out of the window. "Just as they said," the Deputy called. "A bloody stinking mess. And that's a horse cock on the door." He laughed. "I would love to have seen their faces."

Gibb watched Tonneman watching Nessel-Vogel. "That's not funny, Nessel-Vogel."

"Yes, sir. I know, sir. Sorry, sir." The Deputy choked off a laugh. His face vanished from the window. It was difficult for Tonneman not to smile. This was serious stuff, and it was his wife who'd seen the horse's works on the door.

But he, too, would have loved to have seen Racqel's face when she saw it. Hell, he'd love to see her face right now. And tell her that he hated when they argued. And that they shouldn't. Ever. But this was man's work, and she should leave it to men.

Cupping his mouth with his hands, Gibb called, "Nessel-Vogel! Where in Jesus' name are you? Where did that yap go now?"

The Deputy showed his face. "Sir?"

"You stay here and keep looking. I want a thorough job of it. And talk to the old lady. There's a blood track leading to the road. I'm going to ride on ahead with Tonneman and follow it."

Nessel-Vogel's mouth opened. "But, sir . . ."

Gibb grunted to Tonneman and hooked his thumb toward the front of the house.

"Which way?" Tonneman asked.

Gibb made a disparaging face. "North, of course."

Tonneman knelt. "You can barely see it, but there's also a bit of blood heading back to the City. You said it yourself: What if he went back the way we came?"

Gibb shook his head. Now the former Sheriff was trying to tell him his job. "The strong trail is to the north. If we find nothing there, we can always come back."

Tonneman glanced up at the rain-laden clouds. "I doubt it. But you're the Sheriff. Carry on."

The Sheriff drove. Very slowly. Whether to spot the blood or ease his back, Tonneman couldn't tell. And he didn't care. He was thinking of Edward Davies. What, if any, connection could be made among the horse killings, this bizarre event with Master Crabtree, and Davies's murder?

The blood marks they followed were faint, but they lay on the dirt for all to see. And whoever had left them was being exceedingly helpful by staying to the roadway.

Tonneman let the lawman concentrate on the trail. Shaking his head at the bloody ruin of his coat, he donned it and looked to the northwest. A flash skewered the dark clouds rolling in. The faint sound of thunder came. His thoughts strayed again to Racqel. He envisioned her sitting at home with the children and hoped she had forgotten their quarrel. After all, a man had to put his foot down.

"You know where this is leading us, don't you?"

"The Devil's Boulder," Gibb answered as a matter of fact.

All at once two horses came pounding up behind them. A dun and a white.

"God's blood and piss," Tonneman shouted. "That's Ten Eyck's stallion, Snow. And my horse, Venus."

"Ridden by Mistress Ten Eyck," Sheriff Gibb said. He rolled his eyes at Tonneman. "And your wife."

Chapter 29

❧

Man Who Walks Like a Fox stood on a slight rise. A clump of pines masked him from the man he was watching and any other who might come off the road. His deerhide shirt and trousers blended into the bark of the trees. Even if he danced like a fool who had drunk too much spirits of fire, Europeans would not notice. He knew he was as invisible to them as if he were deep in a cave. He stood perfectly still.

The sword at his side, encased in the blue baldric, was the trophy he'd found in Shellpoint.

He'd made his camp on mossy ground near an underground spring, one of the many that bubbled up on this Island to feed Shellpoint. The white man—cursed be his name and the seed of his loins—was relentlessly pushing northward, encroaching on Foxman's domain.

Here only the Five Nations once walked and hunted. Here, no mewling pink faces. Only the Mohawks, Oneidas, Onondagas, Cayugas, and Senecas. And of these the Mohawks were the mightiest.

But all that was yesterday. Today, more and more white men were not only here, they were invading Mohawk River country, long the home of his tribe, the Mohawks of the Iroquois Five Nations.

Still, for over ten summers and winters, more than any other member of his tribe, Man Who Walks Like a Fox had been coming back to the City, over and over. To sell his pelts. To steal from the white man. To kill the white man.

And to see the woman.

The tall, black-haired, black-eyed woman. The woman who had chosen the Dutchman over Foxman.

Since the early hours of the morning, when he was disturbed by the cries of the dying animal, the Mohawk had been watching.

A COACH OF no little refinement drove down the Broad Way toward the City. It came to a sharp stop near the Devil's Boulder. The coachman had been half-asleep when he felt the horses, a bay and a chestnut, shy, then bolt, but not together, and not in the same direction. He came to his full senses with a startled oath. The coach rattled and shook as if in a storm, then fell over on its side, amidst sounds of wood cracking and creaking and the cries of the passenger within.

The coachman at the top went flying. When he landed in a bed of nettles, he screeched like a woman. But then, thought Foxman, the white man did not know how to deal with pain or other manly things.

THE HORSES, SNORTING and whinnying, dragged the overturned coach down the road while the lone passenger attempted to climb out of the side window, which was now on top, and kept losing his balance with every tug of the two panicked beasts.

Finally, the coachman, whimpering, and stuck head to foot in nettles, freed the horses. The bay, a high-strung mare, ran straight into a massive oak, shook off the blow, and calmed down enough to stop. The chestnut gelding tossed its head, blew blaring breath through its nostrils, and nibbled at the sparse March grass.

Meanwhile, the coachman was paying no heed to his animals. Silvester Higgins's concern was with plucking painful nettles from his body. One had pricked him on the left cheek, which was already swelling mightily. He cursed with great vigor.

At last, however, Higgins remembered his duties. He stopped swearing and assisted his employer, Leland Merrivale, from the coach. Together the two men attempted to right the vehicle.

"No use," said Merrivale, who'd been on his way home from doing business in Albany.

"We can do it if we bounce, sir," the coachman insisted, picking at himself. The nettles would be the death of him. He reached for the coach. "All right?" The merchant nodded. "One, two, three. Heave!" Again they did not succeed.

Almost crying from his pain, the coachman shook his head. "I'll need help."

While the chestnut continued to graze, the bay panted and shook, and walked little steps in anxious circles. Merrivale brushed dirt from his fine clothing and looked about.

"Something at the Devil's Boulder scared the Jesus out of those horses," the coachman said.

"What?" Merrivale demanded. The merchant looked back to the massive stone. The sky flared with lightning. Clouds overhead darkened and swirled. Rain came down in sharp pelts. "Let's have a look. Might be we'll find somebody there who can help with the carriage."

The coachman, still complaining and plucking nettles, followed the merchant back toward the Devil's Boulder. Immediately, they were forced off the road by a pair of riders—women, they were, with their skirts billowing around them—galloping hard from the City.

As soon as the merchant and the coachman stepped back into the road, they were obliged to leave it again to make way for a wagon. This, too, came from the direction of New-York. The coachman wiped rain from his face as he watched the procession of riders and wagon. All pulled up at the Devil's Boulder.

"That was the Sheriff," Merrivale said. He removed his low-crowned, wide-brimmed crimson hat from atop his full-bottomed wig, shook off the water, and ran a neatening finger over the silver-buckled black band before restoring the hat to his head. He nodded at Higgins, and they set foot on the road, this time with more caution.

The Devil's Boulder had gathered quite a collection of people: two women, the Sheriff, and Pieter Tonneman. Merrivale and Higgins followed in the wake of the wagon. Coming closer, they observed the women bending over the huge rock.

What they saw shocked them to the soul. Across the Boulder lay a man covered in gore, head back and arms outstretched like the Savior himself. He was held almost upright by a pitchfork driven through his bare feet. Jesus Christ, indeed.

Chapter 30

"Lord save us," Antje said. "It's Master Crabtree. Look at his poor feet. The world has gone mad."

Racqel placed her palm under the schoolmaster's nose. "He's still breathing." Gently, she peeled his lids back. Mad eyes blazed at her. "He must be in considerable pain," she said.

Tonneman glared at his wife fiercely. Even under all that blood it was obvious that Crabtree was stark naked. Seeing Tonneman's look, Racqel's back stiffened. The man was hurt. She was not about to leave.

Tonneman put his mind back to his work. This was the very spot they'd found the heifer. A coincidence or . . . ?

"Mercy, mercy," Higgins prayed, darting furtive glances at the women. "The witches have cast their evil eye on us. God save me." At that, the coachman fell into a deep swoon.

Rain poured from the sky as from a high ocean wave, wetting them all to the skin. It made Crabtree's nakedness more flagrant as the rain washed away the cloaking blood. Gibb braced his feet on the stony ground. He placed both his massive hands on the pitchfork. "Hold him, Tonneman." Speaking to Racqel but glowering at Tonneman, he shouted, "Get back, mistress. This is no place for you. Go home."

Tonneman held on to the victim's shoulders. Racqel shuddered and stepped away. She had seen more than she wanted to. Had the others not noticed? The poor creature. He was so small. Like a little boy . . . She drove it from her thoughts.

"Ready?" Gibb asked.

A grim-faced Tonneman answered, "Yes."

Gibb braced his feet again, spat on both his hands, and gripped the pitchfork. He gave a vigorous pull and almost lost his balance, so startled was he at how easily the fork came free, scattering stones and pebbles.

Crabtree let out a piercing scream.

"Antje," Racqel cried. "Mud. After I wash the surface blood away, I must cleanse and stanch all his wounds. The earth here has too many stones; I need thick mud. A stream is close by." Racqel looked about. The coachman was awake, sitting on the ground, rubbing his injured cheek. "Use him to carry the mud. His hat."

"Sheriff." Merrivale stood at Gibb's shoulder. "What can I do to help?"

"Take these women back to town."

"I'll have nothing to do with Devil worshipers," Higgins insisted, still sitting on the ground. He held up his hands to form a cross with his fingers, and, on his knees, backed away.

Crabtree was whimpering. Blood oozed from the schoolmaster's body and washed away in the rain. New blood ran from his wounded feet. "There, there," Racqel whispered. "You're going to be all right." She lifted her head for a moment to Tonneman, then shifted her gaze to Antje. "Antje, hurry. Coachman, help her."

Tonneman, anger fading, and a little in awe of his wife beneath the outrage, said, "The stream is there, but a short way. We'll take him to the mud." He gestured toward the woods, then lifted Crabtree as if he were a baby. "I'll take him."

The stream was barely ten feet off. The rest filed after.

Only the coachman remained behind. He found a large damp pine to hide under, offering dire predictions of the Apocalypse.

Wet pine needles slapped them as they entered the forest. The world smelled of wet earth and wood. The rocky ground gave way to grass, then moss, muffling their footsteps. A ceiling of green protected them from the downpour. Except for the sound of the stream and the rain on the trees above, it was quiet, even peaceful.

The stream meandered, feeding Shellpoint, going in and out, shallow and deep. Narrow as a trickle here, and wide as five feet there, it sprang from among rocks and roots, the amber-green of the pine needles that created natural dams and little falls.

Tonneman laid the schoolmaster gently on a slab of stone and covered his personals with his coat, already bloody from Davies. Crabtree moaned pitifully.

First Racqel took handfuls of mud and packed Crabtree's feet to stop the bleeding. Crabtree's wounds needed to be washed clean, but then, the rain had done most of that for her. She scooped water to finish the job the rain had begun, cleaning away the more stubborn crusts from his body. All the while Antje was tearing strips from her petticoat.

"Move away, gentlemen," she ordered. "This is now women's work." She put Tonneman's coat aside, and she and Racqel got to their knees and continued cleaning Crabtree's body. Antje's soft sigh and meaningful look told Racqel she had taken notice of what Racqel had seen, but this was not the time to comment on it.

" 'Twould be easier to simply dip him into the creek," Gibb grumbled to Tonneman. "But I'm past arguing with these two."

"As am I," Tonneman agreed. He couldn't help but admire his wife's deft hands at work, still she *was* a trial.

Racqel made a poultice from winter grass, pine needles, and mud and coated Crabtree's wounded feet.

"Done," said Racqel, wrapping Crabtree again with Tonneman's coat.

"Well?" Gibb asked. He inclined his head to look down at Racqel.

Racqel and Antje washed up in the stream. Racqel shook her head. "His only serious wounds are those of the pitchfork in his feet. Those on his body are like razor nicks, when a man shaves."

"But all the blood!" Gibb tilted his neck left and right.

"I don't believe it's his."

Tonneman lifted his hat and scratched his head. From the softening sound against the trees he could tell the rain was letting up. "Whose blood, then?" But he had the answer almost as soon as he asked the question. The horse's thing nailed to the door. Of course. The horse killer. It had to be. The horse killer had bloodied the schoolmaster and dragged him to the Devil's Boulder. Then he had pinned him with the pitchfork, the Devil's own weapon.

"Gibb, how much will you wager that not far from here there's the rest of that horse?" Tonneman picked up the schoolmaster's limp body and headed back to the road. The Sheriff followed close on his heels.

Antje, Merrivale, and Racqel came after. Racqel was deep in thought when she realized she'd left some pieces of cloth at the waterside. She was tired and tempted to abandon them. But she was her father's daughter. Returning to the stream, she sat on the stone where Crabtree had lain, mindful of the blood but too exhausted to care. She wrung the strips of cloth free of water.

The rain had stopped. Pebbles of many colors glowed in the rushing water that played a sweet melody against the rocks. She leaned over and scrubbed her face with her petticoat.

A distant peal of thunder made her raise her head. She spied brown moccasins trimmed with yellow and blue quills not three feet from where she sat. She did not move.

"Racqel." Tonneman's call floated over the pine trees.

Her eyes flew up, past the deerskin pants, the open shirt, the hairless chest, the fierce face, head clean of hair but for the skein at the top. Black eyes held hers for only a moment. Cautiously, she stood, her gaze never leaving his.

"Racqel!" She could hear Tonneman's running footsteps, muffled sound against the spongy moss.

Gathering her courage, she called back, "Here." She moved toward her husband. Evenly she called, "Tonneman—hurry."

Only at the first sight of Tonneman did she dare to look back. Man Who Walks Like a Fox was gone.

Chapter 31

The stink was bad, and getting worse. Nessel-Vogel held the lamp closer to his face so the smell of the burning tallow would overcome the blood stench in his nose.

Books were everywhere, heaped on a trunk, on the bed, stacked askew on the floor, their leather covers once ornate with gold and red embossment now torn, bindings broken, brown with water damage and freshly spattered with blood. On a writing table, more volumes, papers, three or four scattered quills, an overturned pot of ink.

Underfoot, as in a slaughterhouse, gummous purple blood.

He picked up a loose page from the floor; on it were the first few lines of a Greek poem he seemed to remember: *Batrachomyomachia. Battle of the Frogs and Mice*. It was a joke of sorts, a mock heroic poem.

But frogs and mice aside, there had been a powerful struggle here.

Nessel-Vogel left the room. As he closed the door the horse cock nailed to it moved as if it were still alive. The Deputy shivered and gave his own member a reassuring pat.

He then inspected the rest of the second floor, which consisted of two more chambers, both shuttered and dark, with a musty smell, which was preferable to that of blood. From the footprints he made in the dust across the painted floorboards he could see that both were obviously uninhabited and had been so for some time.

To make doubly sure, the Deputy knelt to feel the inside walls of the fireplaces. Each was cold and free of fresh soot.

Down the creaking staircase he went, observing spots of blood but nowhere near what he'd seen in Crabtree's chamber. Mistress Jones's bedchamber was on the other side of the great chamber; there were live embers on the hearth here. The room was clean and had a fresh sweet odor to it. Mint, Nessel-Vogel thought. He'd been fond of the fragrance before, now even more so.

A bright wine-and-blue Turkey rug lay across Mistress Jones's narrow bed. On the small round table was a woven grass basket filled with balls of yellow yarn. The open shutters let the dim gray light through. Lightning streaked across the gray. When he closed the door, Nessel-Vogel heard the thunder boom. Then the rain came, hammering against the treen shingles.

The great chamber was snug, with no evidence of blood anywhere. Mistress Jones displayed silver candlesticks and a pewter tea service. On the walls were sconces with spent, unlit candles, and a painting of a fine-looking couple. The mantel held a large oil lamp.

He squinted at the portrait. A much younger Mistress Jones. Not a bad-looking woman in her day.

His nose had gone through a trial thus far, from blood to mint. Now a smile broke his face as he became aware of the aroma of sweet cakes coming from the kitchen. He let his nose lead him.

The old lady had set the plate of cakes on the cloth-covered table, and sweet strawberry jam and butter. She beamed at him as she set out mugs for tea. When she picked up the stoneware teapot, as if the idea had only just struck her, she asked in the loud voice of the deaf, "When is Sheriff Gibb coming down?"

Nessel-Vogel answered at the top of his voice. "I'm afraid he's already left."

"Ridiculous. I have important information for him." She was quite upset; the teapot trembled so that Nessel-Vogel seized it from her hands. Unfortunately, Nessel-Vogel touched the bowl. He groaned with pain and dropped the hot pot on the table. Sheer chance guided it to the plate of cakes, cushioning the crash. It did not break, it did not spill. The only damage was the crumbling of some of the cakes.

The woman sat down on a stool next to the table to calm herself while Nessel-Vogel alternately stared at his tender palms and nibbled the broken bits of cake. "Oh, dear," she moaned, "oh, dear. What shall I do?"

"Tell *me*," the Deputy replied through a mouthful of crumbs.

Mistress Jones beckoned to him with gnarled, floury fingers.

Her mouth had the reek of long-dead fish. This house was a garden of stinks. He snapped his head back, but the old woman would have none of that. She took hold of his neckband until she had his right ear to her fetid mouth. His eyes teared.

Her coarse whisper doused his face with spittle. "Someone was in Master Crabtree's room with him last night. *All* night."

"Ah," cried Nessel-Vogel. In spite of his discomfort, he relished such moments when his otherwise dull work became stimulating. "Who?" He would solve this matter and show Gibb what a younger, more educated man could do.

Mistress Jones pushed him away. Her eyes were crafty now. She pointed a bony finger. "You are not the Sheriff."

"No, but I'm the Deputy," he shouted, unsettled. He should have been the Sheriff. But that was of no moment now. What was important was the old lady's information. "You remember me. I'm Eric Nessel-Vogel, the fellow who painted your house for you last autumn."

She was peering up at him doubtfully, taking his measure. God's love, he longed to shake it out of her. Rain pounded on the roof. His belly gnawed at him; he also longed for more than crumbs of the sweet cakes.

"Tell the Sheriff," she said, "that I know who was in Master Crabtree's room. But I will tell no one but him." She wore a sly smile as she lifted the teapot from the plate of cakes, pushed the plate to him, and poured him a steaming mug of tea.

Nessel-Vogel grabbed two cakes, made fast work of one, and then was out the door, cramming the other into his mouth, feet flying as he ran north up the Broad Way Road in the pelting rain.

Chapter 32

What with the rain, there was no blood track left to trace. All Nessel-Vogel could do was follow his beleaguered nose. Finally, drenched and craving the warmth and dry comfort of a jail cell rope bed, he spied the Sheriff's wagon at the Devil's Boulder. This side of the wagon the Sheriff and Tonneman and a man with a fresh boil on his cheek were just righting a coach. Like him, all the men were dripping wet.

"What are you doing here?" Gibb demanded.

"New information," Nessel-Vogel told the Sheriff.

"Not now."

"It's important."

"So's this."

To the left, at the stone marker, was Mistress Tonneman kneeling beside a man lying on the ground. Nessel-Vogel approached. God in Heaven. The schoolmaster, Crabtree.

Mistress Ten Eyck mounted her white horse and rode toward the City in a shower of wet pebbles.

The coach was up on its wheels. Nessel-Vogel endeavored again to gain the Sheriff's attention. "Sir—"

"Not now, man. Don't you see we're busy?"

Nessel-Vogel closed his eyes to Gibb's scowling face and the rain and imagined his hands around Gibb's neck, squeezing.

As thunder rumbled, Racqel climbed into the coach. Tonneman and Merrivale lifted Crabtree, now wrapped in Merrivale's thick brown traveling cloak. Tonneman's intention was to place the wounded man on the narrow seat, but the merchant guided the schoolmaster to the floor. Crabtree's head rested against Racqel's knees.

Tonneman reached in and caressed his wife's face. His hands and her face were freckled with spatters of blood, and wet strings of Racqel's usually faultless hair were hanging down. But none of that mattered. Her eyes told him what he wanted. She was all right. Their argument was done with. As frightening as Foxman's appearance was, the Indian hadn't harmed her. Tonneman withdrew, and closed the door of the coach.

Meantime, Merrivale walked around the coach and sat on the other side of Racqel. The coachman had hitched the horses.

"City Hall it is, Higgins." Gibb turned to Tonneman. "We still have your dead man at Mendoza's place. Are you with me?"

"Give me a moment," said Tonneman, wiping Venus's drenched muzzle. The mare shivered at a sharp clap of thunder close by. "Steady, girl."

"Higgins, wait." Gibb now spoke to his Deputy. "Well, Nessel-Vogel?"

"Yes, sir?"

"Talk fast. I'm wet as a drowned rat. My back will complain to me all night about it."

"Mistress Jones says she heard someone talking to Crabtree in his room. She'll tell who it was only to you directly."

"Pig shit," said Gibb. "If it's not one thing, it's another. Well, she'll have to wait. As soon as Tonneman is done singing love songs to his horse, we're going to Staple Street. Get on back of the coach and be of some help to Mistress Tonneman with Crabtree."

Nessel-Vogel nodded, then added over the sound of thunder, "I need to piss."

"Get on with it, man. The coach won't wait all day for you, and if this rain keeps up, we'll need an ark."

Nessel-Vogel ran up to the woods, untied his breeches, and,

humming, closed his eyes in contemplation of the anticipated relief.

"Who the devil do you think you're pissing on?"

Coming up from the ground, wielding a short sword, was a stranger. He was quite angry, as he had a right to be.

One hand holding up his breeches, Nessel-Vogel stepped to the side. With his other hand he seized the stranger's wrist and squeezed. The short sword fell to the ground. Nessel-Vogel exerted pressure, and the man, too, went down to the ground, his face in the mud.

"Who the hell are you?" the Deputy demanded.

"If you let me up, I'll break your neck," the stranger roared with a thick Scots brogue.

"Then I'd better not let you up," the Deputy said, anchoring his captive firmly in the mud with his right foot. In this position he refastened his breeches, then picked up the stranger's weapon. "I repeat, who are you?"

"If you let me up, I'll tell you."

"Tell the Sheriff." Nessel-Vogel removed his foot.

The man stood. He wore a mud-smeared yellow shirt, and over his tight-fitting buckskin trousers a tartan kilt of dark blue and green. His beard and mustache and the hair under the dark blue bonnet were the color of a bright carrot. The hair was almost to the man's shoulders.

Nessel-Vogel stared at this apparition. By his carrot hair this man could have stepped out of the grave Tonneman had unearthed. Nessel-Vogel prodded the man with his own sword. Guiding him toward the road, he called, "Look what I found."

"And who might you be?" Gibb roared. "And what the Devil are you doing here?"

"Amos Lopez-Campbell is my name," the carrot-haired man answered in his Scots lilt as he wiped mud from his face.

A pair of blue ribbons trailed down from Lopez-Campbell's bonnet, along with a long braid tied with more ribbon, which hung almost to the halfway point along his back. One of the ribbons was dark blue, the other scarlet. If asked, the Scot would tell you the blue, like the rest of his attire, was for the Campbells; red was the Lopez color.

Tonneman scowled. If he didn't know better, he'd think he'd been drinking again. Even with nature attending the corpse, it was plain to see this man was the double of the body in the grave. Tonneman took the bit of red silk from his pocket and held it against the red ribbon in the stranger's hair. Dry against wet he couldn't tell if it was a match. He returned the scrap of silk to his pocket.

"What are you doing here?" Tonneman asked the Scot.

"Having a sleep."

"In the rain?" Gibb asked.

"It wasn't raining when I closed my eyes. And if a little rain troubles you, you shouldn't be a trapper."

"You're a trapper, then," said Tonneman.

The man nodded. The rain streaked the mud on his face.

"A Jew?" Tonneman interjected.

The man bridled. "What's it to you?"

Tonneman ignored the man's question. "And who is that in the fresh grave in the Jewish cemetery?"

Gibb's eyes went wide. He shifted from one sodden foot to the other. "Now we're back to the Jewish cemetery again."

Tonneman raised his hand. "In a minute, Sheriff. Tell us, Scotsman."

"I don't choose to talk about it."

Tonneman was amazed at the man's audacity. "Well, you're going to talk about it."

"Why the hell did you go there in the first place, Tonneman?" Gibb demanded, growing visibly more and more annoyed with his predecessor.

"My wife told me the dead cow in the field was a Jewish ritual. If an unknown body is found, Jews kill a cow."

Gibb removed his hat, shook off the rain, and replaced it on his wet head. "Heathens. Why the hell for?"

"Don't ask. I reckoned there was a missing body somewhere. That's why I looked in the Jewish cemetery."

Gibb groaned.

"And," Tonneman continued, "the body I found looked a lot like this chap here." He tapped the Scot on the arm. "Brother or cousin?" he asked the stranger.

"Cousin."

"Did you kill him?"

"It's my job to ask him that." Gibb was losing his patience. "Tonneman, you've got a great deal to answer for. Nessel-Vogel, forget what I said before. You get in the back of the wagon with the prisoner—"

"Prisoner?" Lopez-Campbell cried, fists clenched. "Why? What did I do?"

"Shut up," Gibb ordered. "Did you kill your cousin?"

The Scotsman glared and did not answer.

Gibb waved a hand in disgust. "Tonneman, you coming?"

Tonneman was of two minds. If the injured schoolmaster recovered his senses quickly, Tonneman wanted to be present to hear his story. If the solution to the horse killings rested in Crabtree's mind, he could complete his commission to De Sille and be done with the oily bastard. Thus, he should go with the coach.

But then there was Davies and the way he died. And this new man, obviously one of the two trappers he'd learned about at Asser Levy's tavern. And quite possibly the murderer of the other one in the grave. A falling-out between cousins? Tonneman weighed the questions in his mind. He elected to go with the Sheriff.

There was a way he could see to both problems. He opened the coach door and leaned in, trying not to bring the rain with him, but failing. Merrivale was yelling to the driver out the far window. Racqel looked up from her patient.

"Stay with him, wife. If he comes to his senses while I'm in Staple Street, question him about what happened."

She nodded. There was a somber smile on her face. Something had changed between them. Nothing they could talk about now. But it was new, it was good, Tonneman was certain of it.

"Tonneman," Gibb called from the wagon.

"Stay with him," Tonneman said again to his wife. "Keep him from speaking to anyone else till we return."

"Are we ready?" Merrivale asked Racqel.

"Sir," Nessel-Vogel said, "are you sure about Mistress Jones? It's not out of our way."

"All right, damn it, Mistress Jones first, then Staple Street. Tonneman. I don't have all day."

Tonneman closed the coach door; the vehicle started forward. He tied Venus to Gibb's wagon and climbed in beside the Sheriff. The horse pulled and the wagon started its slippery journey through the mud.

Chapter 33

❧

The rain had ceased but huge dank clouds hung over them as Tonneman, Gibb, Nessel-Vogel, and his complaining prisoner drove up to the Jones house. Bordering on marsh, the land was now swampland itself; the roads had swiftly turned to mud. The wheels of Gibb's wagon groaned against the undertow of the muck, while Gibb groaned his protest with each new effort of the gray gelding. Venus, bringing up the rear, whinnied her encouragement. Or perhaps it was relief at not having to do the pulling this day.

Tonneman let his eyes roam the countryside. Workmen had come out again to repair whatever damage the rain had done and were getting on with their labor. They were calling to each other. Birdsong filled the crisp, clean air. In the distance he saw a lone horseman hunched low on a brown mount, riding toward them on the Broad Way Road, then veering off.

"Eh, Tonneman? That pitchfork came out awful easy."

Tonneman brought his attention back to the Sheriff. "What?"

"Just thinking out loud. Let's make this quick. Chasing a wild goose is what I call it." Gibb reined to a halt and eased down from the wagon. "Nessel-Vogel."

"Sir!"

"Take the prisoner and lock him up."

"I protest," the Scotsman roared. "You have no cause."

"Shut up," Gibb shouted back. "I arrest you for the murder of your cousin."

"You can't prove that."

"We will. We have laws. This is a God-fearing community."

Nessel-Vogel nodded his agreement. "I'll take the wagon."

"No, you will not take the wagon. My leg is aching me from here to Hades. You have feet, both of you. You can walk."

"Yes, Sheriff." Nessel-Vogel prodded the carrot-haired man with his own sword. "Move."

"Don't push me."

"And don't you give me your sauce."

Without warning the prisoner started to run. Nessel-Vogel leaped on his back and pulled him to the ground. When he pulled the Scotsman back to his feet, both men were muddy from tip to toe.

"See what you've done?" Nessel-Vogel complained, eyeing his filthy clothes. "Try that again and I'll castrate you with your own blade."

"Any man would have done the same," the prisoner grumbled.

Keeping up their argument, the Deputy and his prisoner trudged east, heading for the jail in City Hall on Queen Street.

Tonneman and Gibb had watched the proceeding with amusement.

"What was that with the red ribbon?" Gibb asked. He stretched his neck; pain coursed through his back.

"Just an idea," Tonneman answered dismissively. It was not something he wanted to share with the Sheriff.

Favoring his right leg, Gibb limped to the front door of the Jones house and rapped sharply. When there was no response, he opened it.

Following, Tonneman cast a look whence they'd come. Only the blurring figures of Nessel-Vogel and his prisoner. No sight of the brown horse he'd seen earlier. He shook his head. Gibb was already inside the house. Tonneman went through the door carefully. He didn't fancy being surprised again. Hellfire. He was getting too old for this game. But caution was good. And hesitation was disaster.

The Jones house reeked of death and rot. And butter and sugar. Not a heady blend.

He found Gibb in the kitchen. Sweet cakes and crumpet cakes lay on a blue plate under a linen cloth. They stepped out to the hall. A low humming came from the top of the stairs.

Gibb shouted, "Mistress Jones!" There was no reply. The humming continued. He shook his head. "Deaf as the Devil's Boulder."

They climbed the creaking staircase and found the woman on her hands and knees beside a bucket of water, scrubbing the floor with a rag. The thing on Crabtree's door had been removed. God only knew what she'd done with it. The door was closed tight.

The old woman looked up and dropped her rag. "My word! You boys gave me a start. Don't you believe in knocking?"

Gibb rolled his eyes. Tonneman covered a smile with his hat and offered his hand, which Mistress Jones took. Even with his help, standing up was not easy for her.

"Have you found poor Master Crabtree?" she asked.

"Yes," Gibb answered. "He's not too badly hurt. He'll recover."

"God is merciful."

Twisting his neck left and right to get the kink out, Gibb said, "My Deputy tells me you know who did this?"

"No," Mistress Jones said adamantly. "I don't know who did this. I never said such a thing. Why did he say I did?"

Gibb looked at Tonneman with disgust. "That Nessel-Vogel thinks he's so smart—"

"But I heard who Master Crabtree was talking to in his room." The woman's lined face displayed a benign expression. "Oh, yes, I heard that."

"Of course," Gibb said to Tonneman, not even bothering to whisper. "Deaf as a stone but can hear through a door."

The expression on Mistress Jones's face made Tonneman wonder just how deaf the old lady really was. "Go on. Who was it?" he asked in an ordinary voice.

"Our Savior," she said, "Jesus Christ."

"PREPOSTEROUS."

Tonneman had been counting. This was Gibb's eleventh use of the same word. One more and he'd have an even dozen.

They turned on Staple Street and drove to the Mendoza warehouses. "Witchcraft, religious fanatics, and absolute madmen like Beado and Davies. What's this town coming to? Preposterous."

Twelve. Tonneman did not respond. Though he quite agreed with the Sheriff, he was more interested in the hunched rider mounted on a brown horse who had reappeared about a hundred yards back.

At the warehouse they found Davies much as Tonneman had left him, but the crumpled corpse was already meat for the maggots.

Gibb crouched as if he had no problem with his back and pulled the long knife from the dead man's neck. It came only halfway out. The effort made the corpse's head bob like a child's doll nodding to them.

"Got something to say to us, Davies?" Tonneman asked.

Gibb rocked the knife back and forth. "The butcher killed me," he squeaked in a high voice.

Tonneman smiled. "Which butcher?"

"I don't know," the Sheriff acknowledged. "But this is a butcher's knife."

"Yes," said Tonneman. There were nicks in the evil-looking blade, which eliminated the Jews because of their law that butchers could not use knives with nicks.

But the nicks could have come from Davies's jawbone. That put the Jews back in. He followed Gibb into Mendoza's main warehouse. There they found the merchant on his knees next to a man in trapper's gear. This stranger was a Frenchie by the look of the dirty fawn felt hat with tattered lace trim, threadbare gold taffeta, and grimy gold ribbon loops. Tonneman wondered what the wood creatures made of such a chapeau.

The man's black hair, thick with grease and pulled back at the nape with a piece of rawhide, fell just past his shoulders. Tonneman sniffed. Bear grease. And rather old bear grease from the rancid stink of it.

Standing back, Tonneman let Gibb go to work. The Frenchie was André La Champlaine, and he'd just come down from the north with a load of prime pelts.

It was no surprise that David Mendoza was as surly with the Sheriff as he had been with Tonneman. The Jewish merchant acted quite put-upon for having his business interrupted yet once more.

"I have naught to do with Davies," he said. "I didn't see him. I never knew him."

Tonneman kept his own counsel; he offered no questions. They would learn nothing further from Mendoza, of that he was certain. He pondered the long butcher's knife. Asser Levy had one, or more, he was sure. And Jan Keyser, the tanner. And the ten or so other butchers. And the six or so other tanners.

As he stood just inside the warehouse, Tonneman saw the hunched rider on the brown horse coming slowly down Staple Street. A fit of fury enveloped him. He rushed out and seized the reins of the four-footer with one hand. With the other he pulled the man from the saddle. The rider kicked and screamed, "What? What? What?" Tonneman threw him down into the muddy road.

It was Charles Lanchester, the sail maker who had begged him for work only that morning. Tonneman shook the man. "Why are you dogging my steps?"

"Not me, not me, Tonneman." Lanchester cringed in the mud. "It's a mistake. I can explain." Saliva dripped from both sides of his mouth, down his elongated jaw.

"Explain, then, or I'll toss you into the river in a bag of rocks." Tonneman started toward the North River, dragging the sail maker along by the tail of his coat.

"Please, no," the little man blubbered.

Tonneman set him on his feet. "Then speak."

"He hired me to follow you and report to him."

"Who?"

"If I say his name I'm a dead man."

"God damn it." Tonneman reached again for the sail maker, who ducked and slipped in the mud.

"The First Councillor!" Lanchester cried.

"I should have known," said Tonneman. "The First Councillor be damned, the First Arse-hole himself, Nick De Sille."

Chapter 34

The man was unconscious, but to Racqel's relief, his color was returning. After Nessel-Vogel had set a kettle of water over the fire and stirred up the flames, Racqel sent the Deputy to her house, only next door, to fetch her bag.

Though Antje had promised to look after the children, Racqel felt a pang of concern for them. But first she must see to Master Crabtree. Having missed her midday meal, she was weary. Her clothes were disheveled and damp and her head throbbed. A careful examination told her that in addition to his wounds and his fright, the schoolmaster was feverish, complaining of pain not only in his feet but in his body and his head.

Nessel-Vogel had supplied a straw pallet and two sorry blankets from the cells below. Except for Mad Beado and the Scotsman, the jail was empty. Neither breakers of tapster laws nor breakers of heads were guests of the City this day, a highly unusual occurrence considering the heavy port traffic.

From his stupor, Crabtree cried out, "No! Stop!" He cowered beneath the thin blanket.

Racqel sat on a low stool, wiping his brow with the damp cloth. She dropped the cloth into the wooden bowl on the floor and took his hand. "You're going to be all right. You are among friends."

His eyes flew open. Terror. Then relief. "Mistress Tonneman. Thank the Lord."

"What happened to you, sir? Can you say?"

"Horror beyond horror," Crabtree whispered. He seized her hand and began to sob.

"There, there," Racqel said. The poor man was shattered, quite rightly, too, from his terrifying experience. Who could have done this to him? And why?

Abruptly the sobbing ceased. The man had swooned. His hand held hers so tightly she could not remove it. What was keeping Nessel-Vogel?

"He was a giant."

Startled, Racqel saw Crabtree was again awake.

"Hairy giant." The schoolmaster moaned into the blanket that he had pulled up to cover his face.

It was difficult enough to understand Crabtree under normal circumstances since he spoke with a clipped, up-north, Johnny accent. Now the blanket muffled his words. He released her hand.

Gently, she removed the blanket from over his mouth and leaned toward him. "What did you say?"

"A hairy giant. Black as . . . pitch. As the Devil."

This was no man he was describing. At least no man she'd ever seen in New-York. This was the Devil, if not in life, in Crabtree's feverish mind. The man was mad. Racqel shivered. Had he always been so? Had she sent her son to learn from a madman? She soothed his sweating brow and asked softly, "Can you name him? Is he from these parts?"

"I'm afraid to tell you any more. He'll . . . punish me. With the whips."

"You must tell us," Racqel urged. "We need to know. To protect you. To protect us."

He peered deep into her eyes, then nodded. Even in his troubled state he knew she spoke the truth. He sucked on the end of the blanket, like a child nursing, then began to speak, faintly at first, so that once again Racqel had to lean forward to catch his broken words.

"I had been ill . . . during the night and early morning. I had drunk more than a mouthful of brandy to help me sleep. I left a note on my door. Having had so much spirits . . . at first I thought it was a bad dream. Is Moses well, dear lady?" Crabtree clutched at her with hysterical fervor.

"Yes. Please go on."

His voice grew stronger now. "When I heard the banging I rose from my bed, believing it was one of my students." He stopped, shuddered, looked past her, as if the monster had returned. He screamed, "Dear Jesus, don't let him take my soul!"

Quickly, Racqel turned. Nessel-Vogel stood in the door. The Deputy had returned bearing her bag and a large wicker basket. He said, "Alice sent you some victuals." He dragged a low table from a corner, set it in front of Racqel, and displaced a mound of official-looking papers from it to the floor.

"We shouldn't upset anything," Racqel protested.

"Those are just papers of the Common Council. I'll put them back when you're done." The Deputy grinned. "And if I don't, they'll never miss them, come Saturday." He placed the basket on the low table.

Racqel's patient was whimpering like a babe. She turned to attend him again. "It's only Deputy Nessel-Vogel, Master Crabtree. Don't be afraid."

The schoolmaster began to tremble violently.

Racqel opened her bag.

"May I help, Mistress Tonneman?" the Deputy asked, standing at her shoulder, clearly curious.

"Hot water." She bared the schoolmaster's feet and tended to his wounds, cleaning them, then pouring a mixture of hot water, alum, and myrrh over them.

Crabtree moaned.

After wrapping each foot carefully in cotton cloth, she set about preparing her other medicines. When she was done she asked Nessel-Vogel to prop up the ailing man. She tried to get Crabtree to drink the elixir she'd prepared, but like a frightened dog, the schoolmaster wouldn't open his mouth. At her nod, and with no further explanation, Nessel-Vogel prized open the man's jaw. But when Racqel introduced doses of willow bark and laudanum into his mouth, the wounded man refused to swallow. Racqel gently stroked the schoolmaster's throat, which made him swallow.

Once more Nessel-Vogel laid Crabtree on the pallet and Racqel drew the blanket over his shoulders. The schoolmaster's limbs, contorted with pain and fever, slowly relaxed. Sweat appeared, as if by magic, on his face and neck.

They watched Crabtree slip into a fitful sleep.

Something gnawed at Racqel. Then it came to her. In addition to his awful wounds, surely Crabtree's symptoms were similar to Asser Levy's?

She placed a hand on the schoolmaster's brow and considered her diagnosis. The veil on her memory was lifting. Something her father had told her . . . But the veil fell again, and her tired brain allowed the notion to drift off. She walked away from Crabtree and stood near the door. Nessel-Vogel, ever helpful, stepped forward and opened it.

"Thank you. The cool air is good."

"Yes, ma'am. Is there anything I can do?" There was much respect in the Deputy's demeanor.

Amazingly, she found she was hungry as a wolf. "Bring me some water to wash my hands, please."

Nessel-Vogel was prompt to do as he was bid.

The water he brought was the bowl with the damp cloth she had used on Crabtree's fevered brow. She washed her hands in it and said her prayers. It was not the way she would have wanted, but God understood.

Crossing back to the low table where the basket from Alice awaited her, she pulled the cloth cover off and saw that the Jamaica woman had sent her a fine bit of food. Racqel ate a chicken leg and a roasted potato. She had just finished when a tremendous commotion came from the street. Screaming voices, horses neighing. More shouts. "Sheriff! Sheriff!"

Nessel-Vogel rushed from the chamber to the street. Racqel was more cautious. Slowly she went to the door. Henry Backer, the man who had been awarded the slaughtered cow, stood in front of City Hall. The farmer was screaming like a lunatic. "Where's the Sheriff? I must see the Sheriff! My Beauty is dead!"

"Who's dead?" Nessel-Vogel called. "The Sheriff will be back soon. What's happened?"

"My Beauty is dead. Dead! Mutilated."

"Who is Beauty? Is that your wife? Talk to me, Mister Backer. Did someone kill your wife?"

Backer stopped his ranting and stared at the Deputy. "Are you demented? Who said anything about my wife?"

"I beg pardon, sir. When you said your Beauty I thought . . ."

Backer sneered disdainfully at Nessel-Vogel. "You fool, not my wife. Lord deliver us. My new stallion. Dead and butchered. And written on my stable wall is BURN IN HELL, DUTCHMAN."

Chapter 35

Brook trout, flashing with blue and orange, leaped in the air. Then, sensing his presence, the fish were gone. Flat black stone flies floated on the water, almost hidden under the rotting roots of a winter-beaten birch. Foxman watched the flies. Presently he was compensated for his patience: The flies disappeared under the water, food for the trout.

His hand moved as swiftly as the vanishing black flies; he scooped up a small trout, barely the heft of his hand, and popped the tasty morsel into his mouth. Foxman would have preferred human flesh. But the fish would suffice for now.

A palmful of water quenched his thirst. He spat, wiped his hands on his bare skin, for he wore only an elk-skin cloth about his loins, and walked out of Shellpoint. He had things to do and soon it would be sundown.

Man Who Walks Like a Fox had never ceased wanting the woman. Years had passed. She'd had children and had grown even more pleasing to the eye. He had his own women at home, but his women were not like her. He was convinced that she would realize the error of the choice she had made years before.

He held himself with pride. He could still swim and fight and make sex better than any of the young men of his village. His body was clean of hair and there was no fat on him like on the white man.

His special clothing lay rolled in his canoe; he dressed carefully. Sun-bleached buckskin trousers, a woven shirt of many colors, soft rabbit-skin moccasins adorned with red and yellow porcupine quills. He greased his shaft of hair and wrapped his new sword and baldric with its shiny stones in his bedroll. He would trade the sword for a long gun.

But first he would kill with it.

Chapter 36

Tonneman knew he should sleep on it, but anger boiled inside him like a stew. He would have no rest until he confronted Nick De Sille. Pushing Lanchester aside, he untied Venus from the wagon and was off toward the City even as Gibb yelled after him. The ride over the short distance to the Broad Way Gate spattered him with mud. This served only to swell his fury.

"Halt."

Tonneman wanted to keep riding but was not so crazed as to invite a Musketeer's bullet. He reined in, hoping to know the sentry. Luck was with him again—in the person of Sergeant Frank Nesbitt.

"Why such a dither, mate?" Nesbitt brought the lantern out of the guard shed. Though the sun had not yet set, there was no evidence of it in a sky full of angry clouds.

"Only eager to get home."

Nesbitt raised his lantern. "I should think so. You look like something the dog wouldn't have for supper."

"And I feel the same. I need to talk to you about the horse killing."

The Sergeant lifted his eyebrows.

"No time now." Tonneman was already urging Venus forward. "I'll be back later."

"Say no more. I'm here at the Duke's command and your service till dawn." Nesbitt motioned him into the City. "But no galloping on City streets."

Tonneman could hear the Sergeant's rough laughter over the sound of Venus's hooves digging up the road.

Although Tonneman's mind was filled with loathing and anger for De Sille, his orderly brain reminded him that not only had he passed up the chance to talk to Nesbitt and the guards about what they might have seen Sunday morning when the first horse was killed, he had also not talked to the Night Watch—what was his name? Otto Wersten. God, he must be getting old. He should have talked to those people first off. Why had he gotten caught up with Gibb's shit?

Most men tended to bury simple, everyday facts, believing trivial details had nothing to do with anything. Tonneman knew better. Sometimes the most routine was the most important. The removal of one pebble was what could send a boulder on its downward path of destruction.

Venus plowed along and in no time Whitehall loomed in front of Tonneman, its whitewashed shingles gleaming in the gray afternoon. He leaped from Venus's back with an energy driven by his wrath. Leaving the mare to her own devices, Tonneman all but pulled the British lion knocker off the door with his hammering.

This time the door was opened by a different slave, a young man in courtier's clothing, all fopperied. His dark brown skin shone in the whale-oil light. "Sir?" he inquired with great courtesy.

"I'm Pieter Tonneman. I must talk to your master."

The slave smiled but made no move allowing him to enter.

"Now." Tonneman brushed past him into the entry.

"Good evening, Pieter."

She was preceded by the soft rustle of her green silk skirts. Flipping a green lace fan away from her face, she said, "So sweet of you to call. I have not seen you in such a long time." Geertruyd De Sille had a high voice and spoke with the faint lisp of a child. There was no cap on her golden hair, which hung loose around her pale face.

Completing the picture he knew so well was the black *mouche* on her right cheek. Large pearl earrings hung from her ears. A long strand of fat matching pearls encircled her neck and danced delicately about her full white bosom. He breathed in her heady scent, grateful she did not use lavender. Rose water?

No doubt about it, Geertruyd De Sille was a beautiful woman. And a prime bitch.

"Good afternoon, Geertie. I want to talk to Nick."

"We are having tea. With some very distinguished gentlemen out of Boston and Hartford." From elsewhere in the house Tonneman could hear the soft babble of voices. "You'll join us, of course."

"I will not. Tell Nick I'll be waiting in his office."

As Tonneman moved past her, Geertruyd managed to turn herself so her breasts brushed his body. She was smiling up at him like an English jade. Tonneman shook his head and stamped down the hall.

The First Councillor's office was an elegant room with an ebony cabinet, velvet-covered chairs, and a French carpet. An ornate chandelier hung from the ceiling. None of this meant anything to Tonneman. He paced the spacious chamber, taking deep gulps of air, attempting to compose himself. With each intake of breath, he hated the lavender scent that assailed his nostrils more. A small voice in the back of his mind warned him to remain calm. Another, more insistent voice goaded him to take Nick apart with his bare hands.

"Ah, Tonneman." The First Councillor entered the room as if he were being presented at court. He wore a gold velvet coat, his wig was ornately curled, and he carried an ebony staff. "Pray, sir, tell me, to what do I owe the pleasure?"

"I'm going to break your fucking neck."

"No, you're not, my friend." De Sille watched Tonneman's fury with an amused expression. But he came no closer.

"I am far from being your friend, you devious bastard. You twist my arm to do a job, then you put a spy on my trail?"

"God's blood, Tonneman, use your head. I'm an important man, a representative of the Duke. I can't trust anyone. I was merely protecting my arse."

"God's blood, Nick, I'd like to kick your arse from here to the real Whitehall!"

De Sille smiled. He coughed lightly into the dainty nose cloth that he'd plucked from the embroidered sleeve of his coat.

"I would think that you'd put more care to protecting your own arse." De Sille paused, obviously pleased with what he was about to say. "We've been having trouble with witches of late."

Tonneman's battered brain reeled. "What?"

"As we speak, the Council is debating the fate of Katherine Harrison, the Wetherfield Witch. One Alice Manning has accused Mistress Harrison of doing witchly things."

"Such as?"

"Be damned if I know." De Sille fluttered his hands. "Flying by the light of the moon. Miraculous cures. I understand that has happened of late in this town."

"Say what you mean, you misbegotten shit pig."

De Sille waved his scented nose cloth in front of his face, as if dispersing the odor of Tonneman's words. "A miraculous cure. Yes, indeed. Asser Levy was sick near to death. Your wife paid him a visit, and now the man's as sound as a young bull."

"What are you suggesting, you bastard?"

De Sille allowed his eyebrows to rise. "I'm not suggesting anything; I am saying it full out. And mind your tongue."

"Saying what?"

"Of course I don't believe in such stuff, but there's talk that only a witch could have cured the Jewish butcher. So watch your own arse, Tonneman." De Sille entertained himself with a bit of snuff from the right-hand pocket of his coat. He sneezed and then continued in polite tones, as if he'd said nothing untoward. "Have you found the knave who killed our stallion?"

Tonneman shook his head. His concern for Racqel's reputation had cooled his blood. And while he envisioned himself killing Nick, the stronger image was of falling asleep in his own bed, his arms wrapped around Racqel, comforting her, being comforted by her. "No," he said bluntly. "And it looks like the bastard has struck again."

Dropping his guard completely, De Sille spoke in Dutch. "Where? Whose horse?"

Tonneman responded in their mother tongue. "I don't know. All we've got is the cock and some blood and a terrified schoolmaster."

"A pox on you and a pox on this villain," De Sille raged. "Damn it, Tonneman, the Governor is here. In *my* house. And he wants my scalp."

Distressed as he was, Tonneman did not banish the sudden notion when it came. "Well, *give* it to him," he shouted, lunging at De Sille, his hands going not for the First Councillor's throat, but his head. Off came Nick's lush, curly black wig. The dome beneath was near bald and barely threaded with dingy gray strands of slack, dry hair.

Tonneman's boisterous Dutch laughter filled the chamber and spilled out into the hallway. Still laughing, he bent and picked up the enormous wig and shoved it at the sputtering, ridiculous De Sille.

"One day, Tonneman," De Sille said evenly, replacing the wig, "someone will run you through or put a bullet in your head. And when that day comes, you can believe this, I will not hang him. Most probably I will embrace the man and pay him one hundred pounds."

Tonneman's voice was low. He was clammy and tired and Racqel was waiting for him. "You also have a murder to deal with in Staple Street, De Sille. The deed was done in a warehouse David Mendoza rents to Jacob Roome. Gibb is working on it but—"

"A killing?" De Sille fretted with his wig, attempting to set it right.

"Remember Edward Davies, who went missing a few days ago?"

"That loon. He's always been trouble, roaming the City at night like a wolf. What is his death to me? One less difficulty in this troublesome town."

Tonneman expelled a weary breath. "Davies might have been your horse killer."

"Then the case is closed."

De Sille seemed so pleased with himself that Tonneman spoke without thinking. "Then again, he might not have been the horse killer. Davies had something to tell me."

"What?"

"I have no idea. But it well may be, First Councillor, that your horse killer has moved on to humans."

Chapter 37

At sundown Foxman strolled down to the East River just outside the Water Gate to New-York. Climbing easily, he was soon atop the pier that led, in one direction, out over the East River to Asser Levy's slaughterhouse, and in the other, into town, just inside of the Water Gate. They would kill him if they caught him, but they wouldn't catch him. He smiled at the weak ways of the white man and at the folly of a big iron-clamped door and an imperfect sea fence.

As he was in this place often—stealing, listening, every so often killing a white man simply because it pleased him to—he already knew they were fearful of her because she knew Indian ways to treat illness and was a wise medicine woman.

The night before he had listened at the butcher Levy's window and heard the butcher and his woman speak angry words about her.

Tonight he would listen at *her* window.

Chapter 38

"**H**e insisted that he was well enough," Racqel said. "But he was not. Still, he appeared to sleep peacefully. And Mistress Jones will look in on him."

Tonneman made a derisive noise that sounded like the hoot of an owl. So much so that a real owl in the woods answered him.

Racqel, though bone-weary, managed a smile for her husband. "As will the Night Watch."

They sat on the front stoop of their house, close, Tonneman's arm about her shoulders. The lamp on the bracket next to the back door was turned low. The children were fed and asleep. Alice was also to bed. The house was silent.

As the peace of the evening settled over New-York, only the creaking timbers of the vessels in the East River and the lap of the evening tide came to them.

Tonneman cleared his throat. How to begin? Coward that he was, he broached a different subject. "Are you certain that it was Foxman you saw?"

"Quite."

"I thought the scoundrel would be dead by now."

Racqel's response was a shiver.

Tonneman rubbed her shoulders. There was no way around it.

They had to talk about it. He said it straight out. "Asser Levy is cured."

Racqel, showing no surprise, nodded. "Or so he thinks. It's the way of this illness." She twisted her head to look at her husband. "What I've just said. How do I know that? My father told me about this disease. If only I could remember . . ." She turned front and leaned back against him. He was so strong, so solid.

Tonneman said quietly, "There's witch talk about." She tensed. "I've been hearing," he continued. "And De Sille came right out and said it."

"Said what?"

Tonneman heard the tremor of fear in his wife's voice. This made him angry, but he suppressed it. Now was not the time for anger. He let loose a big sigh. "They're saying you're a witch, Racqel. Because of Levy's cure."

The night was silky black. Silver stars began to flicker in the clearing sky. A breeze stirred the fresh blooming crocus. But Racqel was sweating and cold all at once.

His arm tightened around her. "Don't be afraid, my love. There are always those who want to put blame."

"Blame for what? Oh, dear Lord. And if I'm a witch, you see, then it follows that I'm at the bottom of these horse slaughters."

He didn't answer; he only held her tight.

"I did not cure him, Tonneman." All at once it was clear to her. "Solomon Navarro must be spreading this lie. Levy is not cured. The illness will return. It always does." She shuddered. "They'll probably condemn me for *that* too."

"Take care. A witch is one thing. A Jewish witch and . . ."

"I know," she answered softly. "I will be careful."

They sat silent, listening to the human sounds the night carried. A cough, a sneeze. Somewhere a dog barked.

"The trophy on Crabtree's door?" Tonneman said.

"Yes?"

"Most likely it's from Backer's new stallion."

"Hoy, Tonneman house!" The call came from Queen Street.

Tonneman could sense all his neighbors listening. Perhaps it was time they moved out to the country. He stood, wary. "Around here, whoever you are."

The sound of running footsteps came toward them. "It's me. Jacob de Kees."

Tonneman took the lamp from its bracket. "Jacob? You should be halfway to Boston by now."

The Post Rider appeared, rumpled and out of breath. "When I stopped to change horses at Ladderman's farm . . . just outside of Stamford? I learned a bit of news I figured you had to hear—" The young rider fell silent. He was gaping at Racqel.

"De Kees," Tonneman snapped.

"Your pardon, sir. Mistress Tonneman." Jacob was clearly flustered. "It happened before. Twice. In Hartford."

"What happened, boy? Spit it out."

Jacob de Kees turned beet red. "There was horse cock cutting in Hartford too."

Chapter 39

The early morning had sharp cold teeth but was sweet to the nose. As the sun warmed the air, the blue heavens, so blue they might have been painted, showed not one cloud.

Everywhere spring was in evidence. The dogwood trees had not yet begun flaunting their pink and white buds, but green shoots promised tulips and daffodils. Fruit trees were coming awake after the winter months. Soon New-York would be abloom in color and scent.

A large wagon rattled past him. It was laden with timber from the forests well north of the City, on its way to ships in the Bay and thence to the Islands or to England.

Skirting the gallows in front of the Fortress, Tonneman couldn't help but remember two old friends, one who had hanged and one who should have hanged. But that was another time, and besides, both were long dead.

On the other hand, Market Day was alive and in full tilt when Tonneman arrived at the Market Field just north of the Fort.

Over the years, more and more farmers, Dutch, English, French, and all in between, as well as Indians and Africans from the vast expanse that lay on the other side of the Wall and across the rivers, came to New-York for Market Day to sell, barter, and buy. Tonneman knew many of them—from Breukelen or other parts of Long

Island or up in New Haarlem—as well as he knew his fellow New-Yorkers. Some were even his blood relations.

Today, as most every Wednesday, those with things to sell were setting up stalls to display and vend their goods to the City folk. Tales of the wealth of New-Yorkers abounded. And with a thriving port and worldwide visitors, a pretty penny could be made by farmers, craftsmen, and tradesmen.

New-Yorkers, buyers and tradesmen alike, walked everywhere. People with goods to carry used wagons. Indians didn't cotton to wagons, living in the woods as they did. They came afoot, or downriver in canoes, or on horseback, towing their goods behind them on two poles with skins stretched over.

Tonneman's first stop was at Harry Price's stall for a cup of buttermilk.

"That's good," he said after draining the cup of milk in one draught. "Do you know Edward Davies? From hereabouts."

The milkman nodded. "Just to see, not to speak to."

"Did you see him in your part of Breukelen day before yesterday?" When Tonneman pulled out a penny from his purse to pay for his buttermilk, his fingers brushed the piece of red silk.

"Can't say that I did."

"Ask around for me, will you?" Tonneman set the empty cup on the counter.

"Be glad to."

Tonneman showed him the bit of silk. "This mean anything to you?"

Harry Price frowned and shook his head.

"I'm looking into some horse killings we're having over here. Any trouble like that where you are?"

"Not so I've heard. And I would have heard. Another cup?"

"That's a good idea." Tonneman laid a second penny next to his first on the stall counter and started off, sipping from the refilled wooden cup as he walked.

"Penny extra for the cup," Harry called.

"I'll bring it back."

"And I'll give you your penny back. If you do."

What had happened to trust? These days, what with the City growing, and so many strangers, he granted Price his point, but he was no stranger to Price. Tonneman placed a third penny next to the first two. In the process he dropped the slip of red silk. He sighed, picked it up, and shoved it into his coat pocket.

The sights and smells of food were everywhere; the strongest was the cloy of spiced apple cider. It mixed with the tantalizing odor of frying fish and roasting pork. Everywhere he looked, most were eating.

As he studied the crowd, Tonneman noticed his shadow, Charles Lanchester, the sail maker, finishing off a sausage. Lanchester was toting what seemed to be a sack of clams over his shoulder and was now busy sampling a wedge of cheese from a Dutch farmer's stall.

Tonneman laughed. What else could he do? When he thought of how much the fellow was costing Nick in victuals, he laughed again. Full and loud.

"Agh!"

The scream came from nearby. Tonneman was not alarmed. Over the years he had come to recognize Luigi Castellano's cries of pain and frustration.

For as early as '64, Luigi, from New Jersey, across the North River, had been coming to Market Day to show off his fire-eating talents—which were nil—from the open back of his wagon.

Though the son of a fire-eater, after all these years Luigi still hadn't gained the competence his trade required. But people dropped pennies into his tin plate to watch him just the same.

Whether it was to watch him eat fire or to watch him burn, Tonneman was never quite sure. A thin, dark man, Luigi was a queer sort. As were most, Tonneman had concluded with each passing year.

Burning torches rested in holders on either side of Luigi's wagon. Tonneman slipped in among a group of spectators and watched as Luigi took one of the torches and drank from a long-necked bottle.

A mouthful of brandywine.

And a vigorous spit. A woman gasped.

Flames flared, and flared again and died. The audience murmured its disappointment as the brandywine dribbled from Luigi's mouth. He rubbed his seared lips in anguish.

Tonneman sighed. All these years and the man hadn't learned. Nor had he given up. Tonneman didn't know whether he should be sad for Luigi's stupidity or glad for his bravery.

Someone said, "They steal children and drink their blood."

"No, that's the Jews."

The voices were close by.

"Who is that?" Tonneman demanded. A rock bounced along the ground and struck his shoe. Was that an accident? "Who threw that?" The wooden cup cracked in his angry hand. He cast the shards to the ground. "Face me man-to-man and I'll break your neck."

"Jew tupper!"

The crowd that had gathered around the fire-eater's wagon broke away as if Tonneman were a leper. They quickly dispersed.

Luigi waved his torch at Tonneman. "You've lost me a great deal of money."

"I doubt that. I'm looking into some horse killings we're having over here. Any trouble like that where you are?"

"No," Luigi answered, gently probing his tender lips with his tongue.

Tonneman, chagrined, left him a shilling and moved on.

At once he came upon some of the men he had seen in Asser Levy's tavern the day before. Leading the pack was Asser Levy, looking like his own son. "Good day, Mister Tonneman," the man called.

"Good day, Mister Levy." Tonneman stared at the mark on Levy's left cheek. "That's a nasty bruise."

The butcher's hand went to his face. "Yes, I fell when I was ailing."

"You look fit now."

"A miracle. Thanks to the Creator and the ministrations of your dear wife. My apologies. I have no time to talk. I came out to smell these wonderful cooked meats of yours I can never eat. Good day, sir. I'm off to pray and thank the good Lord for my well-being."

Asser Levy moved on with his quorum of bearded men.

Tonneman was worried about Racqel. There was no way she could prevail. Racqel was right. Next they would be blaming her for the cock cuttings. Even for the ones in Hartford.

The cadence of an old madrigal floated above the busy Market Field. Tonneman nodded to Michael Korbonski, the fiddler, son to Sweet Lips, the whore whose real name or origin he'd never known, and the Polish Jew fiddler, Isadore Korbonski.

The boy was singing about the western wind and rain, and Christ and love.

"How are your folks?" Tonneman called.

"Somewheres west, all I know," the boy responded as he made music on his fiddle.

"I'm looking into some horse killings we're having here. Have you heard anything along that line?"

The boy shook his head and played a new tune. Something like a melody Tonneman had once heard a Russian sailor sing.

Tonneman pulled the piece of red cloth from his pocket. "Have you seen anyone wearing this kind of silk?"

"Pretty. I'd like a coat of it myself."

Tonneman was tired of asking about the silk. Truth was, he didn't know what to ask anymore. Have you seen someone wearing it? Dozens of people—nay, hundreds—could have something made of red silk like this. No, his question was too vague. It might be a clue to the horse killer, but it was barely better than no clue at all. Jesus' hands—even though they didn't wear silk, the horse killer could even be any one of the City's one hundred lobsterbacks in their red soldier suits. Scowling, he pushed the scrap of cloth back into his coat.

"Ho, Tonneman." The young tanner, Raphael Schuyler, Jan Keyser's major rival, had set up a stall and was showing leathers of various lengths and widths and pliability, which could be used to make harness straps, jerkins, breeches, as well as boots and shoes.

A faintly acrid odor touched the air, but young Schuyler and his plump Betty, from a wealthy Jamaica English family, the Hamiltons, were so good-humored that people were not put off by the tanner's stink. Besides, Betty Schuyler always had sweets to give the children on Market Day.

"How goes it?" Tonneman responded, knowing the Common Council was constantly threatening to banish all the tanneries farther north to keep the stench from the expanding City.

Raphael Schuyler grinned. "We bought a parcel of land well past Stuyvesant's Bowery, up along the East River."

"Practically in Albany," Betty said, dimpling, her smile like sunshine from under her bonnet. She thrust a plate at Tonneman. "We're celebrating."

Tonneman helped himself to a sugar cake. "The move?"

She shook her head, and dimpled again. And blushed.

"Ah. And when is the son and heir due?"

The young woman's dimples went deeper as her smile widened.

"By harvest time," her husband answered proudly, his hand resting on his wife's belly.

Tonneman congratulated them and continued on his way, then he stopped short and turned. "One thing. Dead horses are part of your business. I'm looking into the horse killing we had Sunday. Any strange people bringing you horse carcasses?"

"No, Mister Tonneman," the tanner said. "But if I hear, you'll be the first to know."

Betty Schuyler's cake was still sweet on his tongue when Tonneman arrived at the Bikker wagon. The broad table, shaded by a sun awning, held eggs, butter, and milk, with tubs of thick yellow cream.

Anna, the only living child of Tonneman's first marriage, was counting out change for a customer. Tonneman was always confounded when, after a time of not seeing her, he spied his daughter, the grown woman. It always took him a moment to realize that this was the red-faced, bawling babe who had come from his loins and Maria's womb. His first child, now a wife, the mother of his grandchildren. Where had the years gone?

Johan, his grandson, a sturdy lad of eleven, was the image of his father, Johan Bikker. Johan the younger was filling a wicker basket with potatoes. Margrietta, Tonneman's granddaughter, looked like Anna did when she was five. The child was attempting to help her brother but succeeded only in getting in the way.

Johan, Tonneman's son-in-law, stood beside his wagon. Apples, onions, and hot cider were arrayed on the back.

Tonneman missed the old ones, Johan's parents. The Bikkers had died the previous summer within weeks of each other from the summer fever.

"Grosspapi!" Margrietta shrieked, running to Tonneman and clutching him at the knees. He untwined her fat little arms and raised her in the air. Over her delighted cries, he smiled at his other family. "How goes it?" he asked.

"Racqel has been here already, Papi," Anna told him. "She seems so troubled. Is anything wrong with the children?" Anna took the little girl from Tonneman and set her on her feet.

"No. The children are good. Nothing to worry about." But he himself was worried. Never before had he felt threatened by his fellow citizens. This witchcraft nonsense was a Johnny thing, an English lunacy.

He clapped his son-in-law on the back. "We had a horse killed and mutilated on Sunday. Anything like that going on around you?"

"No, glad to say."

Tonneman kissed his daughter and granddaughter, patted his grandson on the head, drank a mug of cider, and was on his way.

He had toured most of the area, visiting with old friends and children of old friends, except for the two most distant stalls. These were around the rear of the Fort, a stone's throw from the windmill.

This last space was by unspoken agreement left for the Indians to trade, separate from the white man. Several years back the free Africans had used the area too, but that had led to trouble. Now if one wanted to buy from the Africans, one went to where they lived, around Shellpoint or in the Village of Greenwich.

Each of the Five Nations seemed to take turns coming to the

Market Field and each kept out of the others' way. Once in a while outsider Indians came to trade.

Today was one of those whiles: The heads of the men trading here today were smooth except for a high middle piece from the front of the pate to the back of the neck. That, and the wood carvings set out on a blanket on the ground, and the blanket itself, told Tonneman that these Indians were not of the Five Nations. They were Algonquin, from up north, past Albany. The Algonquin were a friendlier group than Foxman's people, the Mohawks, who had a taste for human flesh.

Blankets were displayed along with dried corn and herbs, carved pipes and figures—bears, owls, other creatures. All were overseen by two pipe-smoking old women whose gray braids fell well past their hips. Sides of venison hung on a nearby birch. The old women watched Tonneman with hooded eyes as he neared their wares. He could hear voices coming from close by; neither woman spoke.

He recognized his wife's voice and understood that she was asking questions. Racqel was more knowledgeable than any other white about Indian medicine. He smiled and leaned himself against a broad oak. By the spin of the blades of the windmill nearby he knew the wind was blowing strong from the Bay. It meant nothing; with no clouds over the water, there would be no rain. He slipped his hat over his face and waited.

After a while one of the old women made a ratchety sound in her throat.

When Tonneman shoved back his hat he saw Racqel walking toward him. "Come," his wife said as if she'd known all along he'd be waiting for her. "I have learned something."

Chapter 40

❧

When Tonneman stepped into the Devil on a Chain, a man at the bar coughed into his hand. But the sound he made wasn't a cough. It was the word *Jew*.

Tonneman had never seen the man, an ordinary fellow who was big enough and blond enough to be a cousin. For sure he was a Dutchman. But by his eyes he hated Tonneman. And for his furtive one-word remark—or was it a curse?—Tonneman hated him. Sore tempted was he to break the bastard's back. But he had other fish to fry.

He found Pos at a table in the rear, playing the arm game with François Garlic-Head, the trapper. Garlic-Head was not really his name, but no one remembered his true name anymore. All anyone knew was that the trapper ate garlic by the handful. His sweat reeked of it; his breath could shrivel a tulip.

Pos gave Tonneman a knowing wink. Relentlessly, he pressed the trapper's arm to the flat surface of the table.

The trapper let out a stream of invective in French and English and Dutch, threw some coins on the table, and sprayed the room with a scorching breath of brandywine and garlic as he crossed to the bar for another drink.

"There's a good fellow." Pos grinned and flexed his hand, then used it to whisk up the coins. He raised his empty cup to the tapster.

"I want a word with you," Tonneman said.

Pos's grin vanished. "There's trouble in your face, old friend. Sit. A drink for Mister Tonneman too, Dirk."

Young Samuel Hankin poked his head inside the door, as he did in all the public houses, seeking to earn some coin.

"Sam," Tonneman called.

The boy ran to Tonneman, hat in hand. Somewhere over the past four days the lad had found himself something out of the ordinary: a large, red silk shirt with no sleeves, which he wore like a gown over his brown coat.

"Where'd you get the shirt, boy?"

"Captain Pos gave it me."

Tonneman looked a question to his friend.

"Big tear in the sleeve," Pos explained.

Tonneman nodded at the answer and let it stew in his brain along with more information about red silk in this City than he wanted to know. "Sam."

"Sir?"

"You know Otto Wersten?"

"Yes, sir. The Night Watch."

"Yes." He gave the boy a penny. "Find Otto for me. Tell him I want to talk to him. Tell him to send you back with where and when we can meet."

"Yes, sir." The boy smiled wide with his sorry brown teeth and ran off.

Tonneman could not ignore the cup of brandy when Dirk, the barkeep, set it before him. He placed his hands on the cup. He could feel the heat of the brandy within. He lifted the cup to his lips. Each whiff of spirits was a siren's call. One taste. What would it hurt? How easy it would be to drink it in one gulp. And then have another. And then, before having another, attend to that Dutch bastard at the bar who'd coughed "Jew," and break his back.

He could feel Pos's eyes on him. He set the cup of brandy down and shoved it to the center of the table. He knew Pos would drink for both of them.

"You've heard about Backer's stallion?" Pos showed the bright stare he always employed when he was hiding something.

That stare gave Tonneman pause. "Yes. The killer nailed the cock to the schoolmaster's door and just about killed poor Crabtree too. I've got him safe until he recovers. I pulled Michael Pijnenborgh off the road crews to keep an eye on him."

Pos's tongue made a clicking noise, then he sly-eyed Tonneman. "Crabtree told you who did it, then?"

"Nay. The poor creature swears he was set upon by a hairy giant."

Pos laughed loudly and drank his brandy.

"I suppose that lets you out," Tonneman said. "Though I have seen you carry on like a gigantic fool."

Pos laughed again. He pushed aside his empty cup and brought Tonneman's cup to his lips. After an almost dainty sip, he grew quite serious again. Setting the cup down, he put a finger in the brandy, tasted it, then spoke softly. "They say Racqel has used witchcraft to cure the butcher Levy. There's even talk that she is to be brought up before the Common Council on witch charges."

Tonneman's fist hammered the table; it shook the brandy from Pos's cup, spilling it. "I want that stopped. De Sille can end it now. Tell him he'll get naught from me while this threat continues."

Absently wiping drops of brandy from the table with his fingers and licking them, Pos was silent for a moment. Then he drank what remained of the second brandy. He shook his head dismissively. "A few fanatics, that's all." To the barkeep he called, "More brandy-wine."

"And tell him that this cock-cutting business has happened elsewhere. One of my people found—"

Pos's face fell. He said, "Then you've heard about Boston."

Chapter 41

Tonneman slept like a bear in winter. He did not dream. But in his sleep that night he did form two theories that came to him full-blown before he awoke. Not a difficult task, since both theories were fairly obvious. Theory One: Whoever mutilated and killed horses in Boston and in Hartford had to be the very man who was now doing the same in New-York. And Theory Two: The Scots trader, Amos Lopez-Campbell, knew a lot more than he was saying.

The caress of the morning sun on his face brought him full awake. Blinking back the light, he rubbed the sleep crusts from his eyes. When he moved to embrace his wife, he found instead an unmovable object.

Racqel was sitting up in bed, her shawl around her; the unmovable object, a tooled leather box, sat on her knees. The box contained her father's records and recipes for treatment. Tonneman had not seen the box or its contents for years, not since Racqel had placed them in the attic soon after they were married.

"Are you awake, husband?"

"I am." He put a low growl in his voice to tease her. "Thanks to you, woman."

But she took no notice. "I believe," Racqel said, "that I now know what Levy's illness is. I kept going over and over it." She held a paper out to him.

"No, read it to me." He sat up and placed his arm about her.

"My father arrived at a diagnosis years ago. I was reminded of it when I talked to the Indians yesterday. They suffer from the disease too." She made a small noise meant to be a laugh. "My father called the ailment butcher's disease. People get sick from dead livestock."

Tonneman grunted.

"What do you think?"

"I think I'm proud of my physician wife," he said, nuzzling her neck. "She has the brain of a man, yet is very beautiful."

"I should have been a physician."

"Yes, of course. But that would mean you would be a man. How lucky I am that you are not."

She frowned and looked distracted.

"This is wonderful news, then, for Levy is cured, is he not?" His hands caressed her shoulder.

"No!" She took his hands in hers. "I know of no cure for this ailment, husband. The symptoms come and go according to God's whim. The only safeguard I know of is for the patient to stay away from the carcasses of dead animals. And if I'm right, Crabtree has it too. I must go to Asser Levy and advise him that he is not cured."

Tonneman groaned. He yearned to say "I forbid it," but knew such words would only sharpen her resolve. He lay back and pulled the bedclothes over him, knowing full well that his scrupulously honest wife would now also be condemned for causing Levy's illness to return.

The morning held none of the usual comfort found in the Tonneman household. Moses and Maria had eaten early and were now outside with Benjamin, doing their chores. Under Alice's watchful eye, Daniel slept.

Two things were on Tonneman's mind. Racqel's well-being; he knew what she was going to do.

And then there was Solomon Navarro, the physician.

He was worried about Navarro's reaction should he learn that

Racqel had visited his patient again. No, Tonneman's mind had to be on De Sille's problem and, therefore, his own. He must find out who killed and mutilated the Governor's stallion, and who did the same to Backer's horse, and who attacked the schoolmaster. And perhaps, just perhaps, who killed Edward Davies. If Tonneman could do this, no one would talk witchcraft and his wife in the same breath.

Tonneman knew that Navarro's red silk cravat and Pos's damned red shirt meant nothing at all. In fact, the red silk clue meant nothing at all. What could it prove? Red silk cravats had been the mode for some time. And red silk fabric was certainly nothing new.

Still, it was all he had.

If nothing else, Tonneman disliked and resented the vain little physician, enough to play the Devil with him. There was benefit in that. If Navarro was the horse killer, perhaps unsettling the man would prod him into showing his hand.

But first Tonneman had to stop at the jail. He had to talk to Amos Lopez-Campbell.

The City Hall building seemed unusually quiet. The Sheriff's office was empty. Suddenly cautious, Tonneman placed his hand on his sword. Slowly he advanced on the door to the big meeting room and pulled it open.

"Yes?" Nick De Sille, at the head of a long table crowded with the members of the Common Council, glared at Tonneman. As did the members of the Council. "Yes, Tonneman?"

"Nothing," Tonneman replied softly. And then even softer he added, "Wrong door." Quickly he closed the door and headed to the cellar for the jail cells.

It had been years since he was down there. He took a lamp from the round table in the front hall. As he remembered, the rotting steps were slippery with scum and rat shit, and the air was rancid.

When he reached the foot of the stairs, he raised his lamp and called out. "Hoy, anybody home?"

No answer.

He drew his sword. Then he edged his way carefully around the bags of salt stored in the cellar.

Every shadow his lantern threw on the dank walls made him stop and listen. Was that breathing he heard? Perhaps it was his own. He held his breath. There. He heard it again. Slowly he advanced. After the time in Mendoza's warehouse, he wasn't about to take any foolish chances.

The doors to all four cells were open. And three of the cells were empty.

The last cell stank worse than the others. Cabbage soup. Very old cabbage soup.

Tonneman went into it and held his lamp over the form on the cot, expecting to find Amos Lopez-Campbell.

The figure moaned and turned. He did not have red hair.

It was the Deputy, Nessel-Vogel.

Chapter 42

"I'm a more than passing strong fellow," Nessel-Vogel declared.

"I know that. What happened?"

"It takes a lot to put me down."

"Get on with it."

"Amos Lopez-Campbell and Mad Beado were our only residents, and I was bringing them some cabbage soup. Mistress Ray makes it for us."

"Go on, go on." Tonneman's patience was wearing thin.

"Well, so Lopez reaches for the soup. It was in a clay bowl." The Deputy kicked at the shards of clay at his feet. "And then he hits me with it." Nessel-Vogel wiped at his leather vest. "Got hot soup all over me."

"That's too bad," Tonneman said. "And where's Mad Beado?"

"Bloody hell, not him too?"

"Flown the nest, both of them, I'm afraid," Tonneman told him, starting back to the stairs.

"Gibb'll skin me. Two prisoners lost." Dolefully, Nessel-Vogel wiped at his garb again. "First mud, now soup."

"You're fortunate soup was all you got. Lopez-Campbell probably killed that man in the Jewish cemetery."

"Wait for me," shouted the Deputy. "Gibb is going to have my arse for this."

"I'm afraid so."

"Talk about biting the hand that feeds you."

"More like cracking the head," Tonneman replied.

"That's not funny, Mister Tonneman."

YOUNG SAM HANKIN was sitting on the stoop of City Hall.

"Looking for me, boy?" said Tonneman.

"Yes, sir." The boy seemed to have second sight, always there when and where he was wanted. Sam pointed a finger at the yawning man waiting across the road. Even though it was a warm day, the man was hugging himself in his worn duffel coat, there were mittens on his hands, and his rabbit hat was pulled down about his head. "Otto Wersten," Sam announced with pride.

Tonneman slipped the lad a penny and crossed the road.

"Good morrow, Mister Tonneman." Otto's next yawn was wide and noisy.

"Mister Wersten. Forgive me for getting you up so early."

"Not been to bed yet."

"Then I'll make this fast. You know what I want to talk to you about?"

The Night Watch Man nodded. "Already told Mister Gibb all I know, but I'll be glad to tell you."

"Talk with me while I saddle my horse."

In the shed, Venus and Racqel's sorrel, Deborah, were nibbling stray foodstuff from the ground.

"Otto, tell me what you remember of that morning."

"I was making my rounds. Nothing uncommon. When I came to the old Stuyvesant place where the First Councillor lives now, I heard this terrible ungodly sound. Came from the carriage house. It must have been the horses. The gate was open wide. The screaming stopped. Just like that. I heard the horses, neighing and kicking out their stalls. Before I could go farther I was hit in the face with blood. So much blood it made me sick, I'll tell you. I was on my arse when the horse galloped by. Then I got to my feet and I hied myself to the carriage house. Smythe was already there. You know him?"

Tonneman nodded.

"Man's useless as tits on a bull. I shook my rattle to bring help. Lord knew what we were going to find inside. What my ears had heard my eyes now saw. Two poor creatures were screeching and kicking holes in their stalls." Otto wiped his sweaty face and removed his coat. "It was terrible, I tell you. Like a slaughterhouse. The Governor's beautiful horse, the one he got from the King, was on the ground, its insides outside and all over."

Tonneman liked barns, stables, horse places. He filled his lungs with the pungent smells in the stall, as if to ward off the horrible image Otto described. The image that was strengthened by his own experience at the carriage house.

Horse sweat was good, mixed usually with hay and grain. Leather was good too. He liked the smell of leather. And the oil used to make it shine.

Tonneman patted Venus, then set the saddle on her. "You didn't see the rider?"

"Not a hair." The Night Watch Man rubbed his eyes. "If you have no further use for me, sir, I'm off to bed."

"Thanks for your trouble, Otto." He gave the Watch Man two pennies.

The pennies disappeared into a pocket of the coat Otto held in his hands. "Thank you, Mister Tonneman. Always at your service." The Night Watch Man put his fingers to his rabbit hat in salute, slung his coat over his shoulder, and yawned again. He shuffled off to his bowl of hot corn porridge and his cold bed on Beaver Street.

Tonneman made the cinch secure and gave Venus a reassuring pat. As he led the mare out on Queen Street, he saw Sam Hankin dashing toward him, his small face flushed with excitement.

"Did you hear, sir?" the boy yelled. "It's all over City Hall."

"Hear what?"

"They found Mad Beado floating in Shellpoint. Dead. What's more, they say somebody cut him the way was done the horses."

Chapter 43

As Tonneman rode up the Strand to the Water Gate, he considered Mad Beado's death. The connection to the horse killings was clear because of the mutilation. Or was the cutting just a trick to make everyone think there was a connection? What had Beado known? And what, if anything, had Davies meant to tell Tonneman when he beckoned to him at Mendoza's warehouse?

He weighed Otto's account. It wasn't much. No matter. It would all fall into place. It had to.

Luck was with him. Sergeant Frank Nesbitt was just stepping away from the Water Gate.

"Ho, Venus. Frank, a word, if you please."

Nesbitt turned and walked the few paces to Tonneman. "What can I do for you?"

"Which of your men had the duty on Sunday?"

Nesbitt laughed. "You mean the morn of the cock?"

"If you like."

"I don't even have to consult my roster sheet. Brown on this Gate and Hart at the Broad Way."

"I'd like to talk to them."

"You can if you like, but I'll save you the trouble. Both swear no one got by them."

Tonneman frowned. "The horse killer isn't a ghost who comes and goes without a trace."

"Hart swears no one came in his Gate. And Brown said the only sound he heard all night was that of a cat lost in the woods."

"What?"

"A cat. Keep your bowels tight. I didn't say a great angry bear. You think the cat came into town and butchered the horse?"

"No, but I'll wager Private Arse-hole Brown went after the cat and—"

Nesbitt groaned. "Oh, shit. Say no more. You're frolicking number one right. The horse cutter lured Brown away with cat sounds and outflanked the stupid yap."

Tonneman sighed heavily and reined Venus toward Wall Street. Jacob Roome lived on the Broad Way Road, just outside the Gate. And Roome and his wife were next on Tonneman's list.

"Tonneman, did you hear about Beado?" Nesbitt called.

"I did." Tonneman brought Venus to a halt and looked over his shoulder.

Nesbitt caught up with him. "Here's some good news for you. My men saw nothing coming in. But going out is another story. Hart saw your killer. Rode right at the Broad Way Gate. Knocked Hart over."

"When were you going to tell me? Christmas?"

Nesbitt mocked Tonneman by forming his lips into a kiss.

Tonneman sighed. "What did the man look like?"

"Couldn't see."

"And the horse?"

"Couldn't see. I figure that was the animal they found later at the Devil's Boulder. It was so crazed, they had to put the beast down."

"You call that good news?" Tonneman prodded Venus and continued toward the Broad Way. "You tell Gibb all this shit?"

"Yes, sir," the Sergeant called after him. "He didn't think much of it either. Not even when I told him Hart was knocked out for a while."

"Ho." Tonneman jerked Venus around. The horse neighed. "Sorry, girl." He glared at Nesbitt. "You silly bastard."

There was a glint in the old soldier's eye.

Tonneman allowed himself to smile. "Having fun, are you? All right. Tell me the good stuff."

"I just did. Hart was out for a good while. He doesn't know how long."

"He told you this?"

"After a few drinks, and when I told him if he didn't give out with the truth, I'd break his arm and transfer him to Africa."

"Does Gibb know this?"

Nesbitt nodded. "Told me not to tell you. I compromised. I decided not to tell you until you asked."

"You know what this means, don't you? We don't know if the rider rode out of town or got off inside the City and sent the horse outside on its own."

"That's the truth of it."

TONNEMAN RODE THROUGH the Broad Way Gate, wondering what good witnesses were anyway. Where one man saw a flood, another saw a stream. No one could be trusted to tell the exact truth.

The Roome house stood out from the rest on the street because of the wagons and carts in front and by the very sturdiness of its structure. Behind the house were a good-sized garden and a big barn. Chickens and pigs fought for yard space with two sturdy, crawling baby girls. From the other side of the barn came the lowing of cows.

Tonneman entered the vast ground-floor store, which was crowded with patrons.

A broad-shouldered woman with red and swollen eyes was standing over the bins of dried beans. She wore a brown sackcloth dress and a white apron. There was an air of industry about the place, but also an ineffable sadness.

"Mistress Roome?"

"That's me."

Jacob Roome was taking payment. His coat and breeches were black and he had a black band on his left arm. "Thanks for your custom," he said to a woman with a mole on her nose.

The nine-year-old Roome triplets, Jan, Dirk, and Willem, whose shirts were sackcloth, were packing items into baskets for customers.

Standing to the side, Tonneman waited patiently for the Roomes' attention.

Jacob Roome looked about the chamber filled with casks and boxes and bins of food, satisfied himself that his wife and three sons were taking care of business, and hurried to Tonneman. "Yes, Mister Tonneman?"

"If it's all right, I'd like to talk to you about your son, Edward Davies."

"Of course," Jacob Roome replied.

Eliza Roome's hand lifted to her mouth. She squeezed her lips, then dropped the hand to her side. "We thank you, sir, for the care you gave my boy Edward as he lay dying."

Tonneman had done nothing of the sort. Obviously Gibb had left out the rough parts. Well, he wouldn't add to the Roomes' burden.

"My Edward was a good boy." Eliza Davies Roome rubbed her hands on her apron as if drying them. "A bit choleric, but he had the call. He would have been a preacher."

Shaking his head, Roome said, "He had spells."

"Yes," his wife agreed. "God saw fit to mark him. But Edward found a friend and teacher in Master Crabtree."

Roome bit at his lip. "I don't know that Crabtree didn't fill his poor head with all kinds of book nonsense."

"One question," Tonneman said. "About a year ago, sir, you traded for some red silk from David Mendoza." He showed the storekeeper his bit of cloth.

Puzzlement creased Roome's face. "That's true. But I don't see . . ." His attention was drawn to two women who had entered the shop.

"Please, sir," Tonneman said. "I won't be a moment. What happened to the cloth?"

"I sold it, of course. That's what I'm in business for."

"Who to?"

"How can I remember? I did trade a good amount for beaver pelts with an Indian."

"Would that be the Mohawk known as Foxman?"

"They all look alike to me."

"His hair. Was it just one lock hanging down?"

Roome, irritated, shook his head. "Enough, sir. I have customers, and my family is in mourning. I have just lost my son."

Tonneman shrugged and was ready to leave when, unexpectedly, Mistress Roome spoke. "I used some of it to make my boy a coat. A fine red coat for my Edward."

"Indeed?" Tonneman almost shouted. "And what happened to that coat?"

The woman shook her head. "It's nowhere in the house." Her eyes filled with tears.

Tonneman, at a loss, backed away and took his leave. Davies and Crabtree. There was a pair to conjure with. Perhaps Davies was the horse killer. But if so, who killed Davies? And who killed Mad Beado? And why mutilate the madman?

SOLOMON NAVARRO LIVED on the Broad Way near the Fort in the house Nick De Sille and Geertruyd had owned when the English arrived years before.

Tonneman circled round the tall Dutch-style house to get the lay of the land. Of course, Nick had to own one of the few brick houses back then. And now, the more Tonneman thought about it, the smug Navarro would, by nature, choose one of the finest Christian homes to call his own.

The branches of the peach trees in front of the house were already greening. Come summer, the smell of ripe peaches would scent the air all the way to Queen Street.

In the rear the formal herb garden the De Silles had planted was gone. Evidently Navarro didn't think as much of the curative power of herbs as Racqel did.

An apple tree in the center of what had once been the garden stood alone next to a latticework bower intertwined with climbing vines.

Determined, Tonneman strode up to the large double door, the upper half of which was paneled in the form of a cross. Tonneman wondered if Navarro appreciated the significance of the design that was Christ's cross. He rapped on the door.

A gnarled black woman opened the top of the door and stuck her head out. She startled Tonneman, for she looked just like Annabella, Geertruyd's old servant woman who had supposedly died at sea on her way to Jamaica. Was it she? Most African women looked alike to him, particularly the old ones.

"Is Mister Navarro in?"

The old woman responded by opening the bottom door and stepping aside. An Amsterdam scene Tonneman remembered well was painted on the upper inside panel of the door. Spreading tulips adorned the lower panel.

Tonneman followed the African woman as she shuffled into the great chamber. "God's blood," he whispered, echoing Nick. Navarro had apparently bought the place lock, stock, and barrel from Nick. It looked just as it had when De Sille owned it.

A new question tantalized Tonneman. Where had Navarro come from? Had the physician bought the house, or had the Jewish Community bought it for him, as was often the custom? Or merely leased it? Whatever way, the house was remarkably as it had been when it was Nick's.

The green plush couch was even in its old place opposite the mullioned window facing the Broad Way. In front of the couch was the carved table. A fire burned in the orange-tiled hearth.

The old woman tapped on a door at the back of the chamber.

When the door opened, Tonneman heard a woman say, "He'll be out soon."

There was no mistaking that lisp. The woman who entered the

room wore red, which set off her smooth white skin. On her right cheek was a *mouche*. Madame Geertruyd De Sille.

"Ah, Tonneman," Geertruyd said softly, "we meet in the most unlikely places." She raised her voice. "Thank you so much Señor Navarro. I feel *so* much better now." She minced to the door, stopped to retrieve her red parasol from the blue China urn, and stepped out into the bright sunshine.

Geertruyd's rose water scent lingered behind her.

"Patient here," the old black woman announced. She even sounded like Annabella.

"Yes?" Now Navarro appeared, a suave and patronizing smile on his face. The man was dressed in black again. Today it was silk breeches and coat over a scarlet shirt. When he spied Tonneman, however, his smile faded. His black owl eyes went rounder, if that were possible. "What are you doing here?"

"I've come to talk to you."

"I'm surprised you didn't send your wife. She seems to think she can do anything she pleases."

Very clever, thought Tonneman. Goad me about Racqel and perhaps I'll forget why I came. "Where were you Sunday morning?"

Navarro laughed. "In my bed, of course. But that's none of your business." His eyes widened. "You don't honestly believe I had anything to do with that damn horse business? I was in my bed all that night and all that morning. And I can prove it if I have to. But I don't have to, not to you. Get out."

Tonneman shrugged and left the physician's house.

Was Navarro in black an imitation of a younger Nick, before Nick gave up his dark attire in favor of looking more English?

Save for the red cravat, of course.

If Navarro bought his home from Nick and clothed himself like Nick, were there further connections between the two men?

But that would be ignoring the obvious. Considering all the players in the game as he knew them, the connection surely must be between Navarro and Geertruyd.

Yes, if she had a new conquest, it would be just like Geertie to dress him up to look like the young Nick she'd met and married.

Tonneman's thoughts about the connection between Davies and Crabtree resurfaced.

Eliza Roome said that Edward found a friend and teacher in Master Crabtree.

Mad Beado was in that friendship somewhere. Hadn't Tonneman and Gibb found him near-dead in Davies's hut at Shellpoint? Now Davies and Beado were dead too. Simple mathematics. Plain as the nose on his face.

The killer was the schoolmaster, Crabtree.

Or was it Navarro?

Chapter 44

Choosing her most modest dress, brown with a crisp white collar, and her plainest bonnet, Racqel prepared herself to meet Asser Levy, praying to God for guidance as she did so. She discussed the midday meal and supper with Alice, then draped a light, black cloak over her shoulders, spread a linen cloth over her basket of medicines, and stopped to kiss the children.

"I won't be long, Alice."

Profoundly sad, she walked out the scullery door around to Queen Street and the Water Gate.

Behind her, along the waterfront, the roadworkers still raised dust. Ahead, the sound of laughter and the smell of rum were strong. As she walked, the reason became clear. A cask had broken, accidentally or on purpose, and the workmen unloading cargo from an English ship just returned from Jamaica were scooping the escaping liquid with their hands and drinking. Sheriff Gibb would have his hands full before the day was out.

There was no sentry to be seen at the Water Gate. Racqel shook her head. Didn't they know there was a madman running loose?

She had four choices: Levy's home, his tavern, his shop, or the slaughterhouse, through the gate and out on the pier. Since it was closest, she chose the house at the Wall.

"My mistress is not at home." The young servant girl spoke haughtily. The girl's stare was a combination of awe and insolence. Quick as her words were spoken, the door was closing.

"Wait. I seek your master."

The girl's eyes narrowed. She studied Racqel with something like fear. "My master is at his slaughterhouse every morning except for the Sabbath and Sunday. I will tell him you called." The door slammed shut in Racqel's face.

"Many thanks," she murmured, turning away. She knew that the girl behind that closed door was no doubt saying a prayer to keep the evil witch away. All Racqel wanted was for her children to be instructed and confirmed. Was this asking too much?

She started back toward Queen Street, her thoughts smoldering. Her problems would be resolved if Tonneman became a Jew.

The sentry, a round man with a huge belly, was now at his post. He was chewing on a sausage.

"Good morrow."

". . . Good morrow, Mistress Tonneman."

Was it her imagination, or had the Musketeer hesitated when he recognized her? No matter, she would not let anything deter her from her mission.

Just beyond the Wall was a pier that jutted straight out over the East River. Racqel nodded to the sentry and stepped through the Gate.

Resting on pilings above the water was Asser Levy's slaughterhouse. The wind coming from the east had a sharp edge, bearing the stench of the slaughterhouse with it. Crows and hawks, and every so often an aggressive gull, vied for position, noisily seeking Levy's scraps.

The slaughterhouse looked as formidable as it smelled, but she set her foot firmly on the planks leading to it, just as a wagon pulled by a swaybacked horse approached from the north. "You can't go there," shouted the man in the cart, which was piled high with canvas bags, some split and spilling salt. He reined in his mottled gray horse and glared at her.

"Halt," another voice called from out on the pier. "You may come no farther."

"Go back," still another voice said.

Ahead, her route was blocked by two husky young men. Both seemed horrified by her invasion. She was, after all, a woman.

"I've come—"

"Let me pass," the man in the horse cart demanded.

The gray was practically stepping on her feet. Frightened, Racqel hovered at the edge of the pier, fearful of falling into the water as the salt cart clattered by.

After the cart had stopped at the slaughterhouse, she called, "I've come to see Asser Levy. This is most important. Tell him Mistress Tonneman must see him at once."

The two youths did not move.

"Please," she cried. "It is urgent."

One young man went off while the other watched her warily.

Everything, Racqel thought, not knowing whether to be angry or miserable, conspired to make her feel the pariah. The wind had died down, yet still she shivered. But she stood firm.

She saw Asser Levy come out of the abattoir. He took off a bloody white duster and handed it to the young man who watched her.

"Mistress Tonneman," Levy called across the distance that separated them. "I tell the world that you are my angel of mercy. But this is no place for you."

His greeting was so effusive, the workman unloading the salt stopped to watch them.

"I have brought you more medicine." Racqel stepped several paces forward.

Levy raised his right hand. She stopped.

"But I am cured. Don't you see that? You have cured me, and I am so very grateful to you. Please come and see me later at my house. I go home for the midday meal. My house is your house from this day forth."

"Thank you, Mister Levy," she called. "But I must talk to you. Now!"

Levy sighed. "And I must talk to you, Mistress, but I would rather not do it here." He clasped his hands together in front of his black waistcoat. "I am so grateful, dear woman, as I luxuriate in my good health, that I have been considering a Jewish mother and her four Jewish children who have been forced to exist without the love and strength of our Community. And I have been thinking, too, of what she asked of me."

In spite of herself and what she knew, Racqel's heart surged with hope. She didn't speak.

"I mean to right a wrong," Levy continued. "Send young Moses to me. I personally will begin his studies. It will be a blessing for me to shepherd a young man as he learns to praise God."

"Thank you." Racqel was overwhelmed. "But please . . . I hope you will feel the same after I tell you what I've come to tell you."

"And that is what?" Levy smiled at her benevolently.

"I'm afraid you've allowed yourself false hope. You are still ill."

The butcher laughed. "If this is sick, may I be sick till the day I die. And I pray God that is not near at hand."

"You don't understand, you are not cured. The sickness has merely gone away for a time. It might come back."

He frowned at her. "So might the Angel of Death. I'll worry about that when it happens. Woe is me, what is all this talk of death?"

"Mister Levy, how long have you been a butcher?"

"What's that got to do with anything?" He was trying not to be irritated. "Most of my life."

"Then you're a very lucky man."

"Tell that to someone in his grave. Again death." Levy spat three times through his fingers into the river.

"I believe you have the butcher's disease. That was my father's name for it. It may come from the dead livestock in your slaughterhouse."

Now she had gone too far. Levy's face was contorted and his voice was cold. "Nonsense, woman. I follow our law. We are pure.

We are clean." He shook his head. "Why did I think a woman could help?"

"Mister Levy, I beg you, don't go to your shop or the slaughter-house, or anywhere near dead animals."

Asser Levy's black eyes glowed with anger, mistrust. This was the lowest insult. "Why not ask me to stop breathing until Judgment Day? I tell you, my meat is the finest. My slaughterhouse is clean. Every lung I examine is smooth and pure. There is no disease among my meat."

She stepped as close to him as she dared. When she was an arm's length away, she said, "If you do go amongst dead animals, you may very well fall ill again. You could die."

Sweat appeared on Levy's forehead. His neck cloth seemed to choke him. He began shouting at her. "Don't try to chase me into the goat's horn. Look at me, woman. So upset my hands are shaking. If I fall sick again, it will be because you have made me sick. Is that what you want? Would that be your vengeance because of your griev-ances against our righteous Community? None of us turned their backs on the Lord. You did. None of us married a Gentile. You did. Blessed is the Lord our God. The Lord is one. You are responsible for your children being beyond the pale because of your sins, not ours. Leave here at once!"

Levy's passion set off a fit of coughing. The paroxysm was so severe, the man brought up blood. He pointed his finger at Racqel, shouting, "Blood. Blood. You're killing me. Oh, my God. The Chris-tians are right about you. You are a witch."

Chapter 45

Each of Asser Levy's words hit Racqel like hot coals, burning into her very being. She had to get away, run, hide her tears, her terror.

Instead of dashing through the Gate and back toward her home, she ran along Water Gate Road, past the Jewish cemetery, stopping only when she dropped her basket of medicines. What good was it? What good was she?

She decided to return to the cemetery; perhaps there would be some solace at her father's grave. The rumble of an approaching vehicle made her look up. A carriage was bearing down on her. She grabbed her basket and ran into the woods. This time she ran until she couldn't catch her breath, and fell against an old pine. Exhausted, she slid down to the ground and cried tears of frustration, and of loss.

HE WAS THE SEARCHER again, but for the first time he was also himself. In spite of the sickness, this knowledge was exhilarating. When he returned to his own bed two days before, the fever had raged within him. It was still raging now. But by force of will he had kept it hidden from those around. Alone, he allowed it to affect him. His bones were like the nails of Jesus, threatening to tear through the skin that held them together. He needed a terrible, sacred strength to strike down the blasphemer.

Once more he would don his fine red coat and do God's work. It pleased him to wear the red coat when he carried the sword of the Lord. A poetic mockery against the English, the redcoats, the God-damners, for the English were the evilest of the blasphemers. But his mission was not against them alone. All would suffer his wrath. The Dutch. The Jews. Even the Indians and the niggers. All were sinners. And because they did not obey God's laws, all were damned.

His eyes blazed with more than the fever. There was a tear in the shoulder of his fine red coat. It could not be mended; a piece was missing. He threw the rag down, cursing. He would do without the sullied garment. Then he picked it up and fondled it. No, he would wear the coat one more time. His work was near complete here, and he would move on again. It was God's will that he go among the sinners, chastising them, as Noah did, warning them against the blas-phemy of wealth, gluttony, and fornication. The flood would come again. Only this time the flood would be blood. He walked down the stairs oblivious to his surroundings, and out, going north and east. His feet found the old path, the Indian trail. He followed it, singing a hymn to God. A new sound stilled the birds and filled his ears. Frowning, he stopped, listened. It was the sound of a woman cry-ing.

The wood was enchanted, he knew. He crept close to the sound. From behind a mound of leaves he saw *her* resting on a boul-der in a clearing.

Was this weeping angel with dark hair the woman Mary, Mother of the Child they called Jesus?

His bowels gripped him. Another test from God, as God had tested Luther with constipation. The Searcher backed deeper into the forest to relieve his suffering. And to pray.

When he returned to his mound of leaves he saw that Mary, Mother of God, had recovered. She had come to him to cure him of his pain. Had she not cured Asser Levy? She understood the dark magic of herbs and the mysteries of the Indians and the night. Blessed Mary would cure him. He stepped into the clearing.

MAN WHO WALKS LIKE A FOX had been following her since she left her house. The salt being delivered to the butcher's pier gave him the idea of capturing a bag for himself. But the angry words of Asser Levy made him pause.

Why was she so frightened by mere words? What could frighten this one? She was not one to show fear.

He drew back his lips in what he believed was a smile, and watched as she ran away from the town, first on the road, and then into his domain. He followed her.

"BLESSED MISTRESS MARY," the Searcher whispered as he stepped into view. "You know how ill I am, and only you can help me, as you helped Asser Levy."

Racqel stared at him. Fever burned in his eyes. His lips were dreadfully chapped and cracked. Surely, he was mad. She had lost the linen cloth that covered her basket, but the medicines inside were there intact. Placing her hand on the thick flask of laudanum, she held it out to him. "Here, this will ease your pain," she said.

He eyed her with suspicion. "No, I was mistaken. You are not Blessed Mary, Mother of Jesus. You are the other one. The whore, Mary Magdalene." He seized her arm. "You are the hidden witch whom I must kill. Come with me."

Shocked, she dropped the basket. The flask fell to the ground. A crack appeared in the thick glass. With a cry of dismay she reached for it. The flask fell apart in her hands. The sharp smell of opium and brandywine pervaded the air as the precious pain-relieving medication soaked into the earth.

TONNEMAN WATCHED NAVARRO'S house for a while, to no avail. Patients came and went, Jew and Christian alike, but no one suspicious. Tonneman was keenly disappointed. The way things stood, the killer was either Crabtree or Navarro. One or the other, but he wanted it to be Navarro.

When the sun reached mid-sky, Tonneman was hungry and thirsty, and he headed home to dine with his wife and brood.

Navarro and Geertruyd. He laughed aloud. Wait, where was his head? Navarro had come to New-York—New Orange then—in '73. From . . . ? Tonneman scratched his head. Somewhere in Johnny land. Rhode Island? Newport?

Rhode Island, Massachusetts, Connecticut. This fit his theory perfectly. If someone were traveling south, what would make more sense than his next stop be New-York? That would mean Crabtree was innocent and that Navarro was the cock cutter.

And Navarro, the physician, the surgeon, certainly knew how to wield a knife with enough finesse to slice a cow's throat.

But, according to Racqel's theory, the dead cow dealt only with the dead man in the field, which in all likelihood was one Lopez-Campbell killed by the other Lopez-Campbell.

What did one have to do with the other?

Nothing.

But Navarro *could* be guilty of both.

TONNEMAN'S BRAIN WAS overworn from all his theories.

He found his children gathered round the table in the kitchen, waiting for Alice to ladle thick potato soup.

Alice set a bowl in front of him and filled it.

"Where is Mutti?" Tonneman asked Moses, who was standing by the door that led to the garden.

The boy raised his hand, indicating silence. Tonneman was distressed until he realized his son wasn't being rude. Moses was in the middle of a prayer as he washed his hands.

Sighing, Tonneman cut the bread. Who would ever have dreamed his life would turn in this most amazing way?

Moses wiped his hands and came to the table. "She hasn't come home yet," the boy told him.

"But she was almost out the door to see Mister Levy when I left."

His knife hovered over the bread. His children were staring at him, as was Alice.

"Papi?"

"It's nothing, Moses." Tonneman set the knife down. "She may have had to stop for—" He looked at Alice. She was frightened. So was he.

They didn't hear the knock at first, not until Maria rose from her chair. "The door, Papi."

"Sit and eat." Tonneman went to the kitchen door.

On his stoop stood a very abashed Asser Levy. "I beg pardon, Mister Tonneman. Your wife . . ."

"Where is she? What's happened?" Tonneman's heart threatened to explode in his chest. He pushed Levy until the two of them were outside on the stoop. He closed the door.

"I must see her. I must apologize to her."

"She's not come home. What happened? What did you do to her?"

"I'm so sorry. She came to see me early this morning at the slaughterhouse to tell me I was still sick and that there was no cure. I didn't want to hear that. I drove her away."

Tonneman's powerful hands grabbed Asser Levy's coat. "She intended only kindness to you."

"As God is my witness, I meant no harm. I lost my composure and shouted at her. She ran away."

"Where?" Tonneman demanded.

Levy wrinkled his forehead. He closed his eyes against the pain of his thoughtless actions. "She ran along Water Gate Road. I thought she would be home before now. . . ."

"You what?" Tonneman roared. "She was going *away* from here and you thought she'd be home?"

Levy nodded. "How can you ever forgive me?"

"I can never forgive you." Forgetting about Levy and casting his children from his whirling thoughts, Tonneman released his hold on the butcher's coat and hurried past the clothesline toward Queen Street and Coenties Slip. He had friends there.

THE SMALL CLEARING revealed a burned-out hut. Perhaps twenty feet away were the banks of the massive Shellpoint.

Racqel stared at her captor. He was shrunken, flushed with fever. He appeared to be mortally ill. If she shoved him, he would fall over.

All that meant nothing when he drew the knife from his waist and pointed it at her. "Cure me," he said.

Chapter 46

❦

The warm sunlight slipped through the trees surrounding Shellpoint. It fell upon the blade of the knife.

For Racqel it was as if everything in the world stopped in that instant. No birdsong, no rustling of leaves, nor the murmur of the springs feeding into the huge pond. Even her breath stopped.

"Take away your curse, daughter of Hecate, and I will see you to Heaven." His fevered eyes caught hers in a fanatical grip; she felt paralyzed with fear. "Cure me as you cured the Jew, Levy."

She took in a fractured breath, surprising herself. With the breath the silence and the paralysis were broken; Racqel assessed her situation. He had a knife and he was mad.

And he was sick. With symptoms very much like Asser Levy's.

Did he, too, have the butcher's disease? If that was horse's blood on his body when they found him . . . ?

But so quick?

Odd, that a schoolmaster would have such a malady.

And then she knew.

Foxman, shadowing Racqel and her captor, did not even stir the leaves beneath his feet. The man with the knife was moonstruck.

Didn't Foxman now wear the sword and baldric that the man had abandoned in the pond?

Foxman circled around in order to watch and listen.

"MASTER CRABTREE. You know me. I am Racqel Tonneman, Moses's mother."

"No, you lie. Moses's mother was the Pharaoh's daughter!"

"I beg you, sir, lay down your knife."

He blinked rapidly, then rubbed his eyes. "Mistress, cure me." He did not lay down his knife.

Racqel set her basket on the ground and knelt over it. The laudanum was gone, but she had the willow bark and paregoric. She held out the bottle of paregoric. "Drink this. It will help you." Her heart beat so, she could hear it.

She wanted to live and she did not want him to die. If he drank some of the medicine, it would make him sleepy. But how much was enough to save her life? Not enough and he could still kill her. Too much and he could die. She was not a murderer. "Just a little."

The schoolmaster took the bottle from her outstretched hand and stared at it. Then he dropped it into the pocket of his red coat.

"It must be taken with water," she said, pointing to the pond. Her voice was firm but her hands trembled. When he bent to drink, she could hit him with a rock. This was the man she had sent Moses to study with. God help her, she could have sent her young son to his death. Fears for her children whirled in her head. *God, protect me*, she prayed. *Bring Tonneman to me. Tonneman, come for me. Please come.*

The schoolmaster edged closer, the knife in his right hand pointed at her. She could smell his sour breath. He pulled her cloak from her shoulders, sniffed it, and threw it to the ground. Next, he grabbed at the hem of her dress. Her first thought was *Good Lord, is he going to rape me?* Then she remembered that he wasn't capable of this, for she had seen him naked. Crabtree had the genitals of a child.

His knife slashed.

He was cutting the cloth of her dress. He pushed her to the ground and held her there with his foot while he tore and tied the cloth. He looped his rope of cloth about her head and tied her by the throat to a tree near the burned-out hut.

Only then did he retrieve the bottle from his pocket, put it to his lips, and drain it dry.

FOXMAN, CROUCHED ON a low branch of a pine as if he were part of it, enjoyed the performance of the little schoolmaster, but he was growing tired of this sort of play.

"MASTER CRABTREE, I beg you. Don't hurt me. Please let me go." She pulled at the noose that held her to the sturdy oak. All she succeeded in doing was tightening the cloth rope.

The schoolmaster shook his head pityingly. He tossed the empty bottle away and thrust his knife into the air in triumph. He began to run around and gather branches, placing them at her feet.

He would burn the witch at the stake, as was proper. A powerful thirst suddenly enveloped him. "Water," he gasped, choking the word. He stumbled toward the pond.

RACQEL FINGERED HER noose, but the rough bark made purchase difficult. She turned her face so her cheek was against the trunk, her arms about its solid mass. If only she could reach the knots before the schoolmaster returned. Try as she might, her fingers could barely grasp them. She stretched her arms and extended her hands again. Her short nails began to dig at the knots.

Tears of frustration stung her eyes. The children would be without a mother, Tonneman without a wife. Again.

She mustn't think of this. She must think good things while her fingers reached and her nails dug.

The Passover was coming. Everything had to be prepared. She and Maria would burn the common bread and bake *massah*. *Mix flour with pure spring water. Now we must hurry. We must roll the dough and have it in the oven before it rises. Otherwise it becomes unfit for Passover. Roll the dough on a long, narrow rolling pin. Good, good. Then prick it and put in an oven.*

"Oh, God in heaven." Racqel raised her eyes, but her fingers never ceased clawing at the knots. "Save me."

FOXMAN WAS NEAR content. The woman was safe, bound to a tree a short way from the one he sat in. Once he rescued her, she would be his. She of the smooth skin, soft as a doe's.

On a branch above, a gray squirrel stared at him, then scrambled high, out of reach.

Foxman considered the madman below. He'd seen him drink from the bottle.

Soon, woman. Soon. Soon you will be mine.

She was brave. Strong. Perhaps she would free herself. His lips drew back into his slight smile.

The madman was lying on his belly to lap water from the pond.

From his post the Mohawk could hear the clamor of white men in the woods. No Indian would make such noise. It would not take them long to get there. He had no more time to squander.

Making no sound at all, he leaped to the next tree, and then the next. The madman was now on his back, singing to the sun.

SHE RESTED HER tired arms from her unrewarding labor and looked up. Directly at him. Foxman.

The Indian was in the tree next to hers. He leaped and was now above her. She turned to look for Crabtree. He was in the water chasing the ducks, cavorting like a child.

MAN WHO WALKS LIKE A FOX slipped down the tree. He touched her hair, so soft, felt her shudder. He lifted her hair and held it against his face, breathing in its perfume.

"Please," she said.

He reached around the tree and cut her bonds with one stroke of his sword.

She fell backward into his arms as he knew she would, and he held her against him.

He didn't feel the knife until it was deep in his back.

Chapter 47

Tonneman opened the door to the Ten Eyck house and howled, "Ten Eyck!" When there was no answer, he ran to the slip.

There he found Antje and Conraet Ten Eyck, sitting on the dock, feet dangling over the side. His partner was unhooking a fish from his line. "Tonneman?" Ten Eyck handed the fish and pole to his wife and stood.

"What's wrong?" Antje placed the fish in a wicker creel and laid the pole on the dock. "Tonneman, what is it?" she cried, seeing his face now, scrambling up, near tripping over her skirts.

"One of the children?" Ten Eyck asked, his sharp eyes narrowing.

There was no need, or time, to talk of wrongs and hurt feelings; Tonneman knew that. "Racqel. She's missing."

"How missing?" Antje shook his arm.

Even as he spoke, Ten Eyck was moving. "Where? When was she last seen? Where?"

"Along Water Gate Road. Earlier this morning." Tonneman was running now, and Ten Eyck with him, step for step. "They're calling her a witch."

"She can't have gone far," said Ten Eyck.

"That's not what troubles me."

They veered around two slaves unloading a flour cart.

"Wait," called Antje, running after them, "I'm coming with you."

"No," Ten Eyck shouted. "Hitch Snow to the wagon. Follow us along Water Gate Road."

To Antje, Tonneman yelled, "See if she's gone to the cemetery. If you don't find her, come back to the Gate."

Jan Keyser drove from Broad Street into the Strand. His wagon was loaded with hides for Europe. When he saw the men running, he called to Antje. "What's the to-do?"

"Racqel Tonneman. She's lost."

"Witches can't get lost," the tanner said. "Everyone knows that." In spite of his words, he snapped the reins and hurried his black gelding after the two men. The tanner was not one to miss the excitement.

"I'm with you, Tonneman," Keyser screamed. He pushed the gelding to the limit and forced the two friends off the road as he raced past them.

When Tonneman and Ten Eyck arrived at the Water Gate, not only was Keyser there waiting for them, so was Asser Levy, along with the two brawny men. The young men were armed, one with a stick, the other wearing baldric and sword.

"I wish to help," Levy told Tonneman. "I'm to blame for what has happened."

Tonneman grunted. "I won't deny the truth. For now I simply want my wife home and well." He marched through the Water Gate; the others followed.

"What is this?" demanded the sentry.

He was paid no notice, except for Keyser. "His wife ran off."

"I wish mine would," the soldier retorted.

Ten Eyck glared at the Musketeer and at Keyser. "Tonneman and I will go through the woods on the left, Levy and his men on the right. Keyser, you go as far as the Stuyvesant place. If you don't see her, come back."

Keyser nodded. Maybe, he thought, if he found the Jewish witch, Tonneman would cast some business his way. He lifted the reins. Still, mayhap he shouldn't be in a big hurry. He didn't expect to find the witch alive.

Chapter 48

She was falling. The Mohawk's grip was strong as death. When they hit the ground, his body cushioned her from the shock. He uttered a jagged sigh and was still. Was he alive or dead? Her nostrils filled with his animal odor mixed with bear grease and the other strange smells he gave off.

Suddenly his strong grip eased. Racqel pulled herself free and crawled on hands and knees. She didn't get far; her sight was blurred; the world spun. She was shaking and was racked with nausea.

Stand up, she told herself. Run. Run *now*. But she could not move.

The red man was lying there, his eyes glazed. What had happened? Blood pooled around him. His sword lay next to his outstretched hand.

She saw the schoolmaster then, not ten feet away.

Run.

She stood and tottered a step toward the trees. Foxman didn't move. Crabtree was kneeling at the edge of the pond, praying. His clasped hands were bloody. At once he groaned, fell over, and lay as if dead. She breathed a sigh of relief; the drug had finally caught up to him. She was free.

Overhead a hawk began to circle.

There was movement at the edge of her vision. Foxman, easing himself up. The Indian's face was contorted but he made no cry. He was dripping blood. He flung his arms out in an odd fashion.

She had thought him dead. She called out her husband's name; she could not move.

But the Indian was not reaching for her. He stretched his arms, his left over his shoulder, the other behind his waist. His body twisted and turned. Racqel gasped when she saw the knife spiking out of his back.

Foxman gave a cry of triumph; his left hand seized the knife and pulled it out, his hand even more bloody than Crabtree's. The Mohawk's face was a mask. Even his eyes did not show what had to be agony.

Racqel took a deep breath. With small, shaky steps, she returned to Foxman. She placed her hands on his shoulders. Blood flowed from the wound in the Mohawk's back, but it was not spurting. That was good. "Don't move," she told him.

Keeping distance between her and the sleeping Crabtree, she walked to the bank of the pond, where ducks splashed in the warm sun. She pulled at the tie that secured her petticoat and let it fall. Swiftly, she made her mud pack, then carried it back to Foxman wrapped in the soft cotton of her petticoat.

Foxman was sitting back against the oak that had so recently imprisoned her. She marveled at his thinking. He was pressing the injured area against the tree to contain the bleeding.

The ground was dark with blood. She tore a section of cotton from her petticoat and used it for a make-do bag in which she wrapped some mud. The Indian understood her intent; he leaned forward so that she could stanch his wound with the mud poultice. He had probably done as much damage pulling the knife out as Crabtree had done in stabbing him with it. She pressed the mud bag against his wound until it stopped bleeding.

Foxman nodded. "You learn our medicine well," he said in Dutch.

Racqel nodded too.

She tore another strip from the petticoat and, kneeling, secured the strip around his chest and back, around the mud pack. This would keep some of the poultice in place until she could get help.

Foxman tilted his head, listening.

She stopped and listened too. She heard nothing, yet it seemed that someone was calling her.

The Mohawk's head fell on her breast, but she didn't cringe. For the first time since they had met at the Mendoza warehouse all those years ago, the Indian didn't frighten her. She lowered him to the ground so that he was lying on his side and moved his head gently to ease his breathing. She recovered her cloak, shook it free of dirt, and covered him with it.

Turning, Racqel shuddered. She had forgotten Crabtree. How could she? The madman might waken and come after her again. As she stood she looked for him at the water's edge.

The schoolmaster was gone.

She wasn't afraid of Foxman, but she was afraid of Master Crabtree.

Again she heard her name. It rustled through the forest like dry leaves. This time when it came again the sound was clearer, the calling of her name over and over: "Racqel, Racqel, Racqel, Racqel, Racqel . . ."

TONNEMAN LED THE WAY, mute, except to call his wife's name every so often. He knew the Indian trails in this neck of the woods. But if she were lost, would she be on the trails or off the trails? On her own Racqel would surely hold to the path. If she were abducted . . . ?

Behind him he knew Ten Eyck was there, would always be there. Their friendship was a bond that had spanned many years, many troubles, many joys, and several wives. He had forgotten that; he would not forget again.

Hand raised, he stopped. "Racqel," he called, then listened. He heard naught but sounds of the forest: wings flapping, air through leaves, claws on wood or earth.

She was gone. Not forever, he prayed.

Despair overwhelmed him. He turned to Ten Eyck, his face sagging with pain.

Ten Eyck grasped his shoulder. "Courage, Tonneman. Racqel is a clever woman, with great resources. A good brain and a good heart."

Tonneman nodded. Ten Eyck was right. Tonneman moved on, his eyes taking in everything on either side of the trail, his lips whispering an awkward, untidy prayer to the God of the Jews and to Jesus Christ.

They were coming close to Shellpoint, where Davies's charred hut still stood. He would circle the pond. The Africans who lived on the far side might have seen something.

A squirrel ran across the trail, and Tonneman stopped.

Ten Eyck asked, "Do you want me to take the lead?"

Tonneman was sick with fear, but he had to keep going. "No, she's got to be out there. Ten Eyck, what would I do without her?"

"Soldier on, my lad. We'll find her."

"If we do, I swear to Jesus Christ, I'll do anything she wants. By Christ, I'll even let them cut me and become a Jew." He reared his head back and yelled, "Rac-qel!"

"Here . . . Tonneman." The call drifted to them like a tender caress.

"Hosanna," Ten Eyck cried, punching Tonneman's arm. "You old dog. She's alive. You spoke too soon. Now you'll have to let them cut you." And he laughed so loud, nesting birds flew off in panic and concealed animals dug deeper into their hiding places or ran to find better ones.

"She's alive," Tonneman repeated like a benediction. "She's alive." He was running now, shouting to the sky, branches slapping his face and arms, the narrow path treacherous beneath his feet. "Racqel! Where are you?" The smell of charred wood grew stronger as he came closer.

"Tonneman, hurry. Foxman has been badly wounded."

"Foxman?" Ten Eyck asked Tonneman.

They were off the trail now, crashing through the brush unmindful of the clawing branches, heading toward the remains of Davies's hut.

When they broke into the clearing, the first thing he saw was Racqel kneeling beside the prone Indian.

Tonneman whooped with joy as she rushed into his arms; he stroked her matted hair. Her sweet face was crossed with scratches.

Ten Eyck crouched beside Foxman. "He's still alive."

Tonneman whispered harshly into his wife's dark hair. "Did he bring you here? I'll kill him."

"No. Crabtree did. He may be your horse killer. . . . He has the butcher's disease, like Asser Levy. He wanted me to cure him." In his arms, she shuddered. "He's mad, Tonneman. I think he would have killed me if it were not for Foxman."

Ten Eyck got to his feet. "Where is Crabtree?"

"I don't know. He drank a great deal of paregoric. It should either disable him with terrible cramps or put him to sleep, I don't know which. Crabtree tied me to a tree and stabbed Foxman as the Indian was releasing me. One moment I saw Crabtree in a swoon near the water, the next he was gone."

Ten Eyck grunted and drew his sword. "I'll have a look around."

Tonneman knelt on the ground. "Foxman?"

Man Who Walks Like a Fox opened his clear eyes and stared at Tonneman.

"My wife tells me you saved her."

"For me. Not for you."

"Over here," Ten Eyck cried. He stood at the entrance to Davies's charred hut. "I've found your horse killer, Tonneman. Curled up like a baby, snoring loud enough to wake the dead."

Chapter 49

"**H**ulloo, Sheriff. Did you hear that? All your killers haven't flown the coop. Tonneman and Ten Eyck have caught your horse murderer."

The Sheriff's voice snapped out from another part of the wood. "Shut up, Nessel-Vogel."

As if he were on a holiday stroll, the Deputy sauntered along a path that led to the colony of freed slaves on the far side of Shellpoint. "Who the Devil is it?" he asked Tonneman and Ten Eyck.

"Lester Crabtree, the schoolmaster," Ten Eyck replied.

Crashing behind Nessel-Vogel came Sheriff Gibb. "So it was Crabtree. I had a feeling it might be him. That pitchfork at the Devil's Boulder came out much too easy. Maybe we can get him to confess to the dead Scot in the Jews' cemetery and make a clean sweep of it."

Tonneman, still clutching Racqel to him, shook his head. "No. One Lopez-Campbell probably killed the other. When you catch up to him, maybe he'll tell you why."

Nessel-Vogel chuckled. "The Sheriff had him all right, but the wily Scot hit him on the head and got away."

Gibb glared. "That was after *you* had him first, Deputy. Locked up in a cell at that, and *you* let him get away first."

Ten Eyck came closer. "What was that again?"

Grinning, Nessel-Vogel said, "After giving me hell and all for letting him get away, the Sheriff tracked the Scot to the Mendoza warehouse, where he was getting supplies. He had the Scot all trussed up in the wagon. And then somebody knocked him on the head and Lopez-Campbell got away again."

"It was that Jew-bastard helped him."

Gibb's deprecation was still on his lips as Asser Levy and his two young minions joined them in the clearing. "And which Jew-bastard was that?" the butcher demanded of the Sheriff.

"Look at this," Nessel-Vogel shouted gleefully. "It's as busy as Broad Street on Market Day."

"And which Jew-bastard was that, Sheriff Gibb?" Levy's olive skin was florid with anger.

Flustered, Gibb said, "Beg your pardon, Mister Levy, Mistress Tonneman, I meant no offense. I can't prove it, but I'll get that Mendoza for this."

"Aren't you going after Lopez-Campbell?" Tonneman asked innocently. Trappers were near impossible to track.

The Sheriff shook his head and rubbed the small of his back. "With my condition I wouldn't last a day on the trail. He'll be back. I'll wait. I'll watch."

"By my reckoning he's halfway to Hudson Bay by now," Nessel-Vogel exclaimed, ever more gleeful. "And he's never coming back."

The Sheriff, taking his Deputy's comment in stride, grunted. "Most likely. So, Tonneman, I see you've had better luck. The Water Gate sentry told me your wife went missing. You've found her. Now where's my horse killer?"

Tonneman exchanged glances with Ten Eyck. Tonneman nodded.

Racqel was safe. With Crabtree's capture, Tonneman would have fulfilled his mission for De Sille. Tonneman and Ten Eyck would be free of any obligation. He offered his partner his hand; Ten Eyck clasped it tightly. Tonneman said, "Not *your* horse killer, Gibb. My horse killer. You tell the First Councillor that. Change that to

Tonneman *and* Ten Eyck's horse killer. You make sure De Sille knows that."

"So you found him and I didn't," Gibb said, offended. "You caught him by luck. If you hadn't been looking for your wife . . . Luck. Cow-shit luck. That's all it was. Pure luck."

Tonneman grinned. "What do you think this miscreant-catching game is? Some thinking, but more going nowhere, sweating, and luck. If you must know, I had it down to Crabtree and one other. I would have caught him sooner or later."

"Whatever you say. How'd you figure it out?"

"Asking a lot of questions. And I remembered what you said about that pitchfork."

Gibb massaged the back of his neck. "Do you think Lopez-Campbell or Campbell-Lopez, or whatever the hell his name was, had anything to do with the horse killings?"

"I doubt it. Ask Crabtree. Ask him about Davies and Mad Beado too. He killed them sure as God made fish in the sea. Crabtree was Davies's teacher, you know. And that lovely red coat? Davies's mother made it for him from cloth Roome traded with Mendoza. Either Davies gave it to Crabtree or Crabtree took it from him. Same difference. Go on," Tonneman said, "ask Crabtree."

Gibb grimaced. "A lot he'll tell me. Where is he?" He cast an idle eye at Foxman. "Is that Indian dead?"

"No," Racqel replied. "He has a serious wound. We must move him to the City Hall, where he can be properly attended."

The Sheriff shrugged. "Where is Crabtree?"

"There." Ten Eyck jerked his thumb toward the charred shell of the hut. "That is, if *he* hasn't escaped you too."

"Don't say that, even in jest." Gibb sighed. He went inside Davies's old hut. After several moments he shouted, "Let's go, Nessel-Vogel. He's dead to the world. You'll have to carry him."

"Of course. If there's an easy way and a hard way, I always get the hard way. As if I were some dumb ox." Still grumbling, the Deputy joined the Sheriff in the hut.

While the two lawmen dragged the snoring schoolmaster out

into the sunshine, Levy tapped Tonneman on the arm. "Could I have a private word with you?"

"My aching back," Gibb cried. "The man's sleeping like the dead."

"That's the paregoric," Racqel explained. "He'll sleep through the night."

Tonneman looked at Racqel.

"I'll be all right," she promised. "I think I'll sit down and rest for a time."

Tonneman led her to the oak where she'd been Crabtree's prisoner and kissed her cheek. "I won't be long."

She nodded. She shut her eyes.

Tonneman noted that Foxman, lying not far from Racqel, his eyes closed, was breathing evenly. He walked back to Asser Levy. "Now, Mister Levy. What is it?"

Levy scanned the people nearby lest they hear, then studied Tonneman for a long moment before replying. "I'd rather the law didn't know of this, but I trust you to do what you must once you've heard what I have to say. Ezra Cohen, who works for Henry Backer as slaughterer, had too much to drink the other day. Cohen found the Lopez body in Backer's field. It is this body I'm told you dug up in our cemetery." Levy could not keep the disapproval from his voice.

Tonneman understood the man's distress. And his condemnation. He didn't take it to heart. "Go on."

"I'm shamed to tell you this, but with what was happening with the horse mutilations and the remarks against us by some, Cohen feared this body would lead to yet more trouble for our people. He went and talked to my idiot son-in-law, Zedekiah. Zedekiah and eight other drunks in my tavern formed a quorum with Cohen. Cohen killed Backer's cow. He used to be in my employ and wields a blade properly. Together these ten bumpkins put the body in our cemetery. The next morning, when that fribbler Cohen sobered up, he became frightened by what he'd done and ran away. That kind of behavior is why he no longer works for *me*," the butcher concluded.

"Amazing," Tonneman drawled with gentle sarcasm. "When I asked about Lopez, none of Cohen's drunken friends knew about the red-haired men being in your tavern."

Levy shrugged. "Jews get drunk too, you know. And do the same stupid, terrible things Gentiles do."

"Good heavens," Racqel cried.

Startled, Tonneman looked toward her.

How could it have happened?

Racqel was still resting by the tree. Ten Eyck was helping Gibb and Nessel-Vogel as they attempted to get Crabtree to walk off the paregoric.

The two Jewish boys were involved in some sort of discussion and had no idea what was happening in the real world.

He and Levy had been talking.

But only the blood-stained earth gave evidence that the Mohawk had even been there. Racqel's cloak and the sword were nowhere to be seen.

Man Who Walks Like a Fox was gone.

Chapter 50

❧

The cloying scent of lavender hung over the First Councillor's office like a fog.

"That's the tale," Tonneman declared. "Conraet and I are quits with you and your damned commission. One hundred pounds, thank you, sir, and the slate is clean."

De Sille picked up a small gold box from his desk and took some snuff.

"I would like to have my money and leave," Tonneman said. "Now."

The First Councillor raised his hand. "Moment . . . ah—" He sneezed, wiped his nose with a red silk handkerchief, and shoved it into the silk sleeve of his fine red coat.

Tonneman came around the desk and looked at Nick's feet. De Sille wore the silk shoes the cobbler had told him about. Shaking his head, Tonneman said, "My money. One hundred pounds."

"You haven't told me why Davies and Mad Beado were murdered."

Tonneman snorted his impatience. "Simple. Davies was going to tell me that his teacher Crabtree was our horse killer. Beado? I think the same reason will do. But he was a madman, so who's to know." Tonneman let out a sound that was meant to be a laugh. "All three were madmen."

243

"And Navarro?"

Tonneman itched to tell Nickie about his horns, but he let the urge pass. Let another tell the cuckold about Navarro and Geertruyd. "Oh, he's guilty of a great many things, but not horse killing and murder."

"What about this cow nonsense?"

"You didn't hire me to find that out."

Nick sniffed and pulled a clay pipe and his bowl of tobacco to him. "But you have opinions. It won't hurt to share them with me. What about the Lopez chap? What did he have to do with it all?"

Tonneman shrugged. "He killed his cousin. You're not going to smoke that shit, are you?"

De Sille actually managed to appear hurt. "I'll smoke whatever I please. Why did Lopez kill his cousin?"

"I have no idea. But after he did it, we caught him. Gibb put him in jail and he escaped. That is the sum of what I know about Amos Lopez-Campbell."

"So many bloody events and all at the Devil's Boulder. Any reason you can fathom?" De Sille flamed his pipe from the lamp on his desk.

Tonneman shook his head, and waved the smoke away from him with both hands.

De Sille said, "I hear talk that Keyser thinks it's the Jews. He claims there was an inverted triangle cut on the face of the Governor's dead stallion. The Devil mark, Keyser calls it."

Tonneman coughed elaborately. "He said as much to me."

"Aha," De Sille said. "Perhaps this is only to cloud the issue? What if Keyser—or even Henry Backer—is involved?"

"Your question confounds me. I have no answer."

Nick smoothed his mustache with the tips of his forefingers. "It is my considered opinion that the trapper Amos Lopez-Campbell helped the schoolmaster mutilate the horses. And that the two of them and Mad Beado, and Davies, and Keyser and Backer were all involved in a conspiracy to destroy me and my reputation."

"Sounds good to me, Nickie."

"What did you say?"

"And the Jews must have had a hand in it."

"My very thought."

"And the Catholics. But wait—James, Duke of York, is a Catholic. So it's the anti-Catholics. That would include James's brother, His Royal Majesty Charles the Second."

De Sille looked at him strangely.

"Actually, Nickie, I've never told you this, but the English don't really trust you because you're Dutch."

Whatever suspicion of Tonneman's motives De Sille might have had was instantly dissipated by the First Councillor's own worst fears.

"And . . ." Tonneman went on serenely, knowing full well the hook was in. He would pay Nick back for oh, so many things, not the least of which was having to breathe his damn lavender stink. "The Dutch have never forgiven you for being the Englishman's toady."

"I am no such . . ." De Sille sputtered, unable to continue. He took a deep draw from his pipe. In control once more, he said, "I've always felt that."

Tonneman nodded. "I've heard that the Quakers mean to do you violence."

"What?"

"To return to the English and the anti-Catholic issue . . . do you think the King is involved?"

De Sille gritted his teeth, snapping the pipe stem. He threw the broken pipe to the desk, suspicion and only suspicion on his mind. "Taking the piss out of me, are you?"

"I've always said you were a shrewd man."

"Mock me all you will, Tonneman. Crabtree did not act alone."

"I disagree. That's why he had to kill Davies and Beado. They wouldn't go along with his demented scheme for killing those horses."

Tobacco coals were falling from the cast-off pipe and charring a document on De Sille's fine desk. He spat on his fingers and hastily extinguished the coals. "Therefore, it is also my considered opinion that you have not fulfilled the terms of your commission, Tonneman."

"Pig swill, Nickie."

"Say what you will. I'll not pay you one hundred pounds for a job not done."

Anger flashed in Tonneman's eyes. "You miserable excuse—" He stopped and considered. "Never mind, Nick. I'll get it from Solomon Navarro."

De Sille's brow wrinkled in bafflement. "Why should Navarro pay you one hundred pounds?"

Tonneman grinned. The itch had won, and Tonneman was glad of it. "Elementary. I'll make it the price for not telling you he's tupping Geertruyd."

Chapter 51

The Ten Eyck table was so laden with food and drink, it showed not one bare bit of space.

Still, Antje was able to shove a platter of cheese aside with her elbow to make room for a bowl of yellow apples. She poured the beer and cider.

Eyeing the feast with immense satisfaction, Tonneman said, "Here we are again." He watched his wife as she moved to the basin of water Antje had set out for her on a small table and said her prayers. In a small prayer of his own Tonneman thanked God for her presence in his life.

They waited for Racqel to complete her ritual before commencing their meal.

Tonneman cut himself a piece of good Dutch Leiden and declared, "This has been the most deranged week of my life. I've never encountered anything more outrageous."

"Amen." Racqel sat back and sipped her beer. Tonneman's problems were all solved. She still had a major one to deal with.

"Yes," Antje said. "Amen."

Silence followed while the four friends ate.

Finally, Ten Eyck swallowed the last of his beer and held his cup out for Antje to fill again. In a near whisper he said, "I'm truly sorry, my friend, for binding us to De Sille like that."

"It's forgotten," Tonneman replied. "But no more secrets between us, partner. Why don't we leave these women now and go fishing?"

"Not so fast," Antje said. "You may be clear on all that happened, but I'm not."

"What would you like to know?" Tonneman asked.

"Crazy or not, how was Master Crabtree able to enlist those two innocents, Davies and Beado, in his bloody scheme, and how was he able to hide what he was from us?"

"We are a simple, trusting lot," Ten Eyck said.

"True," Tonneman agreed. "And news travels slowly, if at all, from the other colonies."

"But you haven't answered my first question," Antje complained.

"There are such people as false prophets," Racqel said. "Have you not heard about madmen who inspire? They seem to have a peculiar knowledge and are able to entice followers to do their bidding in the name of God. Torquemada was such a man. His Inquisition drove my ancestors from Spain."

Tonneman took his wife's hand and kissed it.

"I must tell you something, husband," Racqel continued. "I, too, have kept a secret from you."

"What kind of secret?"

"Our friends, Antje and Conraet, allowed me a bit of space near here. They built me my own *mikvah*."

"Racqel" was all that Tonneman said.

"I thought you wouldn't approve."

"You should have told me." He sighed. "I probably wouldn't have approved." He laughed. "But you would have done it anyway. And so you have. And all's well that ends well, so we'll talk no more of it."

"Amen again," said Antje. "It's time for hurts to be dissolved. Life is too short. We each know that."

Tonneman rolled his eyes at Antje.

She placed a dish of crumpet cakes on the table. "Your favorite, Tonneman."

His answer was to fill his mouth with crumpet.

"Why horses?" Ten Eyck asked.

Tonneman washed the crumpet down with cider. "Baffles the hell out of me."

"Tell us about the respectable physician Navarro," Antje said. "Or even better, dear Geertie De Sille. Is her fine hand anywhere in this?"

"Only down Navarro's breeches," Tonneman said, and roared. His laughter was joined by Antje's and Ten Eyck's. Racqel smiled.

"Apologies, ladies." Tonneman wiped the tears from his eyes.

Ten Eyck was still grinning ear to ear. "We all know Geertie will do anything—or anyone—if there's profit in it."

Antje cocked her head at her husband. "And how do you know that?"

"When one is in business one hears these things."

"Just be sure one only *hears* about these things and nothing more."

"At my age, beloved, you can be certain of it." He kissed his wife lightly on the lips and pinched her round bottom.

Antje slapped his hand away and wiped down the table. She was blushing.

"We'll go fishing tomorrow, eh, Tonneman?" Ten Eyck said.

Tonneman took Racqel's hand. "Come, let's leave these two to their business."

Together they walked up Coenties Alley to Queen Street. He could smell saltwater and rum, seaweed and spices. He could smell his wife's hair, the musky natural perfume of her skin.

Life was good.

Chapter 52

❧

Asser Levy shifted in his chair in the great chamber of his house on Wall Street as if to find a more comfortable position. Tonneman sat opposite. The two men were dressed alike, in black coats and breeches.

The room was large even for a great chamber. On a shelf behind Levy were arrayed more than a dozen seven-branched lampstands of china, copper, and silver. To Tonneman, one elaborate candleholder even looked to be gold.

The butcher eyed the fair-haired Dutchman warily. "First we'll talk, drink some tea, then we'll go to the baths."

Tonneman grunted.

"You won't be allowed to bathe."

Tonneman shrugged indifferently.

Levy drank the hot tea his wife had served them in yellow majolica cups. He wiped his mouth with a large white nose cloth, then carefully tucked the cloth into the sleeve of his black coat. "You, of course, know that today is the Christian holy day Good Friday. The day on which Yeshua, the man from Nazareth, was crucified by the Romans."

"Some say by the Jews."

"Ah, that is Christian thinking. Jews know it was the Romans. Do you find it significant that we meet today? On Good Friday?"

"It's a day like any other day."

"Ah. So we begin. A non-Jew who undergoes formal conversion is thought of as a real Jew. On the other hand, I myself discourage conversion."

"Tell what I must do to lie beside my wife in your cemetery."

Asser Levy sighed heavily. "That is no reason to convert."

"It is for me."

"No. You cannot wish to be a Jew for convenience. You must love *Yahweh* with all your heart."

Tonneman nodded. "That is the truth. I do love God with all my heart."

"And people."

Tonneman nodded, then raised an eyebrow. "God and people present no obstacles for me. But there is the knife."

"I'll give you a big drink and you won't feel a thing."

"I don't drink."

"Then you'll take laudanum."

"There are spirits in laudanum."

"You certainly argue enough to be a Jew. Very well then, you will take nothing and it will hurt."

Tonneman grunted. He had endured pain before. And for less valued reasons.

"As all converts, you will have a new name and become the son of Abraham, patriarch of our people."

Tonneman thought a moment. He smiled. "Since Simon was called Pieter in my old religion, I will be called Simon in my new."

This time Asser Levy grunted. "Simon Ben Abraham. Good."

"I've read that there are six hundred and thirteen Commandments a Jew must obey. Nobody can live with that many rules."

Levy rubbed his fingertips together. "Quite so. But most of those rules no longer relate to everyday life. They pertain to temple worship in the first and second Holy Temples of Jerusalem."

"The Temples were destroyed years ago."

Levy smiled. "Ages."

"I'm to learn rules for which there is no application?"

"No. Study the Fifteenth Psalm of David. It asks and answers who shall be with God and holds the meat of basic Jewish dogma. Except . . ."

"I know the Fifteenth Psalm well from my childhood. I believe I am an upright man, my toil is righteous, and I speak the truth in my heart." Tonneman realized he was protesting too much. "Except what?"

"There is the tale of the pagan who asked the illustrious and sainted Hillel, Rabbi of Palestine: 'Tell me about Judaism while standing on one foot.'

"And Hillel replied, 'That which is hurtful to you, do not do to your neighbor. Everything else is commentary. Now go study.' " Levy rose from the deep chair. "I say the same to you, Pieter Tonneman. Now go study."

A Footnote

The surrender of New Amsterdam in 1664, which we described in *The Dutchman*, was not the end of it for the Dutch and the English.

On August 9, 1673, during the third Dutch-English war, to the astonishment of New-Yorkers, a Dutch fleet sailed into the Bay and recaptured the City once more. It was renamed New Orange.

New Orange had a short history.

On February 19, 1674, Great Britain and the Netherlands signed the Treaty of Westminster. The news didn't reach New-York till July. While Britain was once more ruler of New-York, the Dutch kept their possessions in the West Indies.

The Duke of York appointed Major Edmund Andros as Governor.

The real Nicasius De Sille was neither a villain nor the Governor's representative. In fact, he was a poet and a respected officer of the law. But we couldn't resist the thought of De Sille and Tonneman having to cooperate and at the same time be enemies. Anthony Brocknolls was the real First Councillor and would have succeeded Governor Andros had the need arisen.

Although the 1674 Treaty of Westminster may have made New-York subject to the English King, four out of five people living in the City were Dutch. The 1698 census showed there were 4,937 people in New-York, 700 of whom were Africans. Some of those were free men.

The word *Yankee* wasn't in the language until 1750. But perhaps it comes from the earlier name the Dutch applied to the English in Connecticut, *Jan Kees*—John Cheese. That's where we came up with Johnnies.

There is no yeast in matzos *(massah)*. The question then is: How would it rise? When flour and water are mixed, if the flour stays wet too long, there is a danger of fermentation, which would make it rise. That's why there is such a rush to make matzo for Passover. The law states that no more than eighteen minutes can pass from the time water touches the flour until it goes into the oven.

Asser Levy and Lester Crabtree were suffering from Mediterranean fever, which wasn't named until the early nineteenth century. It was later called Malta fever and undulant fever and brucellosis. The sickness is caused by bacteria found in the flesh of dead animals.

Even in the seventeenth century, in the Jewish Community, the man who performed circumcision of the male child on the eighth day after his birth and of any brave convert was the (kosher) butcher. Asser Levy could have very easily been the *mohel* (the person who performs circumcision) of New-York.

As for the first twenty-three Jewish settlers in the City:

When we wrote *The Dutchman*, all our sources agreed on the same story of how the twenty-three arrived in New Amsterdam. Since then we have read Howard Sachar's *A History of Jews in America*. In it, Mr. Sachar offers a different version.

Sixteen ships left Brazil. One version of the story had all sixteen heading for the Netherlands. Another stated that two ships did not, and that one of them, the Dutch schooner *Valck*, was bound for Martinique.

In both stories the *Valck* was captured by Spanish privateers. In the first version of the story, the twenty-three Jews on board were rescued by a Frenchman, Captain Jacques De la Motthe. In the second, they met him in Cuba.

Either way, De la Motthe contracted with the Jews to transport

A Footnote

them to New Amsterdam. There is also disagreement over De la Motthe's ship. Was it called the *St. Charles* or the *Ste. Catherine?*

This was the argument Tonneman overheard.

Gudezmo or *Judezmo* was the Spanish language the Jews took with them from Spain. It is now referred to as Ladino.

Katherine Harrison was known as the Wetherfield Witch. Accused by Alice Manning, Katherine was declared innocent after a physician's report said she wasn't a witch. By and large, New-York never surrendered to the hysteria about witches. We like to think it's because the City was always tolerant of eccentrics.

And still is.

A.M.
M.M.
New York City